SIZANI FILE

THE RIDER FILES
BOOK 9

CB SAMET

PRAISE FOR CB SAMET

"CB Samet is a master of the craft ..."

— READERS' FAVORITE REVIEW 2017

"CB Samet has a way of bringing you into the hair-raising suspense, keeping you at the edge of your seat."

— VORACIOUS READERS REVIEWER

"There is plenty of romance, intrigue, and drama in this book to keep the page turning."

— BOOKSPROUT REVIEWER

Award-winning author

GRAY HORIZON: 2019 Readers' Favorite bronze winner in thriller category

MASTERS FILE: 2018 Readers' Favorite honorable mention in romantic suspense category

THE AVANT CHAMPION ~Rising~: 2017 2nd place in fantasy EVVY Awards

BEST-SELLING AUTHOR in *Heroes with Heat and Heart Volume 2* and *Heroes with Heat and Heart Volume 3* Charity Anthologies

FREE EBOOK WITH NEWSLETTER SIGNUP

Rick Swanson loves his job as a firefighter, but his world is sent on a tailspin when an arsonist has an agenda of revenge. He needs to deal with this threat if he's going to get his life back on track.

Mackenzie Rivera is falling fast for fireman Rick, until he inexplicably distances himself. When she learns he's trying to protect her from a crazed arsonist, she won't be idle. And she won't back down from danger. But will her determination and his strength be enough to save them both from the fire?

*~~~***<<<SIGN UP HERE>>>***~~~*

Avant Star Publishing, LLC

Cover Art: Circe Corp

ebook ISBN: 978-1-950942-37-4

print ISBN: 978-1-950942-38-1

1

"This place is a security nightmare," Rafe grumbled, shifting his weight as he stood under the scorching Texas sun.

Ten half-buried Cadillacs squatted in a row within clay-moist ground. Laden with layer upon layer of graffiti, the metal carcasses stood in stark contrast to the flat, umber, barren land around them. Beyond that were patches of grass in various pale green and brown shades of wilting.

"I think you've said that at every stop," Jackson, who hung back in the RV parked in the lot, remarked in Rafe's earpiece. "Cadillac Ranch is an American icon," he touted. "The guide says it was created in 1974, and the cars are vintage 1946 to 1963."

"Easy for you to be fascinated," Rafe shot back. "You're in an air-conditioned vehicle reading the brochure, not standing in a cow pasture sweating balls."

Jackson chuckled.

"Does seem a bit eccentric," Dorian noted in his polished British accent as he gazed up and down the row of cars. He stood beside Rafe, looking over-dressed in slacks, a button-down shirt, and a navy blazer. He had bronze skin like Rafe, but the tufts of gray around Dorian's ears and crows feet around a pair of hawk eyes revealed the extra twenty-five years he had on Rafe.

Rafe wished he could dress lighter instead of khaki cargo pants and a zipper vest over his T-shirt, but he needed the outfit to be prepared for danger and to conceal his handgun. At least he wasn't wearing his suit. He had a brand-new bullet resistant suit courtesy of his employer, but a suit in June in Texas wasn't happening.

He turned his attention back to the assets. The family, a mother and her two children, were having a rambunctious time at the tourist site, spray painting on top of the other layers of paint. The mother, Hiba, smiled while she snapped photos as the two children, Ada and Jabari, laughed at their graffiti. They had managed to spray paint themselves in the process—fuchsia pink, vibrant blue, and neon green on dark skin.

"Rafe, climb up!" Jabari, the ten-year-old boy, called out to him.

Straightening and adjusting her headscarf, Hiba guffawed.

After two weeks protecting the family on their cross-country road trip, the boy continuously tried to turn Rafe into his play friend when Rafe's purpose was to be his bodyguard.

"No," Rafe replied.

"Come, it's fun!" Jabari said.

"I'm not here for fun." Rafe knew he was being overly grumpy, but interacting with children wasn't his strong suit. Neither was baking in the heat, even though he'd grown up traipsing hot, humid South American jungles as a child and had worked the odd summer job as a ranch hand in Texas in his youth.

His foul mood could partially be attributed to missing his twin brother. Santino had jetted off with the love of his life, an archeologist, to their next monumental discovery. Meanwhile, Rafe was stuck outside Amarillo, kicking paint cans around a wasteland while families enjoyed summer vacations.

Their three-man bodyguard team, watching the family of the President of Comoro, had afforded Rafe a rare glimpse into American culture he hadn't experienced growing up. The great American road trip.

"There have been more stimulating attractions," Dorian said, cocking his head to one side as if the decorative Cadillacs posed some type of puzzle. Even the suave Brit was breaking a sweat under the blistering sun.

"*Sequro que si,*" Rafe agreed. They'd seen the St. Louis arch, walked the Meramec Caverns, and ate at many iconic diners.

Overall, guarding the Comoro family had been one of the more enriching protection details he'd been on—excluding moments like today, standing in the heat.

Jabari climbed onto the car while the boy's mother took more photos on her smartphone. His sister, Ada, a foot taller and five years older, tossed her head back and laughed when she "accidentally" sprayed her brother's shoe with pink paint.

Rafe smirked, not at her mischief but at how the girl had seemed to unwind slowly over the course of the road trip from pouting, anti-social teenager to playful sibling.

In the distance, the thumping of helicopter blades drew Rafe's attention. He and Dorian both looked to the sky, squinting against the sun.

"I don't like the way it's making a bee-line straight for us," Rafe said.

"Agreed." Dorian's mouth stretched into a thin line as he gazed at the black chopper. "No reason for an unmarked Airbus to be out here. And no reason to be that low in the sky."

Rafe nodded. A news or tourist helicopter would have brighter markings and wouldn't have been dusting the tree tops, risking power lines and cell towers.

He gauged the distance from the Cadillac graveyard to their RV.

The long expanse of open terrain would make their group an easy target. Dorian must have had the same thought, as he gathered Hiba and her children close to one car, keeping his voice calm and reassuring.

Oblivious, a half dozen other tourists still mulled around the cars, painting and taking selfies.

"Jackson, incoming chopper," Rafe said as the noise grew louder. "*Mierda*. That looks like a sniper hanging out the side."

"Did you say a sniper?" Jackson asked, voice incredulous.

Rafe ducked behind a car as a shot rang out, the bullet thudding into metal. Had he been the intended target? If a squad was after the family, they would take out the security team first. Sweat be damned, he suddenly wished he had worn his ten-thousand-dollar bullet-resistant suit.

"Get down!" he shouted to everyone.

Tourists gaped at each other, murmurs of worry rippling through them.

"*Was that a gunshot?*"

"*What's going on?*"

A second shot sounded as the chopper closed the distance, stirring up dirt and spinning paint cans and litter in every direction. Rafe could no longer hear his thudding heartbeat over the thumping blades. Someone screamed, which motivated the tourists to take off at a sprint back toward the parking lot.

Dorian kept the family behind the protection of a green and gray sprayed car. They could have bolted with the crowd, but if the attacker didn't care about collateral damage, the bystanders could be hurt.

Rafe drew his weapon, a Glock, and took aim as the chopper approached for a landing.

ANGLED UNCOMFORTABLY on the rooftop of the gift shop at Cadillac Ranch, Dia watched the tourists mulling about the cars.

Rafe Alonso and Dorian Chaplin guarded the Sizani family—had been for the last several weeks as the mother and children took a cross-country, site-seeing vacation. The president of Comoro was back in his home country, tending to matters of state, while the Rider Security and Investigation team protected his family. Such had been their annual routine for several years.

Dia blinked away the sweat dripping from her forehead as she peered through her rifle site, lingering on Rafe's lean form in pants and a vest, revealing his formed biceps. He'd fashioned his hair in a ponytail, the same as it had been back in Cusco when she'd first met him months ago. Long fingers strummed his hip where one hand rested. She knew those fingers and the tantalizing sensations they were capable of creating.

The drumming of helicopter blades brought her attention back to the present. She took a deep breath, readied her finger on the trigger, and prepared for the impending battle. Her intel had been right; the attack was today.

When the gunman on the chopper fired his second shot, tourists began scurrying toward the parking lot in panic. She had a clear shot at the chopper pilot, but she couldn't risk killing him and crashing the helo either into the pedestrians or the Sizani family. Unfortunately, from her angle, she didn't have a shot at the gunman inside the chopper.

She would have to hold tight for an opening.

RAFE's first shot hit metal. The second clipped the sniper in the chopper.

Before he could congratulate himself on his aim under pressure, three men armed with automatic weapons poured out of the chopper as it hovered a few feet above the ground.

The assailants focused their efforts on him, forcing him to duck behind the Cadillac and hope the men didn't have armor-piercing rounds to penetrate the seventy-year-old metal.

Dorian took the opportunity to step out of hiding and fire. Four bullets—two of them took out the kneecaps of two different men. He ducked back just in time as those standing turned and fired at him while the two grounded writhed in pain.

Two more men climbed out of the helicopter, and the sniper appeared to be regrouping despite his injury.

Rafe's heart pounded as he prepared to stand and fire again. This was some unprecedented firepower for a family vacation. While Hiba was the first lady of Comoros, the tiny African island touted only agricultural commodities. Sure, it was the largest producer of ylang-ylang, but an oil used as a perfume fragrance hardly seemed worth killing over.

What the hell is at play here?

Even South American kidnappers seeking to nab a tourist for ransom weren't so well outfitted with these types of weapons and transportation.

When Rafe stepped out of cover and fired, he saw the Rider-rented SUV ram directly into the helicopter. Rafe's shot took down the closest assailant on the ground as the vehicle knocked the chopper askew in a deafening crunch of metal striking metal.

Aye, Dios.

He hoped Jackson wasn't inside the vehicle when it rammed. Although new to the Rider team, the guy had ten years under his belt in the FBI. He was no amateur.

"Take the family! I'll cover you!" Rafe told Dorian.

His colleague wasted no time getting the family moving. Rafe noted the terrified expression on Jabari's small face and his heart ached for him. No child should have to face this kind of fear.

Rafe winked and gave an encouraging, "*¡Tienes este abucheo!* You got this," before turning to lay cover fire. He only had one spare clip in his pocket, so his shots needed to be strategic.

Off to the side, he saw Jackson shove to his feet, covered in dirt and gun drawn, ready for a fight. He must have dived out of the Explorer before setting it on a collision course for the helicopter. Jackson ran with Dorian, getting the family into the RV.

Rafe scanned the grounds around the chopper. Men were down, none of which appeared to be a threat any longer. He wanted to question them or at least take identification so his company could figure out who was behind the attack, but there was no time. Priority one required securing the family's safety.

Another rifle shot rang through the air and the body of the man who'd been sneaking up behind Rafe collapsed to the ground. Rafe's heart threatened to explode. He hadn't seen the silent attacker and could have died.

His gaze snapped toward the friendly sniper. For the second time this year, a secret gunman had saved his life. He was grateful but also peeved to not know who it was. That was about to change.

2

"Get out of here!" Rafe said to Jackson on their coms before holstering his weapon and dashing in the direction of the rifle shot. As he leaped over the downed barbed wire fence Jackson had destroyed with the SUV, the RV started to move, Jackson at the wheel.

Rafe reached the gift shop and paused, eyes scrutinizing the perimeter for someone carrying a rifle.

"Hey, man, are you a cop?" someone asked.

Cop? Rafe had been accused of being many things in his life but never law enforcement.

"Go get her. She stole my phone." The tourist cowering behind the porch railing pointed to his left.

Her? Rafe wondered.

He spotted a short-haired woman sprinting toward a silver Acura with a case, slender and long enough to hold a rifle, slung over one shoulder. Rafe bolted in her direction.

He'd scoured video tapes from the gunfight at a copper mine outside of Cusco, but hours of scrutiny had revealed no images captured of his mysterious guardian angel. He wanted to get a look at this woman and find out if she'd also been in Peru.

"*Esperas!*" he called.

But the woman ignored him, dumping the gun in the back of the car and moving to get into the driver's seat.

"Wait!" This time, he extended a hand and caught her shoulder to spin her around before she could climb inside the Acura.

With the speed and grace of a fox, she caught his wrist, pivoted, and used his own momentum to sling him against the side of the car.

He let out a grunt.

She pressed her body against him to pin him to the vehicle.

"Hey," he said, panting from his run. "We seem to be on the same side here. Who are you?" Pressed with his chest against the hot metal, he couldn't see her face.

Without a word, she spun away and moved to get in the driver's seat. He wasn't letting her escape so easily.

He reached for her again, and this time, she turned with arms swinging, but didn't catch him off guard. He blocked her blows, never taking one of his own.

As she forced him defensively backward, he saw her face with skin like dark honey, large hazel eyes, high cheekbones flushed from exertion, and long lashes.

"Midnight," he gasped at the sight of the woman he'd met only once before. Images of that night flashed through his mind—her head against the pillow as soft moans escaped her lips. Fingernails raking down his back.

Confused by her presence here, he tried to piece together past events. Instinct screamed betrayal, but that thought clashed with his fond memories of their brief time together.

Did she use me somehow?

With mounting frustration at her unwarranted hostility, he fought harder, determined to get answers. She was fast and agile, with the advantage of not having just been in a gunfight followed by a two-hundred-yard dash.

"Wait... a damn... minute... woman." Finally, he worked his way into her inner circle, hooked a leg around her, and brought her down onto the grassy edge beside the parking lot.

He used the fifty pounds of muscle he had on her to pin her to the ground. She tried to thrash, but quickly became as winded as he was. Her chest heaved up and down beneath him.

"I'm not a threat to you," he said.

She glared at him with a fiery fury he found puzzling, fascinating, and slightly arousing.

Holding her arms at the wrists above her head, his face hovered above hers. "Who are you?" He had a thousand questions but wanted her to start with the most important one.

Each of her exhaled breaths brushed his lips as her eyes roamed his face.

What was she searching for? Trust?

This closeness reminded him of their one-night stand in Cusco. She'd known how to talk the night they'd first met. Talk and moan and gasp. And since a sniper saved his life not twenty-four hours after their night of passion, he guessed that had been her, too.

"You were at the mines, too, weren't you?" he asked.

In lieu of an answer, a slight grin spread across her lips.

"Ah, now there's an expression I recognize," he said. "Now, behave and answer—"

Pain shot through his groin, and he rolled off her. She'd managed to free a leg and knee him. There hadn't been a lot of force behind the blow, but there didn't need to be.

His vision blurred. He lay recovering as he heard her dash to the car and take off.

"Rafe!" Jackson called to him in his earpiece. "Let's go!"

Rafe sat up to see the RV waiting for him by the road. Shrugging off the throbbing pain and blow to his pride, he shoved to his feet and trotted over to the RV.

When he climbed into the cabin, Dorian was scowling at him. His suit jacket was off, sleeves rolled, and sweat pooling under his arms. "What's the bloody delay?"

Rafe understood his frustration. Priority one in a skirmish was to get the clients to safety. Priory two was minimizing exposure in a public area. Rafe had delayed both.

"I told you to leave me." When he closed the door, the RV pulled away from the curb and toward Interstate 40.

"We don't leave our own. Though next time I might make an exception," Dorian snapped. "I'm calling Mica. Go settle the family." He jerked a thumb toward the back bedroom.

Rafe blinked at him.

"Reassure them, Rafe," he said with exacerbated irritation. "They've been through a bloody ordeal."

Rafe was puzzled. "They're alive." He was a bodyguard, not a grief counselor.

Dorian rolled his eyes. "Pretend you have some compassion, Rafe. Better yet, pretend you're Santino. What would your caring twin do?"

"Fine." Rafe turned and walked toward the back of the RV where Hiba and the children huddled on the bed. He glimpsed himself in the mirror—clothes rumpled with dirt and strands of hair sticking out of his ponytail.

Smoothing his hair back, he cleared his throat. "We're safe now," he said. Despite the authoritative tone he used, they didn't look reassured. "You were all very brave. We'll find a safe place to stop for the night. Everyone did an excellent job following protocol."

They had done some emergency drills their first week together. The main purpose had been to build trust and establish the chain of command should something like today's events happen. Though today's events had been completely unexpected.

Rafe looked from one shell-shocked face to the next. His words didn't seem to offer much comfort. He shifted his weight on his feet as he swallowed. Around him, the RV rumbled in motion on the highway.

What would Santino do?

What his brother needed to do was get his ass back on duty with Rafe so he could handle the emotional fallout. The family under his protection was afraid, and he felt unequipped to handle the situation.

But Santino wasn't coming back. He had his own adventures now.

Jabari hopped off the bed and walked solemnly to Rafe.

Rafe knelt on one knee.

"I thought they would hurt you." He stepped into Rafe and wrapped his arms around him.

Surprised by the boy's affection and fear on his behalf, Rafe awkwardly returned the embrace. "No, no. We're the best team, you see? Not a scratch on any of us." Truthfully, he had a few scratches, a bruised scrotum, and battered pride, but everyone was mostly unharmed.

Except he'd nearly been shot at close range. Midnight had saved him—or whoever she really was. Of course, that wasn't her real name, and she clearly wasn't a traveling saleswoman for a medical device company, as she'd claimed back in Cusco.

"It's okay, my man." Rafe patted Jabari's back. "Maybe tonight we can have a campfire with s'mores."

"What's a s'more?"

"A North American campfire tradition. I'll show you." He stood and ruffled the boy's hair. "Anyone need anything?" he asked. "Water? Juice?" *A shot of tequila?* he thought.

Jabari walked back to the bed and climbed on to snuggle with his mother.

"No, we're okay," Hiba said.

Rafe nodded and turned to leave.

"Rafe? Who were those men? Why were they after us?"

He hesitated at the door. "We'll find out. I promise."

WHEN DIA'S heart stopped racing several minutes into her drive down the Interstate, she called her director.

"Sweeney."

"It's Dia. My intel was right. Someone attacked the Sizani family. Since they only fired at their security team and not the family, I'm suspecting they wanted the Hiba and the kids alive."

"And since you're not calling with a high alert, I'm guessing the team protecting the Sizani family kept them safe." Her director was a seasoned agent in her sixties. Her crisp Queen's English rarely betrayed her Cockney dialect from growing up poor on the East End of London unless she was particularly upset.

"Yes. They're safe." With the car's AC on full blast, Dia finally cooled off. Perching atop the rooftop for an hour in the Texas June heat had been torturous.

"Any idea who sponsored the attack?"

"I don't think it was a US government agency. Beyond that, I'm uncertain. They were skilled, well-armed, and well-funded. They brought a helicopter and half a dozen men against three private security team members. Also, you should know I shot one attacker who would have killed a member of the Sizani protection team."

"Did anyone see you?"

"No."

Only Rafe, and he wouldn't tell authorities she'd been there. Couldn't, because he didn't know who she really was.

She'd covered her tracks and had left no bullet casings behind. Still, she had probably killed a man today. Although it wasn't a first and she'd seen no alternative, she didn't take her actions lightly.

Sweeney said, "I need to alert the General Secretariat and the CIA. The violence will only escalate. US authorities need to put more manpower on the Sizani's."

"Perhaps."

"What's your reluctance?" Sweeney asked.

"I know President Sizani." Dia had developed a rapport when she'd been sent to investigate claims of the discovery of palladium on the island nation. "And I know his opinion of the Rider team currently guarding his family. He's been using their services annually for his family's vacation. He trusts them."

"The situation warrants more than a small security team can manage."

"They have an impressive track record." Dia had studied the Rider team extensively since she had a personal interest in one of the team members. Maybe two.

"And you have an in with their company—" Sweeny's voice hung with an invitation.

Dia glanced in her rearview mirror, ever mindful of ensuring she didn't have a tail. "I'm supposed to go back to Africa to investigate the palladium situation with President Sizani."

"I've another team for that. Do you honestly feel Hiba and her children are best served by the Rider team?"

"Yes for now, but—"

Sweeney cut in, "Then maximize their likelihood of success by telling them the situation."

Dia gaped at the phone on the console. "I'll blow my cover."

"Don't you think it's about time you let certain people know what you really do? Who you really are?"

⚜

RAFE WALKED to the front of the RV, grabbing a water bottle from the cooler, and climbed into the passenger seat beside Jackson as he drove. Dorian sat at the kitchenette table, talking to Mica on the phone about the incident.

"Your intervention was timely," Rafe noted. He rolled his shoulder, still feeling on edge after the attack.

Jackson smiled, his white skin still flush from the adrenaline of battle. "I figure if Bruce Willis can kill a helicopter with a car, then so can I. I admit, I was hoping for more of an explosion."

Rafe shook his head, smiling at the pop-culture reference. Jackson's upbeat nature reminded Rafe of Santino.

"You're not hurt after your tumble?" Rafe asked.

"Nah. The soft ground buffered me. I wouldn't have tried that on asphalt, but you have to know how to tuck and roll."

"Do you have experience with that?"

"Nope. Ten years with the FBI, and I've never been in a gunfight of that magnitude. I'm expecting it'll be a miracle if we don't all get arrested after that fanfare." Jackson's tone was all casual amusement. "And fleeing the scene."

Rafe nodded his agreement. "We were fortunate after our last violent mission not to get reported to authorities. That was, however, in Peru. In the US, it's definitely riskier."

"Everybody knows how to press 'record' on their smartphone," Jackson added.

Rafe considered the tourist who had accused Midnight of stealing his phone. Perhaps she'd seen him recording and had taken the evidence.

"Word of the day," Jackson began, cheerfully.

"Here we go again." Rafe resisted an eye roll, though he did enjoy how Jackson wove his word of the day into an applicable event.

"Filipendulous. Hanging by a thread."

"Apt," Rafe conceded.

"What happened back there? Who were you fighting with?" Jackson asked.

"My guardian angel."

Jackson arched a dark blond eyebrow. "Angel, huh? Looked more like one of the four horsemen the way she took you down."

Rafe scowled. "She didn't take me down. She caught me off guard, is all." He shook his head. "I don't know who she is or who she works for. The first and last time I met her was in Cusco. Santino, Dorian, and I were on protection detail of a client's daughter. On my night off, I met the woman you saw me tussling with. We hit it off, tumbled under the sheets, and I never saw her again until today."

Under the sheets, above the sheets, against the wall... Rafe's lower half pulsed with the memory of his body pressed against Midnight's bare skin.

"Is she holding a grudge against you for a one-night stand? Tracked you down?" Jackson chuckled.

"She's the one who left me before dawn." He disliked hearing his own petulant tone.

"Ouch. That's unexpected. I'd have thought with your slight accent and Latino machismo you'd never be alone in bed unless you wanted it that way."

Rafe pinched the bridge of his nose. "You're not making me feel better about the situation. Besides, I can't tell if you're complimenting me or calling me a man whore."

Jackson laughed but offered no clarity in the matter.

"I need to find her," Rafe said.

Midnight, she'd called herself. Obviously an alias.

"Find who?" Dorian poked his head between the two of them, resting an arm on the seat to steady himself as the RV sped down the road.

"An incredible woman," Rafe said. "We slept together in Peru. She vanished only to reappear today, brandishing a rifle and saving my life."

"Today?"

"She was the woman I rolled in the dirt with just now."

"I didn't see you. I attended to the Sizani family," Dorian said.

Rafe considered how Dorian had been in the back of the RV with Hiba and saw nothing of Rafe's skirmish.

Dorian pressed. "So, she seduced you and reappeared mysteriously today. Is she a spy? Did you tell her anything of value when you slept together?"

Rafe knit his brow. Of course, a former spy would think someone with suspicious behavior was also a spy. Unfortunately, Rafe conceded, Dorian could be right.

"I only divulged facts about me," Rafe said, aware his tone sounded defensive. "Nothing about Rider, if that's what you're asking." He didn't like the implication that he'd been manipulated and used. The very suggestion tainted what he considered to be a wonderfully intimate night. One he'd fantasized about repeating should he ever meet her again.

"Where to, boss?" Jackson interjected, breaking the tension.

Dorian turned his gaze to the driver. "Mica Rider, the actual boss, is routing us to Albuquerque. We'll stop and regroup there."

3

$\mathcal{M}$ica Rider, owner and CEO of Rider Security and Investigation, paced Claire's office, repeatedly making international calls to President Abdul Sizani and repeatedly going to voicemail.

"Ugh." Mica forcefully set her phone down on the desktop. Because it was in a sleek, waterproof protective case, it didn't have the dramatic clamor she was attempting. "I need to tell the President of Comoro his family was under attack, but I can't do that if he doesn't *answer my phone calls.*" She roared the last four words in frustration, running a hand through her blonde waves.

Claire Maltisse, Rider's Operations Controller, sat at her console with three monitors in front of her and nodded as she worked, her sleek bob falling forward and partially obscuring her face. "I sent him an urgent encrypted email to call us. I'm trying to scour social media to see if today's incident in Texas was posted anywhere, but I'm coming up empty. How could a gunfight of the magnitude Dorian described *not* be captured on a half-dozen smartphones?"

"Everyone was busy running for their lives?" Mica suggested, running a hand over her thick platinum waves.

She had a mess to clean up, too, what with her team using one of the Rider vehicles to down a helicopter during a shootout amidst civilians. She would need her FBI contact to help buffer her team from local PD inquiries. Even then, she couldn't be sure they wouldn't all be hauled in for questioning.

Claire groaned in frustration. "I'd hoped to catch a glimpse of the attackers and run some facial recognition to find out who they are and who they work for."

Mica chewed her lip, hating feeling blind and ignorant. And outgunned. A helicopter with six well-armed assailants. *What the actual heck?*

She picked her phone back up and called her father. "Hey, Dad, sorry to bother you on vacation, but you're the closest resource I have to clients in danger."

Her father had traveled to a car show in Las Vegas. He'd been working as an auto mechanic since his retirement from the Marines and had taken a restored Mercedes SL 300 Gullwing to Vegas.

"No problem, sweetheart. I've got the Humvee." Noise filtered in from the background—the dinging of slot machines and drumming of hard rock music.

She gaped at her phone. "You... you took your highly illegal, weaponized vehicle across the country?"

He'd outfitted the thing with rocket launchers and even let her test it out several months ago near his North Georgia cabin. It was like driving a tank.

"Relax," he said. "Its firepower isn't obvious from the outside."

Mica pinched the bridge of her nose. "No, Dad. I do not need the Humvee. You're not going into battle."

"You're no fun."

"I've got clients and three men in an RV westbound on I-40 outside of Amarillo. I need a detail job on the RV they're in."

"Sure. What color does it need to be?" he asked.

"I don't care. I've no idea what color it is now, but anything vastly different and unrecognizable is great."

"Okay. Okay." He paused for a moment. "I've got an idea. Say, who's that woman Mason married, tennis player who now does graphic design?"

"Aurora Meridian." Mica nodded.

"Yeah. Does she do wraps?"

"You mean design vehicle wraps?"

"Yeah."

"Uh. Yes, come to think of it, she does."

Her dad said, "Get me her contact, and I'll be in touch on where the RV needs to go. Who's on the team, anyway?"

"Rafe, Dorian, and Jackson."

Her dad grunted. "Eclectic group. How's the new guy?"

"Jackson is good. Everyone likes him."

According to Dorian's debriefing, so far, Jackson had done well under pressure and escalating danger, although she'd have to talk to him about destroying Rider property. Still he'd made a judgment call to save the client and his team and it had worked.

Claire motioned to Mica for an incoming call.

"Gotta go, Dad. Thanks." She hung up. "Abdul?" she asked Claire.

"No, but I'm putting her through to your phone."

Her?

"Hello, I'm Mica Rider. Who is this?"

"My code name is Midnight. I work for Interpol. I was present at today's events involving the Sizani family."

Mica didn't recognize the woman's faint British accent. "Is that so?" Her voice pulled tight.

"On your side," the woman added. "Rafe can attest that I provided valuable cover fire."

"How do you know Rafe?"

"I know about all the Rider team members, but they don't know me. I've been instructed to debrief you on events in Comoros which led to the attempted abduction of the First Lady today."

"Who attacked my team?" Mica demanded.

"I don't have the who, only the why. I've sent images of the attackers to my organization, so I should have this information by tomorrow."

"Okay." Mica motioned for Claire to record the conversation.

Claire rolled her eyes as if to say, of course, she was already recording the conversation.

Mica wished she could get her hands on those images from today's skirmish. "Tell me the why," she said into the phone as she paced.

"I'll need to relay this information to your team in the Midwest. Can we conference you in at that time so I don't have to repeat everything? I need to know where they're stopping for the night."

Mica's voice hardened. "That type of trust has to be earned. Calling me up and claiming to work for Interpol with a pseudonym like Midnight doesn't cut it."

The woman on the other end gave a sigh of surrender. "The island of Comoros recently discovered a cash crop of palladium. Do you know what that is?"

Beside Mica, Claire nodded vigorously at her desk.

"I'm guessing it has something to do with computers," Mica told Midnight. If Claire knew about this substance, it must be tech related.

"That's right. Palladium is used in catalytic converters, electronics, dentistry, and medicine. Ore deposits are rare."

"So, everyone wants to get their hands on the President's palladium?" Mica asked, realizing after she'd said the question how it came out sounding perverse.

"Currently, Russia is the top miner, so they stand to lose money if new competition arises. Also South Africa. However, the top threat is Sizani's own military, who has him under house arrest."

House arrest. Oh, crap!

The Rider team was caught in the middle of a coup? Mica felt the sudden urge to reach for a potent drink. No wonder her predecessor liked hard liquor. This job was one rollercoaster ride after the next.

Mica scrubbed a hand over her face as her mind churned. "Somebody amongst those groups or others tried to kidnap the President's family today. They could use them as leverage in order to force him to sell or negotiate," Mica deduced.

Midnight said, "That's what my intel suggests, and that's why I've been following your team for the last three days."

Mica frowned. Dorian had a tail for that long and hadn't noticed?

"Tracking device?" Mica asked.

"I had it on your SUV, but the blond—Jackson, right?—crashed the vehicle into a chopper. I can't catch up to your team unless you tell me where they are."

At least Mica was hearing two sides of the same story, and they seemed to match.

"I need some verification that you work for Interpol before I give you my team's location," Mica said.

"Cleaning up this bloody international incident wasn't enough, huh? Fine." She spoke the words in a dismissive tone that suggested she'd expected Mica would demand proof of who she worked for. "I'll have it sent to you in five. Then Claire can text me the location."

The call disconnected.

Mica chewed her lip. "She knows a bit about our team."

Midnight knew everyone on the Sizani detail, including Claire who monitored all missions remotely and provided tech support.

"Now we know how the incident was covered up without social media involvement," Claire said. "But Interpol. Pretty cool, right?"

"I don't know. What if they want to take over custody of Hiba and the kids or turn them over to the US government?"

"Maybe that would be safer for them," Claire suggested. "The FBI would have more resources. I don't know how many more SUVs we can afford to throw at helicopters."

Claire was right. A government agency might be better. But a government agency didn't have the personal relationship and emotional investment Mica and her team had with this family.

"Oh, here's a new email. She works fast."

Mica peered over Claire's shoulder at the file on Midnight. She recognized the government-issued photo of the woman immediately.

Her mouth fell open. "Oh my gosh."

"Wow!" Claire said.

"Text her Dorian's location. Right now."

PETER SHOUP BANGED his fist on the desk of his home office in Chicago.

Fucking Rider team, he stewed.

How could such a small band of misfits be such a menace? He had a hundred employees spread out on various jobs across the world with an unmatched success rate and client satisfaction.

Except where his team crossed paths with Mica Rider.

"Today was a complete cluster ," Shoup said, running a hand over his smooth, bald head.

"The Rider team has been a recurring problem," Nick agreed. He stood beside the head of a grizzly bear mounted on one wall.

Shoup thought of all the times his company had butted heads with Rider employees. First, one of the bodyguards protecting rock-star Ethan Storm had killed one of Shoup's assassins hired to elimi-nate her. Then the Rider team outed Poindexter Pharmaceuticals' illegal activity. The Shoup Group had been shielding the company, having been paid handsomely to keep their street narcotic a secret. Well, the drug was killing people, so that particular security job already had a limited shelf life. But during the debacle, The Rider team had nearly incinerated *him* with a bomb.

Next, Shoup had thought the Fernandez brothers would finish off the ragtag security team since they'd shot and wounded his brother. That had proven to be a foolish hope. Shoup should have known Lautaro didn't have the intelligence or spine for the job. When Shoup had learned that the Fernandez brothers had trapped Santino Alonso in Peru, Shoup had flown down to oversee the death of the Rider team member.

Except, Santino didn't die.

Before Shoup had the chance to bend the situation to his advantage and crush the Rider team, they'd launched a decisive attack. Fortunately, Shoup had fled at the sound of gunfire and avoided their bomb. Mateo Torres and Lautaro Fernandez clearly didn't have the situation under control—evidenced by them both dying in the trailer as it went up in a ball of flames. At the time, Shoup hadn't yet arranged for reinforcements in South America, so he'd been unable to do anything but retreat.

"I shouldn't have underestimated The Rider team." Shoup pulled a bottle of whiskey and a glass out of his desk and poured a drink. He'd known Rider SI was protecting the President's family, but they were only three men. His air strike team should have sufficed.

Lifting the glass, he sniffed the liquid, appreciating its potency.

"A rare mistake on your part," Nick said, fidgeting with his tie.

Why the hell the man wore a suit and tie was a mystery to Shoup. They weren't so formal in his organization. But he did like Nick's calm ambience and quiet efficiency.

"Why do you think they're so successful?" Nick asked.

Shoup drank his whiskey. "Part strategy, part wits and innovation, and part luck."

"What will you tell General Passable?"

"The truth. We underestimated the security team protecting President Sizani's family. We're planning our next move."

"Which is what?" Nick asked.

Shoup looked around at the trophies on his wall. The heads were testament to his superiority and success in taking down fierce animals. He would do the same to the Rider team, and maybe he would mount their heads on a wall for the fun of it.

"I've already deployed another team. We'll catch up to them and then set our trap."

⁂

"Now, you slide the hot marshmallow off onto the chocolate between the crackers to make a sandwich," Rafe explained as he created the s'more.

Jabari smiled when Rafe handed him the desert. "Cool."

"Cool." Rafe smiled back, glad his father had taken some time among their crazy childhood to teach his boys a few fun aspects of growing up. "But also hot. Don't burn your tongue."

Hiba gave Rafe a grateful look as Jabari devoured the sticky mess. The poor woman looked utterly exhausted but was staying strong for her children. They didn't yet have answers for who had attacked them or why, but they were safe in an RV campsite for now. Although their assailants clearly knew they traveled in an RV, Jackson had parked them in one of a dozen campsites, each housing over twenty RVs. The likelihood of an attack tonight was low.

Unnervingly, someone had found them at Cadillac Ranch. They scoured the RV and found no tracking devices. Dorian postulated the Sizani's phones could be cloned, so he had everyone turn them off. The other possibility was the SUV Jackson had been driving, but that was left behind at Cadillac Ranch.

Rafe took a seat in the folding nylon chair, joining Dorian and Jackson in staring at the fire. The air rumbled with the quiet murmurs of people talking from the other RV campsites spread around them. Rafe pulled out his harmonica and played a soft, light tune.

Jabari licked the last streaks of chocolate off his fingers as Hiba stood. "Okay, let's get you ready for bed."

Ada was already inside the RV, showering.

"But, *Maman*, I'm not tired," Jabari complained.

"Well, I am, so we will all lie down."

Sulking, the boy climbed the steps and went inside the RV.

Hiba adjusted her hijab. She had dark skin and large, compassionate eyes. She turned toward the three of them. "Thank you all for what you did today. My children are alive because of you."

Rafe paused his harmonica play and swallowed the lump in his throat. He was seldom directly appreciated by clients for the work he did. As uncomfortable as the gratitude made him feel, perhaps it was better that way. He was a competent bodyguard, though he'd broken protocol going after Midnight, and that could have posed a security threat to his team.

Won't happen again.

Not to mention, the gratitude might be premature. They still didn't know who attacked, why, or if they'd be back.

"You're welcome," Dorian said simply.

"Will arrangements be made to fly us back home tomorrow?" she asked.

Dorian nodded. "Mica is looking into the nature of the attack. We need to make sure your home is also safe before we send you back there."

"I understand." Her brow furrowed, as she hadn't considered the possibility home could be unsafe. "When can I speak to my husband?"

"I hope to give you more information soon. Mica has been unable to speak directly to him but did send text letting him down his family is safe and wanting to her from him."

She nodded and went inside the trailer.

Dorian looked at the two of them left around the fire before pulling out his phone and checking it. "Message from Mica. She says 'someone incoming with information.'"

"What does that mean?" Jackson asked.

Dorian shrugged.

Rafe picked up a stick, tossed it in the fire, and sat back down. Resuming his harmonica, he opted for a melancholy tune. He wanted that update, but he also wanted to know the identity of his guardian angel. He had so many questions. Why had she chosen him in Cusco? Why had she been at the mines? Why had she been at the tourist spot today?

Nearby, a branch snapped, and all three men spun to see a slender figure step out of the shadows.

Dorian and Rafe sprang to their feet. Jackson had one hand on his holstered gun as Rafe slid the harmonica back in his pocket.

"Midnight," Rafe said.

"Dia," Dorian gasped.

Rafe's mind sputtered. *Dia? Dorian's daughter, Dia?*

Dorian shot Rafe a menacing glare.

Yup, Dorian's daughter.

La hostia! Rafe silently swore. His mouth went dry as he tried to recall his exact words from earlier today when he talked about sleeping with his mentor's daughter, before Rafe knew his Midnight was Dorian's Dia.

I'm so dead.

Filipendulous. His life was hanging by a thread.

She wasn't his guardian angel. She was the devil in blue jeans and a t-shirt.

4

"*D*ia, what are you doing here?" her father demanded, his voice harsher than anything she'd heard from him in a long time.

"I'm here to tell you why the first lady of Comoros is in danger." She braced herself for a difficult conversation.

"Mica gave you our location?" he asked, the wheels of her father's mind visibly churning. "How could you possibly know about this situation?"

"I work for Interpol."

Her father went absolutely still. This wasn't how she envisioned telling him—around a campfire in an RV park when they were all exhausted from battle and with the last man she'd bedded staring daggers at her.

"How is that possible?" Dorian asked, his tone a mix of horrified astonishment and didn't-I-teach-you-better.

Except, he'd taught her nothing of the criminal world. He'd kept his past a secret. Perhaps he had taught her that much.

"We can discuss my career choices later. Alone." She glanced at Rafe, who looked like he wanted to tackle her to the ground again, but not so gently. "For now, allow me to brief all of you on the situation in Comoros. Several weeks ago, a government-owned mining team discovered a cache of palladium. President Abdul Sizani had visions of improving island infrastructure, transportation, and education. Others see it as a cash cow they can exploit to get rich."

"Palladium," Jackson interrupted. "This is some type of precious metal?"

"More precious than gold," Rafe said, crossing his arms where he stood.

Even pissed he looked good enough to devour. His ponytail was smoothed back, not the disheveled look when he'd tackled her. His biceps bulged from under his shirt—prominent though not overly bulky. His fingertips gripped his muscles firmly, and for an instant, she wished those fingers were grasping her thighs.

Dia nodded, pulling her focus back to the conversation. "It's used also in dental alloys, automobile catalytic converters to convert polluting hydrocarbons, carbon monoxide, and nitrogen oxide in the exhaust to water, carbon dioxide, and nitrogen. Palladium coatings are used in printed-circuit components, and the list goes on."

She shifted her weight. "Abdul Sizani's general seized government control at the presidential palace and placed the president under house arrest."

"As Interpol, you're qualified to help with an international incident involving palladium," Jackson interjected, his lighter tone suggesting he was on her side in this. At least she had one ally.

"That's right," she said.

"Can you give us a minute?" Dorian looked back and forth from Jackson to Rafe.

The two men nodded and disappeared into the darkness.

Her father paced, looking haggard and worn. "How is this even possible? You lied to me. You lied to your mother. Oh, when she finds out." He had one hand on his hip and the other squeezing his forehead.

Dia had never seen her father so flustered. She'd often wondered how she would tell him about her job and what his reaction might be. She'd wanted him to be proud, but deep down, she'd known to expect disapproval, which was part of the reason she hadn't told him sooner.

"I like my job. I help people."

Dorian shook his head. "I thought you helped people by selling medical devices. Not this. Bloody hell. It never occurred to me to investigate my own daughter."

"I'd hoped you'd be proud of me when you found out." She forced herself to stand her ground and remind herself his anger reflected how much he cared about her. She hadn't even finished telling him the whole truth.

Taking a steading breath, she said, "There's one more thing."

"Of course there is," he snapped. "Thwarting the destabilization of a government is a little beyond Interpol." He cast a sideways glance as he lowered his voice. "And you and I both know an Interpol liaison would have neither the skill nor authority to provide sniper coverage for the Rider team. Twice, assuming Rafe's assessment is accurate."

She'd suspected her father would put those pieces together. Squaring her shoulders, she added, "I also work for MI6."

"No. No! Impossible." He pointed a finger at her. "This is madness."

She'd known he would be upset at her working for the UK secret intelligence service, as he once had. After all, MI6 conducted counter espionage, economic intelligence gathering, political covert actions, and even paramilitary operations.

Working for both organizations gave her great satisfaction. Interpol wasn't just a cover—she did legitimate work helping stabilize other countries and their governments.

She quietly bore his seething glare. She could fight men twice her size and snipe an enemy goon without flinching, but facing anger and disappointment from her father brought dread and angst.

"You're putting your life in danger," he seethed. "I didn't raise you for this."

"Of course you did."

"I beg your pardon?" He stopped to stare at her, hands on his hips.

"You've always taught me the high moral road. Loyalty. Defense of those who can't protect themselves. Imagine my surprise when I learned my father was one of MI6's best spies and questioned if I had what it takes to work for an elite government agency?"

She'd known her father from six to sixteen as a stay-at-home dad while her mother was a writer and bread winner. After that, he would leave for weeks at a time on security details. As a teenager with a social life to attend to, she'd thought nothing of his absences.

When MI6 divulged her father's past career title, they didn't have clearance to tell her exactly what he'd done, but she hadn't need additional proof from them. The evidence had been in her mother's quirky romantic spy novels. Dia had read them all and was stunned to realize the male character had been fashioned after her father. The writing was mostly fictional, but Dia had still felt awe mingled with hurt. Her father had been an entirely other person she'd never known. She'd only known the domesticated, doting version. After she'd had time to process this other side of him, she found she respected and idolized him even more.

"Interpol would never let another country's spy work for them," he said.

She blinked at him.

He tossed his hands in the air. "They don't know. Bloody hell, Dia. The web of lies will be your undoing."

"I do help countries. My Interpol cover is a real job. As a biometrics and cybersecurity specialized officer, I install and train users on software for defense, but I also do coinciding jobs for MI6."

"I'm sure England is thrilled to know the exact security systems of every place you've done installations."

Dia shrugged. "That's not exactly state secrets."

"What sector?"

She hesitated, training kicking in on how she wasn't supposed to divulge any of this. Her father may be the one person outside of MI6 she could tell. Besides, he still had the connections to find out anyway. "GS."

He let out a slow breath, shaking his head. "I guess that makes sense."

The Gold Stopwatch sector had been named for one of the first joint operations of the CIA and MI6 in the 1950s when they worked together to tap into the Soviet Union's landline cables in Berlin. The CIA had called it Operation Gold. MI6 referred to the effort as Operation Stopwatch. Later, the two formed a joint sector secretly known as Gold Stopwatch, or GS, with operatives having joint positions in both organizations in order to work together.

Dia's dual citizenship, ability to sound British like her father or American like her mother, language fluency in several dialects, and bronze skin like her father with his partial Indian heritage enabled her to play different roles in different situations.

"We have to tell your mother," he said. Then, as if dreading the task, added, "We can't tell your mother."

"I'll tell her about Interpol. She can't know the other." Telling her mother would be easier than her father. In fact, Dia suspected her mom would show at least some amount of pride for her daughter.

Dorian sat heavily in one of the folding chairs. "Do you like it?"

"I love it. I travel the world and meet new people. I have a pivotal role in helping people and overall contributing to global economic and political stability." At his arched eyebrow, she added, "I help countries establish advanced security systems using fingerprints, facial recognition, and biosensors."

Dorian scrubbed a hand over his face. "This business with the Sizani's will get messy."

"I'd expect nothing less with billions of dollars on the line."

"People will die."

"Some of them already have, Dad." Not only had some attackers from today probably not survived, but the President's personal security team had likely been murdered when General Passable seized control.

"More," her father growled.

"I'm aware. I'm here to help make sure the first lady and first family aren't part of the casualties. And you," she added, wondering if he'd take offense to her suggestion of his needing her help. She braced for him to dismiss her, claiming it was for her own safety.

"You have already been very helpful."

She exhaled at his compliment and the rush of relief his words brought.

"I agree, we need your help," he continued. "I don't like knowing you'll be in harm's way, and your mother will have my hide if anything happens to you. But you obviously have the skill set and resources we need, as evidenced by your sniper work today."

Dia stuffed down her excitement at his reluctant acceptance. While she'd had a variety of combat training and weapons education, she'd only been in a handful of dangerous situations. Still, she felt she could help him and help the Rider team.

Footsteps approached, and Dia knew Rafe was making sulky strides back to the camp with shuffling feet. He appeared with Jackson beside him.

"Can I have a moment with Rafe, Dad?"

Jackson quietly slipped back inside the RV.

Dorian pursed his lips as he stood. He walked to Rafe and brushed shoulders with him. "We'll be discussing my daughter tomorrow."

"Yes, sir." Respectfully, he looked Dorian in the eye and gave a nod of his head. Rafe appeared tentatively relieved, as if discussing something tomorrow meant Dorian wasn't killing him tonight.

When her father entered the RV cabin and closed the door, Rafe paced by the dying fire.

Suspecting this may take a while, Dia pulled a log from a nearby pile and tossed it into the pit. Ambers danced from the disturbance as flames licked at the new piece of fuel.

"You—" Rafe began. "We... How could you—" His face flushed red, and he shook his hands in the air.

He was still as handsome as the first time she'd seen him in Peru.

Strong cheekbones below a pair of dark eyes. Bronze skin covered a lean, muscular body. His deep voice had a hint of South American accent, the way hers was lightly British, but he could make it thicker when he wanted to lay on the charm or hide it to blend in better with North Americans.

Amused by his flustered behavior, she crossed her arms. "Use your words," she coaxed, trying to lighten the mood and failing.

He shot a look of daggers at her. "We slept together."

"I remember." How could she forget? The night had been one of delicious surprises and the first time she'd ever had a one-night stand.

Rafe continued, "And you don't work for a medical device company. You work for Interpol. And you knew your father and I worked together when we slept together."

"An apt summary."

"You used me."

She bristled at that accusation. "As I recall, the evening was filled with mutual pleasure." She had fully intended to coax information out of Rafe about her father that night. Seduce secrets out of him. Something she'd never before attempted. But once the conversation had flowed, she liked Rafe too much to use him for her own gain. She'd decided that if she wanted to learn more about her father's current work, she would have to confront him.

"You left before dawn," Rafe said pointedly.

Dia scoffed. "Because you've never done that to a woman?"

He started to protest and then snapped his mouth shut.

She smirked.

At her expression, his eyes flared with indignation. She probably shouldn't find his frustration so adorable. Of course, she'd left before dawn. They'd had engaging conversation, tantalizing chemistry, and sensual passion—in that order—but she knew little about the man working with her father. Besides, she couldn't risk her father spotting her in Peru when she hadn't been ready to divulge her career choice.

"That was you at the Cusco mines?" Rafe asked when he reigned in his irritation once again.

"Yes."

"Why were you following me?"

"I was following my father."

The hurt expression on Rafe's face surprised her. Truthfully, she'd seen the skirmish outside the hotel in Cusco and went to the mines to protect both Rafe and her father. She'd provided rifle coverage as she had today at Cadillac Ranch, keeping out of view.

"Look," she began sternly, not liking the gnawing sensation in her abdomen that wanted her to take this man's hand and tell him that night meant something to her, too.

They didn't know each other. Not really. The bottom line was, they had a job to do, and she would never have seen him again if she hadn't been told to help the Rider team with the Sizani's.

Liar.

She might have found a way to see him again.

"Let's put aside the past so we can work on this case," she said.

"Why did you run away from me earlier today?"

"I didn't know at the time my gaffer would order me to fill your team in later. A gaffer is a boss," she clarified at his confused look. "I had a tip that an attempt to kidnap the Sizani's was in the works. I showed up to see if it was true or not."

"Why didn't you warn us?"

"I only had a tip. Might have been false." She'd been worried enough to bring her rifle, though, so perhaps she should have trusted her instincts.

He glanced at the fire and then back up at her. His brown eyes were tiger eye stones with streaks of gold in the light. Shadows danced over the faded scar on the side of his face. The scar and his ponytail were the only features different from his twin she'd noted when she'd seen photos of Santino.

"You'll be working with us until the family is safe?" he asked.

"Looks that way."

"Well, I hope you have other sleeping arrangements. The RV is full." With that, he turned and went inside the vehicle, closing the door behind him.

Dropping into a nearby chair, Dia stared at the small crackling fire. She hadn't made sleeping arrangements, nor did she assume she would sleep here. This would be one hell of a working environment —an incensed father, a scorned one-night lover, and a former FBI agent amused with them all.

*M*ica arrived home to quiet darkness. She let herself inside, dropped her keys on the counter, and locked everything back up. After resetting the alarm, she crept down the hall to Allen's room, where she watched her son sleep peacefully for a few moments.

Once in her room, she showered and readied for sleep before crawling into bed beside her husband David. He stirred and rolled over to pull her into his arms. His chest was bare, with exposed muscles, and his brown hair handsomely disheveled. How did he always seem to know how to make her feel better?

"Hey, hon." He nuzzled into her neck. "Rough day?"

"The roughest. President Sizani is under house arrest by his own military—that will be tomorrow's headlines." She stared at the ceiling in the darkness. "His rogue general wants to force him to yield so he can take ownership of the newly discovered crop of palladium in order to make billions in profits. Meanwhile, someone sent a team to kidnap the president's wife and children, who are currently under my protection. Now their vacation has turned into a nightmare, while I'm stuck worrying if we'll be out matched the next time they strike. Whoever *they* are."

"So, just another day at the office." His deep voice rumbled through her.

"Yeah," she said on a sigh.

"Everyone's okay right now?"

"Yeah."

"Before I met you, I never imagined my future wife would have a more stressful job than me."

"Yeah."

David worked as an ER physician. When they'd met, he worked seventy-two hours a week. Before having a son, they both pulled about sixty hours a week while snagging four weeks of vacation per year. Now, David had cut back to thirty-six and she to forty, except for when critical events like today required her to work longer hours than usual.

David placed a hand on her cheek and turned her head so she was looking into his eyes—those soft green eyes. "What else is churning up there?"

"I want to fly out. Be another body with boots on the ground to help."

"Okay."

"Okay?"

"Mica, I knew when I married you that you would have to travel. I appreciate how much effort you've made to stay in Atlanta when you could travel as much as your employees. I also appreciate the days you work from home. I don't sleep well when you go into danger, but I knew who and what you are when I fell in love with you. I'm not here to hold you back. If you think you need to be with your client and with your team, be with your client and with your team. Allen and I will manage a few days without you."

"Who and what am I?"

He grinned. "Baby, you're a superhero."

She chuckled. David had known her briefly in high school when she'd worn her faded Justice League t-shirt and defended those who didn't know how to defend themselves. In her mind, she simply carried out what her father had taught her, looking out for the underdog.

David lightly kissed her lips. "Maybe you don't wear a cape, but you're still a superhero. Still defending others against those trying to hurt or take advantage of them. So go do what you need to do. Tomorrow. Because tonight, you're mine."

He ran fingers along and under the edge of her panties as he nibbled her ear.

She sucked in a breath and smiled as her body instantly responded to his familiar touch. Rolling into him, she pressed her body against his firm warmth. When their lips met in a slow, searing kiss, she forgot about her worries.

DIA SLEPT in her vehicle's back seat and had a crick in her neck the next morning to prove it. She could have rented a motel room nearby, but after the lukewarm reception from her father and downright frigid one from Rafe, she thought they might be tempted to leave her behind when daylight struck.

When Jackson fired up the RV, he waved at her. She cranked her car and followed them to a diner where everyone piled out for breakfast. A light breeze sifted through the air as the waking sun peaked above distant trees.

When Dia approached the group, Hiba was the only one who smiled at her.

The First Lady threw her arms around Dia. "*Assalamu alaikum.*"

"*Wa alaikum salaam,*" Dia said, returning the wishes for peace.

Still holding her, the woman said, "I'm so glad you're here. When Dorian told me you were joining us, I was happy to have a familiar face."

Dia pulled back, saying, "I'm sorry for what you're going through. Let's talk over food." She didn't like lingering in the parking lot where they were exposed targets in the unlikely event they'd been followed.

With a child on either side, Hiba walked inside as Rafe held the door. Dia brought up the rear. She half-expected him to let the door close on her, but he held it despite his implacable gaze, which he leveled coolly at her. He looked polished in a suit, hair pulled back.

She grinned, oddly liking how he'd taken such offense to being a one-night stand. She'd thought perhaps the emotion revealed he cared, but that may have been her own wishful thinking. His anger might reflect nothing more than a damaged ego. Regardless, they currently had a job to do and people to protect.

Dia slipped away to use the restroom and take stock of the layout and all the exit points. In the bathroom, she freshened up as best she could to appear as though she hadn't slept in a car last night.

When she returned, the group had snagged one of the larger tables in the party room, which afforded them some privacy away from general dining. Hiba sat between her children, with Dia across from her. To Dia's chagrin, her father sat to her right and Rafe to her left. Jackson took an end seat nearest the entranceway to the room.

After they placed drink orders, Dia filled in Hiba regarding the mineral people were willing to kidnap and kill to acquire. She kept the conversation somewhat coded to avoid upsetting the children as much as possible.

"Abdul was so excited to find the palladium," Hiba said wistfully.

The server returned with drinks and took food orders before breezing back out of the room.

Dorian spoke, "Here are the next steps. In a few hours, we'll stop at Holbrook. Mica and her father found a custom paint shop available for a rush job. There where we'll have the camper revamped. We'll swap out license plates somewhere in case the men after us have that information. We stay on the move until it's safe to get you on a plane home."

"When will that be?" Hiba asked.

Dia pursed her lips. "Hard to know. The UN will try talks before they escalate by sending troops to protect your country. I can't place a time frame on the stability. One week or one month. I don't know."

The island nation was no stranger to violence and death. President Abderemane had been assassinated in 1989 by rebel forces led by a disgruntled former army commander who had resigned over a dispute with Abderemane. In total, the country had suffered more than twenty coups or attempted coups since French independence in 1974. The First Lady knew all of this and had no doubt been mulling over these facts since hearing about the attack. With the country's history in mind, Dia had little comfort to offer.

The food arrived, with plates of piping hot eggs, sausage, and pancakes. The three Rider team members and Dia picked up their forks to eat.

"We must pray," Hiba said, looking at each one of them as if they were barbarians.

Halted forks around the table dinged onto their plates as they set them down.

Hiba held up her arms, showing her hands interlocked with her children's. "Hold hands," she instructed her bodyguards.

They did so, Dia taking Rafe's in her left hand and her father's in her right as Hiba gave thanks, "Dear Heavenly father..."

Dia's body warred with herself. Half of her brain registered the familiar comfort in her father's grip and the childhood memories associated with it. The other half felt the zing of warmth from Rafe's touch, raising memories of the night his hands had roamed every inch of her body.

When the prayer ended and hands were set free, she could breathe again. She reached for a water glass and gulped the cold liquid.

This would be a long, awkward assignment.

***

MICA PACKED HER TRAVEL BAG, including her expensive bullet resistant suit she seldom wore. All Rider employees had one. As for weapons, she would get a gun from Dorian or her father after she arrived in Arizona.

As she zipped her suitcase, Allen called to her from another room, and she bounded up the stairs, excited to greet him. After unlocking the gate at the top, she took the first door on the right into his room.

"Hey! Good morning, sunshine."

He sat in bed, clutching his favorite stuffed animal, a fluffy blue bear who'd seen his share of the washing machine over the last year.

"Mama!" he squealed with a smile.

She scooped him into her arms, loving his excitement to see her but feeling the sting of worry and guilt at how she would miss him for the next few days.

"How about some breakfast?"

"I want strawberries."

"I bet we can wrangle some strawberries for you." She carried him down the stairs.

When she reached the bottom, he squirmed to be set down.

"Walk," he said.

"You got it." She promptly set him on his feet and let him walk to the kitchen, where David scooped him up.

"Hey, bud. Good morning." He kissed his cheek.

"Daddy."

David plopped Allen into his highchair as Mica fetched strawberries and a glass of milk in a spill proof cup.

After she set Allen up with his light breakfast, she opened her laptop to check email, and David poured both of them a second cup of coffee.

When she read the first email, her stomach plummeted.

FROM: Hoyle
    SUBJECT: LT
    MESSAGE: Favors need to be repaid. It's time.

"Why the long face?" David asked, blowing on his steaming cup.

She swallowed and turned the screen to face him.

He leaned over and read it. "Sounds ominous," he remarked.

"Lucius Titan wants me to break him out of prison."

"A man with his resources doesn't need your services."

"You're right. It's about cashing in favors and forcing me to break the law."

"What will you do?"

She had received valuable information from Lucius over the years while he was caged at a US Penitentiary, but no amount of information was worth breaking him out of prison and risking her own incarceration. Behind bars or not, he would still run his criminal empire—well, more like his criminal *small town* since being crushed by the Rider team under Maxine, David's mother, several years ago.

"For now, I'll stall. I need to handle the Sizani family first. I can tell you I'm not breaking Lucius out, but I don't know an alternative yet. I won't sacrifice everything we have for that devil."

"Devil," Allen echoed.

"One crisis at a time," David agreed. "What time is your flight?"

"Eleven."

He gave her a kiss on the cheek. "Text me when you land. After that, I know you'll be busy, but touch base once a day, okay?"

"Will do." She turned her attention back to her computer, where she confirmed her flight was on time.

As she stared at the screen, her stomach churned with dread. How would she handle Lucius' request? She couldn't ask any of her employees to risk such an egregious breach of law, either. If Lucius considered her failure to act as a failure to uphold repayment for favors, then he might send his corrupt ex-military forces against her, her family, or her team.

His wrath might be a risk she'd have to face.

Rock, meet hard place.

And she was crushed between them.

6

After the awkwardness of the group meal, Dia drove her car in welcomed silence, following the rest of the group inside the RV. The three and a half-hour drive from the breakfast restaurant in Albuquerque to the small shop on the outskirts of Holbrook had been uneventful. Short, bushy vegetation seemed to span for miles with a backdrop of mountains.

At the shop, Jackson remained in the RV, awaiting instructions on where to park, as Dorian took a walk around the perimeter.

Dia joined Rafe and approached a broad man pushing sixty dressed in jeans and a 'What happens in Vegas, stays in Vegas' t-shirt.

Rafe shook hands with the man. "Jim, good to see you again."

"Mica told me you were in a bit of a scuffle." His pale blue eyes glittered with intrigue.

"Something like that." Rafe rubbed his neck.

"That suit seems fancy for Arizona in June."

"It's hot, but it is also bullet resistant. Seems prudent to wear it under the circumstances."

"Which are what exactly? Mica didn't give me a lot of details."

Both men turned towards Dia. "Dia can fill you in," Rafe said. "She's Interpol. Dia this is Jim McMillan, Mica's father."

She was Mica Rider now, Dia knew, so McMillan had been her maiden name.

"So, it's Agent or Inspector?" Jim shook Dia's hand, giving her a warm smile.

"Just Dia is fine. How about we get the RV started and I'll update you on the situation?"

Dia processed this new information with Jim's arrival. Mica's father—who she recalled from MI6's file was retired military—supported the Rider team. She hadn't known Rider SI had allied with civilians. Perhaps this was common in private security.

"You work for your daughter's company?"

"Nah. I'm enjoying retirement."

"By retirement, he means working on classic car restoration and displaying them at shows," Rafe added.

"No point in being idle." Jim shrugged.

"You must be proud of your daughter's entrepreneurship."

Jim beamed. "Very proud of her. Though she's been in charge for several years now, and this is the first time she's asked for my help." He put his hands on his hips. "I'm an under-utilized resource."

Dia gave him a conspiratorial smile. "A good security agent knows to save her secret weapon for times of emergency."

Jim chuckled.

Rafe shot her an inquiring look, as if wondering what Dia's secret weapon was.

She arched an eyebrow at him. Wouldn't he like to know?

The gleam in his eye told her he'd taken their exchange as if she'd been flirting.

Her cheeks flushed.

Damn, I was flirting.

Jim glanced between the pair of them. "Pull the RV around back.

I've already checked the place out, but I'm sure you have your protocols to follow. There's a nice breakroom the family can hang out in until we're done here."

Rafe turned toward her. "I'll do a walk through if you tell Jackson where to park."

She nodded.

AFTER THE RV rested in the shop, Dia left with Jim to update him, and Dorian remained with the Sizani family. Rafe and Jackson walked the perimeter of the car detail shop as the camper underwent its makeover. Both he and Jackson wore their bullet resistant suits despite the increasing heat.

"Kind of crazy how a summer vacation turned into an international incident," Jackson said.

Rafe twirled his harmonica between the fingers of his left hand. "They'll try again. If not whoever sent the last team, then someone else. Dia said there were billions of dollars at stake."

"Hmm... Dia." Jackson's mouth twisted conspiratorially.

"What?"

"You like her. I saw the way you glanced at her throughout breakfast. If I noticed, her father probably noticed."

"I don't like her," Rafe grumbled. He had watched her warm greeting with Hiba and admired Dia's body as she strode past him into the diner. He'd also noted the way she carefully arranged her silverware at the table as she'd put her napkin in her lap. Curious.

Jackson interrupted his thoughts. "Oh, I see. You don't mind then if I—"

Before he could control himself, Rafe's hackles raised. "Don't you dare think about making a move on her."

Jackson chuckled. "Yeah, you definitely don't like her."

Rafe wanted to smack the smug look off his friend's face, but he was angrier for allowing himself to be baited than by Jackson teasing him. Admittedly, he'd glanced at Dia during breakfast, wondering when he'd next have an opportunity to talk with her alone.

"Word of the day. Canoodle. Kissing and snuggling."

Rafe kicked his toe at a tuft of grass growing from a crack in the concrete. "I don't know why I like her. She's obviously indifferent to me."

"That's one conclusion." Jackson slid his hands into his pockets.

"What else could explain how we sat next to each other throughout breakfast and she never spoke to me?"

Jackson shrugged. "She was doing her job, talking to the client's wife. You were doing your job, engaging with Jabari so the boy didn't start dwelling on the shootout. Besides, how much can Dia say to you with Dorian on the other side of her?"

Rafe nodded and grudgingly appreciated Jackson's support. He also appreciated him not pointing out the other obvious alternative—that Dia wasn't romantically interested in him.

"Gentlemen," Dia greeted them and stepped between the pair when they parted to make room for her to join.

She wore the same clothes as yesterday, and Rafe knew she'd slept in her car. He felt mildly guilty about that, but there actually hadn't been room in the RV. Besides, he'd barely slept. He'd been too close to her father for comfort after the man learned Rafe had been her lover and she had a secret other life.

Walking in the middle between Rafe and Jackson, she kept pace. "The RV is underway. Mica certainly has her connections."

"How are you holding up?" Rafe asked.

"What do you mean?"

"You told your father you work for one of the world's most prestigious international agencies. And he knows you go headlong into danger. Must take some adjusting."

Dia glanced at Rafe and frowned. "He's the one who needs to adjust. My adjustment already happened when I found out a few years ago that my father used to be a spy. And, oh, by the way, my mom's spy romance novels? Yeah, all about him."

"You read them?"

"Of course I read them. I was a teenage girl and had been told they were off limits. Now, I wished I'd never turned the first page!"

Rafe laughed, and Dia smiled at him in surprise.

Jackson squinted up at the sun. "If you want to compare unusual father stories, Rafe has you beat. I'm going to cool off indoors in the AC." He peeled away, oblivious to the glare Rafe shot him. As Jackson walked away, he whistled *That's Amore*, a song Rafe had played on the harmonica more than once on their cross-country trip. The sound trailed behind Jackson as he disappeared.

"What's Jackson talking about?" Dia asked.

"My father was schizophrenic."

"Oh. That night we met at the bar you mentioned he'd passed away, but I didn't know he had a mental illness."

"Neither did I. Not for a long time. He was convinced the apocalypse would happen in his lifetime. My brother and I spent our childhood traveling around the southern US, Central and South America, learning how to survive—everything from combat to planting crops to delivering babies."

"You've delivered babies?" She blinked at him.

"I have many talents. Some of them useful. Some of them superfluous."

"Unless there's an apocalypse." She stuck her hands in her pockets.

He chuckled. "Yeah, unless that."

"You seem like you've adjusted to living in the pre-Mad Max era."

"My brother and I spent a few years as rebellious teenagers after our dad died, but, yeah, we adjusted. Still didn't wind up with a normal job, but this is better. Security suits our adventurous personalities and... unique qualities." Rafe had almost given up thinking he'd ever find his tribe. Then his grandfather had reached out to his friend, Jim McMillan, who'd asked his daughter to take a chance on two men with an unconventional rearing and unusual skill sets.

Dia bumped her elbow playfully into his. "Normal is overrated." She gestured at the harmonica in his hand. "Was that part of your survival training, too?"

"This was my father's. He played it on road trips and around campfires. Seemed appropriate to bring it along this trip." Rafe tucked the instrument into his breast pocket.

Dia fell silent.

"Why me?" he asked. At her puzzled expression, he added, "Why me in Cusco?"

He glanced down at her long lashes and dark honey colored skin.

Her throat bobbed in a swallow. "I didn't mean to hurt your feelings. When I learned my father was in Peru at the same time I was on an assignment there, I tracked him down, wanting to see what his job really consisted of. I saw you and your brother protecting Ava Sharp. I followed my dad and you from Lima to Cusco. That evening when I introduced myself at the bar, I was drawn to you. My actions weren't premeditated. You intrigued me. I wanted to meet the man with the enviable relationship working with my father. I didn't know I'd like you. I certainly didn't expect to go to bed with you. But I couldn't hang around after that in case my father showed back up."

"You like me?" Visions of canoodling filled Rafe's mind.

Damn Jackson and his subliminal words of the day.

She snorted. "We had an incredible night together—including but not exclusive to the sex. I've never done that with anyone. Yes, I like you." She shifted her gaze down to the pavement as she added, "And we have two very different lives."

He didn't like the finality of her last sentence and scowled at the harsh implication. She admitted to an incredible night but sounded as though she had no intention of repeating it with him.

He found this entirely unacceptable.

"Give me the status," Shoup demanded from Nick.

They sat in the back of Shoup's Lincoln as his driver sped him to his private plane. Shoup stared out at the watery Chicago streets on a rainy day. He needed the boatload of cash he would earn for bringing in the Sizani family. Rent for his building wasn't cheap. State of the art security equipment and weapons wasn't cheap. His salary sure as hell wasn't cheap. His private jet and the fuel to fly it wasn't cheap. He hadn't become a millionaire by shirking his duties to deliver the client's demands.

He wouldn't start now.

Nick sat calmly, legs crossed in the spacious back seat. "The last blip we got was in Albuquerque. They've been off-line ever since."

Because General Passable, who was behind the coop and desired the kidnapping of the Sizani family, had access to President Sizani's security, he could trace the family phones, which were all monitored as part of security protocol in case anyone was abducted. Shoup had been given this access to track the family in order to abduct them. Almost poetic.

Meanwhile, the family flitted across the country completely unaware. Except now that his strike team failed and the Rider team likely suspected they'd been traced somehow, phones were off.

When Shoup had learned they were in Albuquerque, he didn't have a new team in place in time to pounce. "The new team is ready?"

"Almost. Some are still in transit."

Like me, Shoup thought. He would be on site for this encounter to ensure the kidnapping was a success.

"You doubled the size?"

"Trippled. Most are flying into Vegas since the family seems to be headed west. When a phone's activated, we'll close it on them."

"As soon as we're close enough, we'll pounce. Attack. I don't care if it's the middle of the night and we have to swarm a hotel. I don't care if the family is cruising down the interstate. The clock's ticking."

Nick tilted his head contemplatively. "Yeah, we can make this work. We can do it like the Lange job where we forced the hotel reception at gunpoint to identify the target's room. If they're on the road and we have a little extra notice, we can shut down the road like the Mitchell job."

Shoup smirked. He'd liked the Mitchell one. His team had called the state highway patrol through false routing, claiming to be the NSA and alerting them to a terrorist in a U-Haul carrying a bomb. The cops shut down a stretch of road, blocking every entrance ramp.

Shoup didn't care about civilian casualties when they blew up the target they were after, but he didn't want other cars on the road to add unpredictable, panicked drivers who might interfere with his plan. By the time authorities had figured out they'd been duped, Shoup's men and all the evidence had been evacuated.

"Good. Good," Shoup said. "Let's run through a few more contingencies, including how we're going to cover major airports in case we don't get any further signals from one of their phones."

Mica arrived in Phoenix, picked up the rental car Claire had arranged, and began the drive toward Holbrook. On her way, she let David and Claire know her progress and checked on some of her other employees on various jobs.

After three hours of driving, she reached the detail shop where the Sizani's RV was getting a makeover. She had debated simply renting a new one, but that would create the same paper trail this one might have. Whoever they were up against had the resources to hunt them down with choppers. Because they weren't dealing with typical adversaries, Mica needed to think outside the box on this one.

When she had to return the rental, she could worry about restoring the RV to its former appearance. Alternatively, she may have to add the purchase of an RV to the Sizani's bill due to the "defacement" of property.

When she parked and exited the car, her father waited outside to greet her. He was a stout man in his late sixties who still retained large upper body muscles, having kept in shape after military retirement over two decades ago. Despite his age, he had a full head of hair, although its salt and pepper color was more salt than pepper.

He wrapped her in an embrace. "How are you, sweetheart?"

She felt like a child in his arms, a little girl without a care in the world for those brief seconds and not a woman in over her head protecting a family against greedy men while weighted down with angst about how she would deal with Lucius Titan once the Sizani's were safe.

"I'm okay."

When her father broke off the hug, he said, "The family's in the break room, watched over by Dorian and Jackson. Rafe and Dia are walking the perimeter."

"Thanks for your help, Dad."

"Anytime. What's your next move?"

"Today, we'll finish the RV and get the family tucked into a hotel. Tonight, I'll convene with the team and review the plan. I need an update from Dia concerning where things stand with President Sizani's house arrest."

Dorian stepped outside from the detail shop, and Mica squinted up at him.

"I'll give you two a minute," her father said, stepping back inside the shop.

Dorian's lean figure towered over her, and she noticed a tension around his eyes she'd rarely seen.

"So, Dia is Interpol."

"Quite right. So she tells me. And that makes me the boob who thought she worked for a medical device company." He ran a hand through his locks of hair, dark except for gray around the ears.

"Anything else about her occupation you want to share with me?"

"No."

She thought not. Although his single word answer was resounding and final—and spoke volumes—he didn't pretend to not know what Mica was asking. They both knew Interpol didn't give its liaisons power to gun down criminals. Something else was at play here. For now, Mica didn't need the details so long as Dia was on their side and keeping authorities from arresting her team for violence in public places.

"I didn't see that career choice coming." Mica had met Dorian's wife Katie, a sweet and witty woman, at a summer cookout once but hadn't yet met his daughter.

"Nor did I." His tone suggested he somehow considered Dia's surprise employment as a short-coming on his part as parent.

"Perhaps you should see this as a credit to you as a father rather than a failing as a former spy."

"How so?"

"As a father, you gave your daughter independence and therefore you didn't know her secrets."

"I trusted her. Trusted that she wouldn't lie to her mother and me."

"What does your heart tell you? That she lied to deceive and manipulate you? Or that she lied to protect you—and maybe to protect herself because she feared your reproach?"

He frowned, but Mica thought he would consider her words and find comfort in them eventually. She didn't know Dia's character, but being the daughter of one of the men Mica most respected and having helped her team even before obligated to do so meant Dia had already earned Mica's respect.

"Back to business. How do you think the helicopter team found you?" Mica asked.

"Family phones. Their personal home security detail would have ensured they could track the family for safety purposes. With the coup, the military could access their tracking software."

Mica nodded. That had been Claire's supposition as well.

Turning a corner a block away, Rafe and Dia came into view. Rafe looked polished in his suit and ponytail while Dorian's daughter wore black stretch pants, a white blouse, and a fitted vest. The pair of them conversed with the familiarity of friends, and... and Rafe was smiling at her.

Mica blinked. Since hiring him, she hadn't known the man was capable of smiling. He was an exceedingly competent employee whom she trusted, but not a smiler.

Beside her, Dorian made a disgusted sound.

She peered up at him and was shocked to see an unprecedented amount of negative emotion. The man who remained unfazed in life-or-death situations was rattled by the sight of his daughter with man.

"Is this something I should be concerned about?" Mica asked as Dorian's jaw tightened. "Are they dating?" she pressed, though she wondered how that could be possible with so short an acquaintance.

"I don't think so."

"But you object to the idea of it. To Rafe?"

"I have no objections to Rafe. He has commendable character. I object to knowing they've slept together."

"Oh." Mica couldn't fathom how that was possible. Dia had only joined the team last night.

As if reading her confusion, Dorian said, "They met when we were in Cusco, and—" he exhaled, "—and Rafe let slip what happened, not knowing the woman he'd bedded was my daughter."

Mica suppressed a smile at the awkwardness of the situation that lent credence to the phrase 'never kiss and tell.' Dorian wasn't amused.

"At least you know the merit of Rafe," she offered. She knew the Alonso brothers' loyalty and dedication but not Dia's. Mica wondered whose emotions were really at stake here.

When they were within speaking distance, Dorian introduced Mica to Dia.

"We appreciate your help," Mica said as she shook the woman's hand.

"I've been assigned to help until the president and his family are safe." Dia's voice had an airy British accent. She flicked a wild strand of her short chocolate hair out of her dark eyes and shook firmly.

Assigned by Interpol or whoever she actually works for? Mica wondered.

Rafe's gaze darted to Dia then away, as if keen to note how her joining them was both limited in duration and not voluntary.

"Any news from Comoro?" Mica asked.

Dia replied, "So far only intelligence gathering. Today, the British ambassador will attempt peace talks. That process could take days or weeks. If they can't persuade the general to relinquish his control of the government, the next steps will be UN troops taking back control."

"Hope for peace, prepare for war."

"Yes."

Mica nodded. "Let's wrap up the RV—pun intended—go to the hotel Claire arranged for us, and we'll discuss the next steps to keep Hiba and her family safe."

***

RAFE WOKE AT FIVE AM. He glanced over at Jackson who slept in the other queen bed and checked his phone for any notifications related to movement outside the Sizani family's room where they had small, mounted, motion-censored cameras hanging out of plain view. All still and quiet. His room was directly across the hall and his phone app would have alarmed at an intruder, but he liked to check anyway for peace of mind.

Restless, Rafe tossed off the covers, dressed in shorts and a t-shirt, and pocketed his phone. He scrubbed a hand over his face as he took the stairs down to the fitness center. Maybe he should have had coffee first, but a workout would wake him up also.

After sliding his key card over the sensor, he tugged open the door. The "fitness center" consisted of two treadmills and a few weights. He glimpsed one other person in the room doing yoga by the mats. Halting, he did a doubletake to look at the woman.

Dia was face down with her butt up in the air.

And now he was awake. All of him.

"I remember that pose the first time we met," he said, sauntering over to her.

"I bet you do." She raised her leg, bent her knee, and stretched her quadriceps.

"We haven't tried that one." He rolled the ball over to her and began doing crunches, noting the arrangement of items on her mat—hand towel folded in a tidy square and aligned at the corner of the mat with key card and phone symmetrically beside it.

"You were a lot more charming in the hotel bar than you've been since."

"You found me charming?" he asked.

She alternated legs. "That's the message you took from my observation?"

"I wasn't working that night, and I didn't know you were my mentor's daughter. And I didn't know you were lying to me."

"You're only happy when you're not working?"

Instead of pointing out that he'd listed other reasons for his disgruntlement, he opted for flirtation. "I was happy spending a night with you. Could be again." He wriggled his eyebrows.

She shook her head and stretched up into mountain pose. "Happiness is choosing to live in the moment."

Because he sensed she had more to say on the subject, he dropped his attempt as seductive tactics. "Enlighten me," he said simply.

"People seek happiness like it's a tangible object in the future. It's the next job, the next promotion, the next relationship, the next romp in the sheets. Happiness is achieved by finding something in every moment to be happy about."

He frowned as he moved over to the weights. Did she think he only wanted to sleep with her? Maybe he could see how his playful behavior would be perceived that way. What did he want if not just sex? More nights of long conversations over drinks? Something deeper?

"Are you telling me I only have to choose to be happy?" He thought of his brother, Santino, who seemed to do just that. Rafe wasn't sure his own personality could simply flip on the happy switch.

Dia rolled the ball closer to where he did arm curls and began stomach crunches. "As long as you don't bypass emotions."

"What do you mean?" he asked.

"Happiness isn't a fake-it-'til-you-feel-it thing. You have to digest emotions—allow yourself to feel them, experience them. Acceptance, not dismal."

"Give me an example." Even as he asked, he wondered how they happened on a philosophical conversation this early in the morning.

"Okay. I was perched on that sweltering roof above the Cadillac Ranch gift shop, baking like a fried egg on a pan, watching you and my father protect the Sizani's. I chose to find happiness in the fact that I'd help protect the men and the family I cared about. I didn't deny how I suffered under the sun, sweating like iced tea on a picnic table. I found something I felt grateful for and found happiness in the moment."

He wanted to be playful and tell her he was grateful for the opportunity to see her contorting for yoga in tight clothes, but he appreciated she was sincere in her advice. Continuing to objectify her body was counterproductive to trying to have a relationship with her. The problem was that he'd always relied on that angle—suave and suggestive flirting—to bed a woman. The more time he spent around Dia, the more he contemplated something more than just another romp between the sheets. He had no moves in his repertoire for that. Besides, he had no idea what that 'something more' might be.

"I'm grateful you're on our team," he said, feeling lame.

She paused her crunches to stare at him. "You are?" Beautiful, wide, brown eyes blinked at him.

Finally, an easy question. "Of course, you're an asset. You bring combat skills, intelligence, and information."

She smiled. "That's an incredible compliment."

He smiled back, hoping he could figure out how to earn more of those lovely expressions, when her phone dinged.

She plucked it off the mat and read the text message. "Dad says breakfast at seven in the diner down the road."

Right. Dad.

If Rafe couldn't even convince Dia he was dating material, how would he convince Dorian not to outright shoot him when he told him he had feelings for his daughter?

Rafe walked to the treadmill, climbed on, and set the pace to run.

And what are those feelings, exactly?

Maybe he didn't need to sort those out, because his time with Dia was limited. When this mission ended, she would go back overseas with Interpol, and he would move on to the next job... with her father.

Yup. Better to drop the whole notion of entanglement with Dia.

RAFE SAT in the passenger seat of the RV as Jackson drove west on I-40 toward Flagstaff. Mica wanted them to get to Las Vegas where they could bury themselves in the populated area with a major airport.

As per usual, the Sizani family rode in the back of the RV. Behind them, Dia drove her rented Acura with her father riding shotgun. Mica drove her rental car behind them.

Rafe wondered what Dorian and Dia talked about. Him? Was Dorian calculating even now how he would eliminate Rafe?

"You're a little morose," Jackson commented. "I'm guessing it's not from the gunfight."

"Morose? Is that the word of the day?"

"Actually, it's flummox. To confuse."

Rafe shook his head. "I can't help wondering if Dorian is plotting my death. I never would've mentioned sleeping with Dia if I'd known who she was at the time."

"You survived two nights. Perhaps that bodes well for your future." Jackson's tone was all amusement.

Rafe would bet Jackson wouldn't sound so smug if he was in Rafe's place.

Jackson gave him a light punch on the arm. "Lighten up, man. Dorian probably has other things on his mind. Like the fact he only now found out his daughter works for Interpol and how on at least two occasions she'd been a sniper picking people off." He hesitated, as if he had more to say on the topic but clamped his mouth shut as he glanced at Rafe.

Rafe rubbed at his hand where it had held Dia's at the breakfast table briefly during the prayer the other morning. "Thing is. I like her. My emotions don't seem to give a damn that her father probably knows a dozen ways to kill a man."

Jackson grinned.

Rafe sighed. "Do you think it's ridiculous for a man to be so enamored after spending so little time with a woman?" The escalation of his feelings baffled him. He'd gone from intrigue at a one night stand to despising her for lying to him to interest in dating her. He'd clearly lost his mind.

"Oh, no. And I don't mock your emotions." Jackson's tone and expression turned serious. "I know what it's like to crave the forbidden fruit. To want to take what you can't have. And I don't mean just sexually."

Rafe took a long look at Jackson. "There's a story there I think I'd like to hear."

"Maybe I'll share it someday. It's not something I open up about to just anyone. Besides, we're discussing you right now, not me."

"Okay, me. Let's say I wanted to pursue a relationship with Dia. How do I do that without pissing off her father now that he knows what he knows?"

Jackson shifted his weight in the driver's seat. "Fathers want three things for their daughters. Emotional safety, physical protection, and financial security." He held up a hand and counted one by one on his fingers as he spoke. "If you want to prove you're worth dating his daughter, show him you have the moral character for all of those things." He put his hand back on the wheel. "Specifically, show you know how to support her emotionally without trying to control her. That you won't be a financial burden. And that you not only pose no physical threat to her but would stand up against physical threats."

Rafe considered his words. "When you summarize it that way, making a good impression doesn't sound particularly difficult."

Jackson continued, "The world is full of selfish bastards—men and women. Dia's father has seen more than his fair share over the years. I'm certain of that. Even if you don't account for the darker world we deal with, the US divorce rate is fifty percent. So, clearly, those three little things are not so easily achieved."

Rafe knew Jackson was divorced and wondered who had been the selfish bastard in that scenario. Based on what he knew of Jackson's character, Rafe couldn't imagine he'd been the one to screw things up.

Perhaps that would be a conversation for another time.

"How do you know so much about fathers and daughters?"

"My previous father-in-law was a take-no-crap, confrontational trial lawyer. He wasn't convinced my ex and I were a good fit. I think he secretly reveled in our ultimate demise. But mostly, I know because I think about what I want for my younger sister—"

"Emotional safety, physical protection, and financial security."

"Exactly."

Rafe fell silent, watching the vast horizon stretch out before them.

Word of the day: flummox. Rafe was certainly flummoxed by his ill-defined feelings for Dia.

8
_____

*D*ia drove her rental behind the recreational vehicle. With the new wrap, it had transformed from waves of various brown colors overlaid on beige to ocean blue with whales and sea turtles. The kids had loved the new design. Behind her, the morning sun hovered in full view above the horizon.

Beside her, her father stared ahead out the windshield, with a frown as the only sign of his displeasure. He was a good father, a caring father, who'd been playful and doting in her youth. From the ages of six to sixteen, he'd made her feel like she was the center of his universe, and he'd been equally attentive to her mother.

When Dia had distanced herself, testing her role as an independent teenager, her father had gone back to work. Private security, she'd been told. When she'd probed with questions about what made him qualified for something like that, she'd always received vague answers. At first, she had thought he was some type of night security guard strapping on a uniform and watching TV monitors or letting people through a guard gate, but her mother had explained it was more of a direct bodyguard role.

He kept the name of the organization he worked for a secret, which at the time, Dia thought it perhaps made logical sense. She came to understand later that he worked for Rider Security and Investigation off the record and often used an alias as a man of many identities.

"When I learned the truth about who you were," Dia began, "I wondered if I'd known you at all, if everything had been a lie. Another secret identity."

"A job isn't my full identity. I was every bit the father you needed me to be. Still am. Always will be."

"I understand that. I came to understand that when I considered our relationship and all of our time together. The shock at first learning you'd been MI6 had me questioning everything. I felt a sense of betrayal because you had this whole other side to you I not only didn't know about but you had no intention of ever telling me."

"Is that why you didn't tell me your real job? A sort of vengeance for my own secrets?"

"Maybe a little at first, if I'm being honest. But then I thought knowing might hurt you, since I knew that pain firsthand. Then I wanted to tell you, but I didn't know how."

Her father shifted in the passenger seat. "Would you have told me if you hadn't been forced into revealing it?"

"Truthfully, I would like to think so. I told myself I would."

"Your mother will be angry with me, knowing that my past influenced your career choice. At least with Interpol."

"I don't see it that way. Mom always admired what you did. I think she'll respect my choices, too, especially as it's generally not dangerous. The Interpol part, anyway. Truthfully, I've never been in as much danger as I have in overlapping work with the Rider team. With you."

That earned her a brief grin before he turned his gaze out the window. "If your mother doesn't know what you do and doesn't know you know I was a spy, how do you know she'll accept any of this?"

Her lips quirked. "Mom adored you. *Adores* you. Oh, it's evident in her spy novels the sun rose and set around you. You were suave, debonair—somehow killing the bad guy and morally incorruptible all at the same time."

A silence settled, like he didn't know what to do with her compliment.

"Are you happy?" Dorian asked.

His question held bottomless depth and feeling, like his life depended on her answer.

"I like my job. It makes me happy."

"And Rafe? Does he make you happy?"

Her eyebrows shot up as she glanced over at her father. The last time they'd discussed the opposite sex, they'd talked of high school boys and how ninety percent of them wanted one thing from high school girls. Despite her father's warnings, she'd found that out first-hand through a series of crushes and fleeting broken hearts. She'd suffered those in silence to avoid the inevitable parental 'I-told-you-so.'

"I am attracted to Rafe. I think his heart's in the right place. But I'm not looking for happiness in a relationship." She wanted to add that she hardly knew the man, but with the tension sparking anytime the two men stood in the same room, she suspected her father knew they'd been intimate.

"Fulfillment, then?" her father asked.

She frowned and bit her lip. Maybe fulfillment was something she wanted, but she didn't know if Rafe was the man for that role. Besides, she had a career plan outlined in detail, and a relationship hadn't been factored in to that.

⁂

RAFE AND DIA walked around the perimeter of the rest stop. Rafe was catching his breath after running and kicking a soccer ball with Jabari. Rafe had taken off his suit jacket and rolled up his sleeves. The exercise was invigorating, albeit hot.

"You're good with him," Dia said. She wore jeans and a t-shirt, with her short locks combed to one side. Her expression was a little more relaxed, making Rafe wonder if she'd reconciled with her father.

"He's a good kid. Worried about his dad, understandably."

"Nice of you to distract him with games."

"How are things between you and your dad?" Rafe asked.

"Nothing cuts quite like the disappointment of a father."

He regarded her. "Disappointment because you didn't tell him? He can't be disappointed in your career choice."

"Yes, disappointment in the lie." As she walked, her foot placement was deliberate, avoiding cracks and seams in the concrete.

"Then that should pass quickly."

"Oh, I don't know. We hold honesty among family in high esteem."

He cleared his throat. "So long as he doesn't have to be honest about who he is? Sorry, I'm overstepping."

"It's okay. Life is filled with double-standards. You told me a little about your father—the survivalist. Did he value the truth?"

The survivalist, Rafe thought. Dia framed it nicely. His father had been a paranoid schizophrenic off his medication who'd thought the apocalypse was eminent. He'd dragged his sons around the US and Central and South America, learning survival techniques for that inevitable end which never came. They had lived off the grid until forced into foster care at his untimely death.

"Lies are part of survival, so, no. He didn't value the truth. Santino and I learned the weakness of lies among family and friends, though, and pledged to the truth with each other."

"You went after Santino at the Cusco mines to save him."

Rafe shrugged, recalling flying the plane with Dorian as his co-pilot while enemies shot at them from below. "He's my brother. I'd always risk my life to save him. That's truth *and* loyalty."

For a brief moment, the quick jolt of fear he'd felt worrying for the safety of his brother pulsed through him. The abduction had been terrifying for Rafe. He'd passed the hours anxiously planning the rescue and not knowing if the South American drug dealer would decide to put a bullet in his twin's head.

Needing to focus his thought elsewhere, he watched Ada and Jabari kick the ball—a rare moment of brother-sister bonding—and avoided looking at Dia as his emotions swirled. He sensed her looking at him, not critically but in a puzzled manner—*flummoxed*—as though trying to make up her mind about something.

She opened her mouth to say something, but before she spoke, Dorian summoned everyone to load back into the caravan of vehicles.

MICA SAT in the back of the RV with Hiba at the small kitchenette table as they drove away from the rest stop. The children played on their tablets behind the closed door, and given Mica had worried either a social media post or tracked phones had allowed the family to be traced to Cadillac Ranch, she made sure all devices were disconnected from Wi-Fi. Of course, she discovered Dorian had already taken care of that detail as well as instructing Hiba to keep her phone and her daughter's phone off.

At the rest stop, Mica had decided against Vegas in favor of driving directly to the Phoenix airport, wanting to get them to the Rider safe house in Georgia as soon as possible. Since they'd already passed Highway 87, they would take I-17 at Flagstaff in the next mile.

Dorian walked back from the passenger seat to join them. Rafe piloted the RV while Jackson drove Mica's car, Dia in her car, and behind her, Mica's dad drove his Humvee.

"I'm sorry for what you're going through," Mica said.

Hiba nodded solemnly. "Abdul and I discussed the implications of finding the palladium. We talked about modernizing the islands, bolstering education and health care. But we knew the discovery was a dangerous thing as well. Such a desired commodity. We wanted to keep it out of public knowledge for as long as possible. We talked about other governments taking control, mostly Western, industrialized nations with firepower. I didn't think our own military would turn against us, but it is not the first time in our history."

"The UN will step in. Help out."

"So long as one of them doesn't decide to take control for themselves," Hiba countered.

"The UN wouldn't stand for that." Mica added a wry smile. "Don't mistake my comment to imply they are somehow altruistic in nature. They wouldn't allow another country to take control of a valuable commodity and tip the economic scales."

Hiba gave Dorian a sad smile. "I am so grateful to have you both through all of this. There is no team I would feel more comfortable protecting me and my children. Wherever this path takes us, I would like at least one of you by my side."

"I don't have any objection to that," Dorian said. "But so you know, I trust any member who's working with us right here, right now, with my life."

"That is reassuring to hear, because I have detected some tension."

"Ah. That's my fault. I'm quite tense over the new discovery that my daughter works for Interpol. She's been lying to me. I thought she worked for a medical device company, which would explain her world travel."

"Oh, my goodness." Hiba's eyebrows rose. "I have known Dia for over a year, but as Dia Abbot. Her mother's name, I'm guessing. I didn't know the two of you were related until I saw you at breakfast, and then it became obvious."

"I'll adjust," Dorian said. "I'm still reeling a bit, but I promise you this does not affect my ability as a member of your protection detail."

Hiba;s smile returned. "I would never have thought otherwise. You have been ever diligent and attentive. And, I am sorry to say I now know firsthand, an impeccable shot."

"*Maman! Maman! Baba* sent a message!" Ada burst through the back sliding door separating the kitchenette/living room from the bedroom and bounded out, phone in hand. As soon as she saw the three adults gaping at her, her delighted smile morphed into an expression of sheer disgrace.

"*Fille*, what have you done?" Hiba snatched the device out of her hand.

Tears filled Ada's eyes. "We wanted Wi-Fi for a few minutes to upgrade our game," she stuttered. "And then a message came through from *Baba*."

Mica considered their current location—I-17 just south of Flagstaff. Phoenix was the logical next stop, given their trajectory south. The enemy kidnappers would be able to deduce their destination if they had picked up on their location from the phone.

"We need a new plan," Dorian said.

Simple, Mica thought. Change course to Vegas where she'd initially planned to go. Or... her mind churned. Or lay a trap for whoever was targeting Hiba and the kids. If Mica could take their pursuers out of the equation, her job of keeping the Sizani's safe would become more manageable. On the downside, setting up a trap also risked putting her team members in danger.

"Keep the phone on," Mica said. "Jackson," she called to the front, "get off at the next exit. We'll stop at a gas station and talk."

"Okay, boss."

She pulled out her phone and called her dad who was brining up the rear of their caravan in his Humvee. "Hey, we're making a new plan. I need to know what weapons you have with you. And... uh... do you have an C4?"

9

Heat simmered off the dark road, making it look like an obsidian lake waiting to devour vehicles who dared trespass. Surrounding the road was red and tan dirt mixed with surprisingly vibrant patches of green trees.

Dia sat on the rocky hillside beside Rafe as the bright blue RV sped down the highway like a drop of ocean water in the distance. Dressed in khakis, she blended in with the terrain, as did Rafe. They wouldn't be visible to vehicles in the valley.

MI6 had passed intel to Dia earlier today that the team who had been hired to kidnap the Sizani family was known as The Shoup Group—security experts based out of Chicago. Mica had seemed more irritated than surprised when Dia shared this information, making Dia wonder what history the security teams had.

"Rafe, how are things looking up there?" Mica asked in their earpiece. Mica had been quick to pivot and make a new plan with the possibility of their pursuers having learned their location through Ada's mobile phone. They'd kept the phone on to lure out the Sizani family pursuers.

Now, they would see if the plan worked. The Shoup group might not even show. They might not have a second attack team on hand. They could be planning an attack in Phoenix.

Rafe told Mica, "Like the RV is about to run the gauntlet. If Shoup's men are hiding in the hills, I might not see them."

Dia considered all the scenarios they had discussed: Shoup could ambush them on the road, from the hills, or from the air. The Rider team's main advantage was Shoup needing the Sizani family alive, so they couldn't simply destroy the RV. Disabling it meant spikes on the road—which would be dangerous at high speeds where the vehicle could be difficult to control and end up off the safety of the highway. They could disable it by shooting out the tires, but that was a difficult task at high speed by car or helicopter.

"Explorers," Rafe said, binoculars to his eyes. "Three of them heading to intercept the RV."

A ground attack, Dia thought.

She moved into position, lying flat on her stomach and aligning her body with her M24 Sniper Weapons System she had already assembled and adjusted for wind—four miles per hour south by southwest. This was the same gun she'd used in Cusco and Cadillac Ranch.

"Claire?" Mica said.

"We're recording."

On the opposite hillside, unseen by Dia, lurked Jackson.

The black Explorers came to a halt two miles from the RV. The three vehicles angled themselves to block the entire road. If the RV didn't slow, it would crash head on with Shoup's cars. Men poured out of the SUVs and took up positions by the vehicles, weapons aimed at the oncoming RV.

Jim's Humvee swerved around the RV and sped up past it. A rocket shot off the top, ripping toward the SUVs.

Shoup's men screamed and scattered as the rocket exploded into the ground in front of the Explorers, sending debris, smoke, and flames flying in all directions. The high explosive round shot from the Bur launcher packed the equivalent of 6 kilograms of TNT of power and a potential kill area of fifty meters square. Striking the ground ten meters in front of the attackers meant less threat of loss of life, though still risky.

Dia peered through the lens of her scope to see the mercenaries all flattened on the dirt ground but still moving, still alive. The Rider team wanted to stop Shoup, but no one wanted causalities on their conscience... or their rap sheet.

Never slowing, the RV plowed through the remaining wreckage of the destroyed SUVs. Flames licked the sides of the RV as it shuddered over the debris, but it kept going.

The sound of pumping helicopter blades filled the air.

"Land attack is neutralized," Rafe said. "Birds are in the air, coming in from the west."

No sooner had the announcement been made than one chopper fired at Jim's Humvee.

"Missile at your three o'clock," Rafe warned.

The Humvee swerved, but the rocket struck near the back tire, sending an eruption of dirt and fire into the air as it knocked the vehicle onto its side. Dia's stomach knotted, knowing her father was inside that small, now flaming, tank.

"Jim and Dorian are climbing out," Rafe said.

Relief swept over Dia. She couldn't monitor the Humvee because she'd focused her aim at the chopper. Firing, she took out the tail rotor, and the chopper instantly began a tailspin. It would be forced to land, and not a gentle one.

The second chopper, gunman hanging out the side, lined up to the RV. Bullets shredded the right front tire, causing the vehicle to jerk and dip off the road at fifty-five miles per hour. Hitting a dip, then a rock, it flipped onto its side before exploding, the blue shell of aluminum bits flying into the air. The remaining helicopter in the air circled the wreckage. Seeming to decide nothing was salvageable, it flew back west, leaving behind all the other team members.

"Status?" Mica asked.

"RV and Humvee are down," Rafe said. "Jim and Dorian are heading toward me. Shoup's men are evacuating."

"Round up. Reconvene at HQ in two days."

BY THE TIME Mica's heart stopped threatening to pound out of her chest at hearing the valley showdown relayed through her phone and Bluetooth ear pods, the overhead announcer declared boarding time. While she'd sent her team on a dangerous and expensive diversion through Sedona, she'd taken Hiba and the kids to Las Vegas for a nonstop commercial flight back to Atlanta.

With Claire's guidance, Jackson had rigged the RV for remote control operation, but there had been no remote way to operate her father's weaponized Humvee, which required more than simple automated lane correction and speed.

Mica had put her father and Dorian in a great deal of danger, but she'd seen no suitable alternative. One Marine to drive, one spy to fire the weapon. They had to push Shoup's team to extreme measures to try to stop the RV. She needed it to crash so Jackson could trigger the internal bomb they'd planted. Shoup would think he'd accidentally killed the family he was supposed to be kidnapping.

The ruse should buy Mica at least a few days to hide Hiba and the kids. But could she keep them hidden and safe until the UN freed Comoros? And how many times would the Rider team clash with the Shoup Group before one of her own became a casualty of their war?

THE FOUR OF THEM—RAFE, Jackson, Dia, and Dorian—converged on a hotel for the evening. Jim had returned to his car show, lamenting the loss of his Humvee but revved up about the action of the day. Rafe and Jackson returned to their shared room, while Dorian and Dia headed to their separate rooms, Dorian nursing a sore back and neck from the crash.

Rafe didn't know what Dia was up to but imagined it involved debriefing Interpol on today's events. Mica had said she would need Dia's help tidying up the highway showdown in a way that would appease state and local authorities.

They had caused serious vehicular damage on a civilian highway, illegally using a Bur rocket launcher and C4. Rafe hoped the backlash on the Rider team would be manageable if police or FBI found out. And hopefully the Rider's connections and reputation combined with extenuating circumstances would be enough to exonerate them. So far, Mica's vast connections seemed to always mitigate situations.

When Rafe stepped out of the shower, towel around his waist in search of clean clothes, Jackson had his phone on speaker.

"Mica and her damned messes," the man on the other end was saying.

"She kept the Sizani family alive," Jackson countered mildly.

"From what you described, any number of things could have gone wrong. What if bystanders had been on the highway? What if shooting a rocket off a Humvee had killed people?"

"Only bad people," Jackson mumbled. He winked at Rafe and mouthed *Eddie*.

Ah, Eddie Finch, Rafe realized. He was Mica's FBI contact—a polished bureaucrat who capitalized off the arrests the Rider team fed him while bitching about their unconventional methods.

Eddie sighed into the phone. "I didn't recommend you for a job with Rider SI so you could turn into one of them—gray morals and breaking the law."

"I was kidding," Jackson said. "They're a great team, and we were careful."

To Rafe, he winked, shook his head, and mouthed *not kidding*.

Rafe smirked as he pulled clothes out of his bag and dressed.

As careful as a group managing explosives could be, anyway, Rafe thought.

"I'd be more impressed if you'd given me hard evidence to make an arrest," Eddie grumbled before the call disconnected.

Rafe frowned. That had been the hope, but he'd watched everything through the binoculars. Shoup never showed himself. For all the action and explosions, nothing incriminated The Shoup Group specifically.

"I'm grabbing some ice. You need anything?" Rafe asked.

"I'll take a Coke," Jackson replied.

Rafe picked up the ice bucket and key card before heading out the door. At the machine, Dia bent over, filling a plastic bag. She looked scrumptious in shorts and a t-shirt, hair wet slicked back after a recent shower.

She smiled at him. "Ice for my dad." She tied off the bag.

"He's okay?"

"Bumps and bruises from the Humvee crash, but he's okay."

Rafe filled his bucket, noting how she lingered and toyed with the top of the plastic bag. They'd parted ways after the incident on the hill together, Rafe holding binoculars and her holding a long, sleek rifle. He hadn't known he could be turned on at the sight of a woman who knew how to handle deadly weapons. He also considered his previous encounters with her. She'd shot and killed men.

Was saving his life the first time she'd shot someone, or had she killed before? Rafe had only ever taken one life, and it had been in self-defense. He'd been in plenty of fights, though—fists, guns, and knives—growing up in the rough environment amidst the trouble his father sought.

"You were an amazing shot today," he said. He filled the ice bin before leaning against the wall.

He recalled how she'd set up her weapon with smooth precision and a meticulousness that mirrored the way she lined up her silverware at meals and carefully avoided cracks in the sidewalks when she walked. Tidy precision. She probably liked everything in her life just so. He had the urge to show her how much fun messy could be.

Whoa. Simmer down. She doesn't want your hands on her in a hotel hallway when she's thinking about her father's car crash.

Rafe had felt less in the action, as he'd been the eyes to watch and communicate everything while Dia had the rifle, Jackson controlled the RV, and Jim and Dorian rode in the Humvee. After the firefight at

Cadillac Ranch and knowing there would always be more harrowing events during his work with Rider SI, Rafe had been content to be on watch duty and back-up this time.

Dia smiled. "Thanks. I've used that rifle more in the last six months around the Rider team than in my few years at Interpol. Then again, my job description there isn't as a sniper."

"You like it?"

She nodded, bangs falling forward. "Love it. I get to travel and enjoy the respect of the position while honoring the responsibility that comes with it. I enjoy helping protect countries against crime with software they might not otherwise know how to use."

He moved closer, reached up, and brushed a wet bang off her face as his body thrummed with delight at their proximity.

"Where are you traveling to next?" he asked.

She blinked a few times as if as dazed as he felt. "I'm not sure. I talked with my dad about staying with the Rider team until the Sizani family is indisputably safe."

He couldn't stop the smile that spread across his face. *Staying. Not leaving immediately.* He had more time to sort out his feelings. No. He knew his feelings—he liked Dia. Really liked her. He had more time to help her feel the same way about him. More time to get messy.

He said, "I enjoy working with you. I like you in proximity to anything I'm doing."

Her throat bobbed in a swallow. "Like getting ice?"

He also liked the way he could make a woman with nerves of steel and able to wield a rifle in the heat of battle breathless, as her cheeks pinked when he flirted with her.

"Especially getting ice." He leaned closer, anticipation heating his core. He couldn't wait to get his lips on hers.

"Dia?" Dorian called as he came around the corner of the hallway.

Straightening, Dia took a step back. She held up the ice pack as she walked toward her father. "Got it."

Rafe caught Dorian's furrowed brow when he saw him and perhaps realized he'd interrupted something. Dia cast a quick look over her shoulder at Rafe before she disappeared around the corner with her dad.

Reaching into his bucket, Rafe plucked out a piece of ice and popped it into his mouth to cool his fervor. He would spend the rest of the night thinking about that view of her backside in shorts as she shot a longing glance in his direction.

IF HE'D HAD HAIR, Shoup would have been pulling it out right about now. He strummed his fingers irritably on the armrest of his private jet en route back to Chicago. He glanced at Nick—maybe Shoup could pull *his* hair out. But his assistant hadn't failed him and didn't deserve punishment. The Rider team did.

Shoup was lucky to be alive. Maybe he should count that as a blessing, but the whole situation pissed him off.

"I've now lost two helicopters and several vehicles because of Mica Rider," he seethed.

"Quite a few injured men," Nick added mildly as he sat, legs crossed in his seat.

Shoup shrugged off Nick's words. His men knew what they signed up for, and the health insurance cost Shoup an arm and a leg, so he might as well be putting it to good use. He would have to hire more replacements, though. Every downed man would cost Shoup three months of orientation and training for someone new.

"I'm lucky her sniper didn't take out the chopper I was in. And where the hell did Mica Rider get a missile-launching Humvee?" He rubbed aching temples as the images of the RV explosion seared through his mind. The family had gone up in flames, and with them, the other half of his payment from General Passable.

"What do you want to do?" Nick asked.

"Regroup and kick some ass." His vehicular insurance premiums would skyrocket when he filed the totaled vehicles and choppers. "I'll have to think about it. Dead people can't repay debts, and the Rider team owes me a shit-ton of money."

"Monetary options include extortion—"

"—if I can get any dirt on them."

"Ransom—"

"—I heard Lucius Titan tried that, and it backfired on him."

"Hacking financial accounts."

"That's a long game move," Shoup grumbled. "I don't know that I have patience for that. Besides, we looked into their lifestyles. No one seems to be rich." Even the business wasn't impressive. No private jet. A bland office in downtown Atlanta.

"Maybe you're left with killing them and cutting your losses."

"Something." He scrubbed hands over his face before turning to look out the window at the clouds below. "There must be some way to destroy them. I'll think on it more."

10

____

Mica slept late the next day and woke to the smell of coffee.

Last night, after landing in Atlanta, she'd tucked the Sizani family into her father's cabin in the north Georgia mountains. She'd used the place, not listed under any name affiliated with the Rider team, on more than one occasion as a safe house. After leaving Hiba and the kids in the capable hands of Ryan and Reece, Mica drove back to her house. After the long day of stress and travel, she'd spent time tucking Allen into bed before crashing herself.

With the morning sun streaming through her bedroom blinds, she dressed in jeans and a t-shirt and arrived downstairs to find guests in her house.

"Maxine," Mica stammered. She gave her mother-in-law a brief hug before turning to Vladimir. "This is a surprise."

Maxine's brown and gray hair was curled back from her face, and she wore the same cargo pants and lose top she always had at Rider SI. Always ready for action.

The large Russian man wrapped her in a hug. "Mica, wonderful to see you." His baritone voice rumbled through her.

When Mica stepped back from Vladimir, she braced for the inevitable kiss on each cheek. He wore his usual jeans and a white t-shirt. Mica wondered if he'd donned a suite since relinquishing his title. He had the same full head of salt and pepper hair from the first time she'd met him several years ago. Despite his retirement, he appeared to have kept in shape, evidenced by large biceps extending from his shirtsleeves.

David handed Mica a cup of coffee, like a sort of peace offering, before he turned back to finish wiping down the sink. "I called Mom the other day and let her know about the trouble with Lucius. She came to help."

"Help?" Mica asked.

Maxine, as the former owner and operator of Rider SI, had enemies. Vladimir, as the former head of the Russian mafia, had more. They were supposed to be lying low in retirement in Antigua, sipping Coronas and lime while enjoying an ocean view from their cushioned lounge chairs on the shore as waves lapped lazily under a warm sun.

"She's restless," Vladimir said. "Let your *svekrov'* help."

David dried his hands and approached Mica, looking worried. "I didn't mean this as a reflection on you. You have a lot to handle with an international crisis. I thought Mom would have ideas on how to deal with Lucius while your plate is full."

Lucius. The man threatening her and her team unless he was released from jail was an absolute menace.

David pulled her into a hug as Mica battled her feelings. She glanced at Maxine, who'd tanned in the tropics, though still had that head of wiry, untamed, brown and gray hair.

Mica wanted to be angry at the three of them conspiring to help her as if she couldn't handle these dilemmas. On the other hand, she was in way over her head and their actions stemmed out of love and concern. Besides, Maxine had effectively dealt with Lucius before, so perhaps she was the best person to involve again.

After David's reassuring embrace, Mica turned to add more cream to her cup of coffee as she bought time to shift from surprised betrayal to grateful acceptance.

"Our daily stress is keeping the resort financially afloat," Vladimir said. "Retirement's been good, but I think Maxine finds the tranquility... stifling at times. David called during one of her restless moments. Missing the days of danger."

Mica chuckled. "Living with the former leader of the Russian mob isn't dangerous enough for you?"

Vladimir laughed. "'Dis is what I asked her, too."

Maxine shrugged. "I miss the intellectual stimulation of finding my way out of danger—my client's danger or my team's danger. I don't miss the worry I endured over everyone's safety."

"I'll drink to that." Mica raised her coffee mug in mock toast.

"She needs one last adventure to scratch the itch she has," Vladimir said.

Mica scrubbed a hand over her face. "Are we seriously considering springing Lucius from prison?" *What's one more illegal act added to my ever-lengthening list of crimes?*

"We need to play it right where it benefits us. Benefits Rider SI," Maxine said.

"I might have some ideas about that," Mica said.

RAFE STARED at the pages of his book as he sat at the airport terminal beside Dorian, waiting for his flight. He hadn't seen Dia since the ice machine and had an odd craving to see her now, even knowing he would soon. She was taking a different flight back to Atlanta and would meet up with them at headquarters.

"How are your injuries?" Rafe asked Dorian.

The man had bruises on the side of one cheek, which Rafe suspected had been from the impact against the passenger side door or window when the Humvee rolled. For those sixty seconds, from the time of the explosion to the time Dorian crawled out of the vehicle, Rafe hadn't taken a breath, hadn't moved.

He'd known Dorian only a year now but held him in the highest esteem and would have been devastated if the man had been injured. His mentor was cool, calm, and collected at all times. During the downtime of any protection detail, he read classical novels. On his off time, he spent his days with his wife, who had her own career as a novelist. Rafe suspected a long vocation of serving his country stretched behind Dorian. Rafe didn't have a country, despite being a US citizen, but he had his Rider family, and he could envision a long career in service to them.

"A few more days and I'll be right as rain," Dorian said. "I don't bounce back as fast as I did in my twenties and thirties, though."

"What do you suppose is next?"

"We still have the Sizani family to protect until their crisis subsides. Our ruse of their demise in the crash will only last so long. I'm thinking Mica is about fed up with Shoup's shenanigans and might be motivated to take some direct action. She's a bit like Maxine that way."

"What do you mean?"

"Maxine and Lucius Titan, another security guru who abused his power, had been adversaries for years. They crossed paths enough times on cases and clients that it all came to a head. We took down Lucius, his team, much of it to do with Claire's ingenuousness and her use of nanoparticles. Titan has been in prison ever since. Now, there's Peter Shoup to contend with."

Rafe nodded. He would support taking down a man with Shoup's track record. The asshole who tried to kidnap a family. He'd subjected a young boy and his sister to being involved in a gunfight. Who does that?

Shoup had also been involved in Rafe's brother's kidnapping. And more, he'd killed people to protect the illegal sale of narcotics. Not to mention, one of the bombs his men had planted had exploded in proximity to Santino. His brother had been fortunate to only have suffered partial hearing loss in one ear.

Yes, Shoup needed to be stopped. Rafe hoped he would be part of the scheme to put the ruthless criminal behind bars.

"I like your daughter," Rafe blurted.

Dorian winced and gave a resigned frown, as if he'd expected this conversation but still dreaded it. "I would hope so, since you've been intimate with her."

It was Rafe's turn to wince. "Would you be opposed to me dating her if she is interested in me?" His mouth went dry and his palms wet as he waited for a response. *Ugh.* He wasn't this nervous in a gunfight. He wasn't asking for her hand in marriage, just to date the woman.

"As you can see, my preferences toward her life choices are not something she takes into consideration."

"I'm sorry she hurt you. But I respect you as my mentor and friend. I wouldn't want my pursuit of your daughter to be seen as any form of disrespect."

Dorian gave him a long look. "You're a good man, Rafe. I've no objections with you dating Dia if she consents."

Rafe was speechless. He had imagined—worried—about many reactions from Dorian, but calm acceptance wasn't one of them. The boost to his self-esteem at a father-figure's compliment had his heart swelling. Taking a shaking breath, he tried to process all of his feelings of pride, joy, and self-worth.

Now, Rafe only had to convince Dia he was worthy.

⁂

DIA ARRIVED in Atlanta but made a stop in Roswell to see her mom. She didn't need to reconvene with the Rider team until tomorrow, so she opted to use the time to tell her mother the truth—*er*—part of the truth.

She had texted her mother about her imminent arrival, and before she could knock, Katie swung open the front door and ushered Dia inside the house.

A house full of memories, Dia thought. She'd spent school years here and summers in the UK until she shipped off to university in London.

Her mom had a newer same mounted TV on the wall but same soft, worn sofa where Dia had watched movies as a child, wedged between her parents, with a bowl of popcorn. The kitchen boasted the same sunny yellow cheer with light streaming through a broad window over the sink. The floors were newer—her mom had pulled out the old carpet and installed polished hardwood. The stairs led up to her childhood bedroom, still preserved with purple walls lined with posters of teen heartthrob bands and video game characters.

Katie wrapped her in a hug. "Good to see you. I'm so glad you came to visit."

After they entered the kitchen, Dia's mother placed a steaming cup of tea before her. Katie had fair skin and long brown hair she had twisted in an up-do that Dia had always suspected was more about creating a thick nest to hold the woman's reading glasses and less about any sort of fashion statement. Her mom's eyes were soft and light and a little distant, as if she was always thinking of the next fun fictional scene she would write for her characters.

"How are the book sales?" Dia asked.

"I have three book signings over the next six weeks. Wish me luck. How are you doing?"

"I'm well. I've been spending a little time with dad."

"Oh? I thought he was on an assignment."

"He is. I've been helping with his assignment."

Her mother, about to take a sip of her tea, set the cup back down on the counter. "How so?" She narrowed her eyes at Dia.

"I work for Interpol, Mom," she rushed out the words, bracing for a harsh reaction like the one she'd received from her father. When her mom didn't reply during Dia's pause, she continued, "There was an international incident involving the family Dad is protecting. I know the family because of a rare metal their country discovered that falls in my wheelhouse of cyber security."

Truth, but not the whole truth. Her father, a former MI6 agent himself, could know Dia worked for the agency. Her mother couldn't. Too much was at stake if her mom let slip her daughter was a spy after a few drinks at Bunko night with the neighborhood ladies. Dia didn't think her mom would ever be so careless, but why add the burden of Katie having to keep such a secret?

Her mother's mouth turned down into a frown. "Interpol. I can't say I'm entirely shocked. You were such an adventurous child. I was surprised when you said you worked for a medical device company, but I thought travel with work would fulfill your adventurous side. Instead, it's crime-fighting?"

Dia sipped her tea and shifted her weight on the counter bar stool. Her emotions warred—guilt and angst. "In a way. I help countries build an infrastructure against crime using state-of-the-art technology. I teach them to implement software for facial recognition, electronic fingerprinting, and cyber security." She gauged her mother's reaction to be some mixture of hurt and understanding.

"Cyber security. So, all of those gaming hours of Marian Brothers, Crafting, and Destination turned into a career?"

Dia chuckled. "It's Mario Brothers, Mine Craft, and Destiny. And, yeah, I guess they did." Truthfully, Mine Craft, with the coding involved, may have played a part in her understanding of computer programming at a young age.

"Your father knows?" She shook her head. "Of course he does."

"I only just told him, and he wasn't happy with the secrets."

"Why the secret? I've never told you to hold back on your dreams. I always only ever wanted you to be something that would make you happy. I want a fulfilling life for you." Katie reached over and touched her hand in a familiar gesture of motherly love. "If that's Interpol, then that's Interpol."

Relieved her mom was much less put out than her dad, some of the tension in Dia's stomach eased. "Dad is upset with me about the secret. I don't know why I felt I needed to keep it. May be a combination of reasons. When I learned about who dad really was through work contacts—" her MI6 contacts, not Interpol, but she wouldn't divulge that "—I was devastated he'd kept those secrets, and some childish part of me wanted to get back at him for that. Following those thoughts was the equally childish challenge—could I keep a secret as well as my dad?" She took a deep breath. "Lastly, I feared his rebuke at my career choice." As strictly an Interpol liaison, she rarely entered in dangerous situations, but her MI6 work was a different animal.

She'd also started her career within MI6 and put the medical device company lie in place at that time. Interpol began after her MI6 training. She'd decided to keep the medical device company lie in place indefinitely because, one, she didn't know how long her role at Interpol would last before another assignment, and two, she had never expected to work with her father.

Dia let out a humorless chuckle. "I've actually been in the most danger since working with Dad."

"Did you satisfy all that need for payback by keeping secrets from your father and me?"

Ouch. Mothers can always stick little barbs of guilt into their words.

"I learned I don't like secrets and lies. Hurting your feelings and Dad's feelings—I'm sorry for that. When I have my own relationship, someone I love, I don't want secrets."

Silence settled a beat as Dia thought about Rafe. Indulging her dual jobs to a potential boyfriend would be a huge risk. One she couldn't take. If she ever had a serious relationship, like that of her parents, she wouldn't keep the hidden truth of MI6.

11

Rafe took the city rail system, MARTA, to his apartment building in Atlanta. Walking inside, he dropped his keys on the counter and pulled his phone out of his back pocket. The place seemed desolate ever since Santino left months ago. Rafe would much rather be somewhere on assignment than in the space he no longer shared with his twin.

He texted Jackson, letting him know he'd made it back to his place and received a *ditto* text in reply followed by, *Word of the day: wanderlust. A strong desire to travel.*

Rafe gave him a thumbs up. He hadn't even spent the day around Jackson. How had he known his word of the day applied to Rafe? Wanderlust was his brother Santino these days.

Next, Rafe called his boss.

"Rafe, you back home?" Mica asked when she answered.

"Reporting for duty."

"Meeting in person tomorrow. I'll text you the address."

"Copy that." He knew the address to Rider offices, so perhaps they were meeting somewhere different. "How bad was the fallout from yesterday?"

"Having an Interpol agent and friend in the FBI involved helped. Hopefully, they'll keep other FBI and local law enforcement off of us for this one. You did good work, Rafe. I'll see you tomorrow."

A few seconds after the call disconnected, a garbled text came through from Mica. Rider code only team members would understand. He didn't know this location and wondered why they weren't meeting at the usual office downtown.

Rafe stared at his phone then set it down on the counter in order to reach for the orange juice in the refrigerator. He thought about how without Santino here, he could drink from the jug with no one to scold him. Instead, he poured a glass and drank.

After carrying his luggage into his room, he meticulously unpacked. The surrounding silence was oppressive.

At last, he called Santino. He needed to hear his twin's reassuring voice and absorb some of that happy Santino seemed to possess in endless supply. He also wanted to talk to his brother about Shoup events and Dia. Maybe not Dia, yet. She befuddled him, tangled up his insides, his thoughts, and his tongue. He wasn't sure he could talk coherently about his feelings yet.

And what if his feelings weren't his own? Maybe Rafe was going soft and doe-eyed because his twin was in love and Santino's emotions were spilling into Rafe's life, muddling everything? As much as Rafe wanted to blame his feelings on an external source, the truth was he liked this woman more than he was comfortable with.

The call went to voicemail, and Rafe disconnected, not wanting to leave a message while knowing his twin would be able to sense Rafe's unease no matter what he said.

He would hit the gym and sweat out his impatience with himself over Dia so he could focus on the next part of his assignment.

DIA WAS the last to arrive in the downtown Atlanta commercial district, pulling her rental car into a parking lot where Rafe, Dorian, and Jackson stood. She joined them, noting the three men were looking across the street at a white-washed brick building. It appeared to be a car detail shop, complete with a grand two-car garage. The exterior was devoid of signs to indicate it was an active place of business.

In this early morning hour, the Atlanta summer heat wasn't yet stifling. Because this was a meeting of the Rider minds, Dia had opted for black slacks and a white cotton tank covered with a light-weight teal blazer.

"Why here?" Rafe asked Dorian. Rafe wore jeans and a t-shirt, hair pulled back in a low ponytail.

She thought of the other day when his hair had been wet and loose. They'd been showering at the same time, and even though in separate rooms, the thought had been arousing. They'd nearly kissed, and, oh, she knew how delectable his kisses were.

"Mica built a lair," Dia's father explained. "She wanted something secret from the main office downtown. I didn't realize it was up and running until she sent us the address."

"We enter this way," Jackson said. "Word of the day. Sagacious. Keen mental discernment and good judgment. Shrewd."

Dia looked to Rafe at Jackson's words but he shook his head as if spouting dictionary definitions was a normal occurrence for his partner.

Following Jackson's gaze, she did a complete one-eighty from the garage, to spy at a tiny, empty parking attendant booth in the middle of the paid lot. When Jackson entered, he punched in a security code and pressed his hand to an electronic pad. When the light turned green, he lifted the latch on a floor hatch to reveal a tight spiral stair-case leading down to an underground room.

He explained, "This is tunneled to the garage. That way, the building stays looking unused and no one can simply wander into it. The signs around the garage parking lot threatening to tow vehicles will keep spaces open. Any cars parked here will look like they are customers of the adjacent law offices."

Dia followed Rafe down the stairs. What looked like an auto shop on the outside was a renovated think tank with high ceilings and state-of-the-art equipment on the inside. Along one wall was a computer console with three monitors. In the middle of the room was a large, oval conference table with rolling chairs angled to face a wide, flat screen.

"You've not been here before?" Dia asked Rafe.

"Never seen this building before now."

At the table sat an older woman with a mix of gray and brown hair and a burly salt-and-pepper-haired man of perhaps sixty. They sat close, and when he looked at the woman, his eyes held a glow of adoration.

Mica was leaning over another woman's shoulder, who sat at the computer console dressed in yoga trousers and a baggy t-shirt. Claire Maltisse. Dia had seen MI6 photos of the slender computer specialist with the sleek bob hairstyle.

Mica straightened as the four of them approached. "Thank you, everyone, for gathering. We're getting the remote team online." She extended a hand to Dia. "Thank you for staying on to help."

Dia shook it. "You're welcome. I'm chuffed to be here. Anything to work toward the Sizani family getting safely home. They are well guarded?"

"I've two other men with them. And I think you've more than proven your value." Mica walked them over to the table. "I'd like to introduce everyone. Maxine and Vladimir, you know Dorian. This is his daughter, Dia, who works for Interpol. Our newer team members are Rafe and Jackson. Gentlemen, Maxine is my mother-in-law and founder of Rider SI. This is Vladimir, her significant other."

The robust man stood, extending a hand to Dia first. When she accepted, he leaned forward and kissed each cheek. Rafe shook hands next, the grip looking firm as his brown eyes met Vladimir's steely pair of blues.

"Vladimir Pronin. Should anyone ask, you've never met me, *da*?" His English was crisp but thick with a Russian accent.

Jackson's mouth fell agape as he shook hands next. "Can't meet the former leader of the Russian mafia who's reportedly dead."

Vladimir gave him a wolfish smile. "Exactly."

Dia shot a look at Claire, who seemed to interpret her 'are-you-serious' expression, because she nodded emphatically with a pair of wide eyes. Mica's mother-in-law was involved with the former leader of the Russian mafia? Romantically involved?

Everyone took seats at the table except for Mica, who said, "Maxine and Vladimir are supposed to be enjoying retirement in Antigua but dropped in for a surprise visit."

"Invited by David," Maxine interjected.

"Yes." Mica forced a smile.

"Everybody's connected online," Claire announced.

Gazing at the large flat screen, Dia absorbed the faces of the other members of Rider SI, whom she only knew from their files. Mason Stone, the retired Navy Seal married to tennis icon Aurora Meridian. Ryan Walsh, the retired Army Ranger married to physician Jenna Masters. Billy Parrish, retired Marine dating rockstar Ethan Storm. Reece Owen, retired Army Ranger married to physician Jessica Ong. Santino Alonso, Rafe's brother, dating the famous treasure hunter, Ava Sharp.

This is clearly a meeting of the minds—of the shrewd, or sagacious, Dia thought.

A brief sadness shadowed Rafe's face at seeing his twin. Fate had swept them on different paths, and Dia wondered if Rafe was taking the separation hard.

Mica began, "I gathered everyone to update you on the latest events. We have a few substantial threats looming. First is the issue of Lucius Titan."

Glancing between the room and screen, Dia gauged a few eyebrows raised and other unsurprised expressions. She'd never met the man, but Jackson had regaled her with stories of Rider's glory during the road trip. He'd shared what he'd learned about how the Rider team had conspired to land him in prison.

Mica continued, "He's been feeding me information on the criminal world since his incarceration. Somehow, he feels this has earned him a break from prison. I disagree, but you should know he is once again threatening to hurt team members or their families."

When Mica glanced toward Maxine, Dia wondered if David Rider calling his mother had to do with Lucius' threats.

"In addition to Lucius," Mica continued, "we have The Shoup Group to contend with. As most of you know, their black ops security group was behind protecting the pharmaceutical company Jess and Reece helped expose to stop the street sale of deadly narcotics. Shoup was also involved in Santino and Ava's kidnapping in Peru. With the thwarted attempt to kidnap the Sizani family, we have now foiled his efforts three times. He'll want revenge, and he has the resources to carry out his will."

"We need to go after him first," Rafe said, hackles raised, the way a man might respond to threats toward his family.

"My thoughts exactly," Mica said.

"Run a con," Ryan said. "Catch him in a criminal act and turn him over to the FBI."

"It's worked before." Mica nodded.

"Who's involved?" Rafe asked.

"Everyone who's not already on assignment. That includes you and Jackson, since I have the Sizani family tucked away for the time being. Shoup knows most of the team, so stealth will be challenging."

"I'll help," Dia offered. "I want him off the streets, too." Because she was part of this team until the Sizani's were safely home, she might as well be useful.

She felt Rafe's gaze land on her, but she avoided returning eye contact. She wasn't joining as a ploy to spend more time with Rafe. Mostly.

"Vladimir and I will help."

Mica gave a resigned nod at Maxine's offer.

"You need Lucius," Maxine added.

Mica's eye twitched, but she looked like she knew this part of the conversation was inevitable. Without enthusiasm, she said, "We break Lucius out of prison as he requested, with the understanding he'll pretend to join forces with Shoup and lure him into a false sense of security."

Mica ignored his comment. "I sure Lucius will double cross us. But with his newfound freedom, he'll want Shoup out of the picture as well."

Vladimir crossed his sizable biceps and mumbled, "If we do this the Russian way, their corpses would not cause problems."

Reece shook his head and stroked his mustache. "In what universe does your scenario *not* end in Lucius double-crossing us?"

Billy frowned. "You're suggesting Titan will feign an alliance with Shoup as he simultaneously plots to destroy both of us?"

"Yes."

"How does that not end in flaming disaster?" Reece asked.

"Careful planning," Mica said, before launching into the details.

12

$\mathcal{R}$afe had spent the last few days studying the files Rider SI had on Shoup and Lucius in between a robust exercise routine. The mental and physical exertion had left little time to dwell on missing his brother and his desire to see Dia.

Now, Rafe stood calmly in one corner of the Atlanta Rider SI headquarters third-floor conference room, watching Mica pace. A few days of planning had passed while Lucius Titan's prison escape had been executed.

"You managed a prison break in two day?" Rafe stammered.

Mica smirked and explained how the right resources had made it seamless. "But a prison break is about more than just stepping outside the walls undetected. You need a new identity the moment you're free."

"You gave Lucius a new identity?" Rafe asked.

"Yes, until we revoke it."

"And he's on his way here now?" Jackson asked.

She continued to pace. Rafe had never seen the petite blonde woman so agitated.

"Yes. I kept the meeting to the three of us to protect the identities of Dia and Dorian. Also, as far as Lucius knew, Maxine is long retired and no longer involved in Rider SI."

Mica fell silent when a broody, hulkish redhead with a matching robust beard rolled a man in a wheelchair into the conference room. Mica stilled, stiff as a board. Rafe knew from the files on this man that the redhead was Lucius' righthand man, Hoyle.

Lucius, in the wheelchair, wore a slate suit. His dark hair was neatly trimmed, and his face was freshly shaven. Despite his physical limitations, he held an air of pompousness about him, as if looking down on everyone, even though he couldn't. His wheelchair was sleek silver with remote control options and a thick cushioned seat, making Rafe wonder if it was custom made.

"Mica Rider," Lucius began, "the woman I dream about." His cool statement suggested those dreams involved inflicting bodily harm rather than anything pleasant one would associate with dreams.

"You should be nicer, Lucy," Mica said. "I visited you in prison and sprang you out of it."

She was taking credit, Rafe realized, to keep Maxine and Vladimir's role in the escape secret.

His eye twitched at her calling him Lucy. "If by sprang, you are referring to my person being stripped naked by two incarcerated Russian mafia lackeys, suited up in grungy overalls, and thrown into the trash. That was your grand prison break idea?"

Mica gave a shrug as if to say 'if the shoe fits.'

"And as for visits, they were few and far between and not conjugal, so color me unimpressed. Now," he blinked casually. "I assume you didn't summon me here for my good looks."

Mica took a seat as far away from Lucius as possible. Hoyle remained standing behind his boss.

"We have a proposition," Mica began. "One that will help both of us. We've exchanged bullets several times now with The Shoup

Group. It needs to end. If you're planning on re-establishing your dominance in the black ops security world now that you're out of jail, you'll want Shoup out of your way."

Lucius gave a slow, languid smile that didn't reach his dark eyes. "I've exhausted quite a substantial amount of money on lawyers' fees with appeals. If I'm to help you, I need financial compensation."

"You can get your financial compensation from Shoup," Mica said.

Lucius picked at a fingernail. "I hardly think he will pay me to destroy his company."

She explained, "We need all of his records in order to incriminate him. Among those dirty deeds will probably be his bank account information. We will simply look the other way should you choose to claim those dollars as compensation for your efforts."

Lucius steepled his fingers, placing his elbows on the armrests in his wheelchair. "I'm considering your offer. And who might the rest of your team be?" He appraised the room.

Mica gestured first to Rafe. "Rafe is excellent at information gathering, as well as blending into the shadows, should the occasion call for it. He's willing to do minor role-playing. Jackson is former FBI and an exceptional addition to our team. He'll be playing a few roles simultaneously. He will be by your side throughout your inter-actions with Shoup so we can ensure you don't double cross us. Meanwhile, from Shoup's perspective, Jackson will be a disgruntled employee, disgraced from the FBI, taken under our wing, and unhappy with the pay and pesky restrictions, such as not killing anyone."

Hoyle smirked, as if to convey he found those limitations entirely believable reasons to betray the Rider team.

"Are you disgraced from the FBI?" Lucius asked, suddenly more interested in the conversation.

Jackson shifted in his seat. "Anyone who goes digging will discover the circumstances surrounding my departure were not favorable. I won't say anything else on the matter."

Jackson's impersonation of an unhappy former agent impressed

Rafe. He'd known the man for months now. He was too content with his work at Rider to dwell on his misgivings with the FBI.

"And you're copasetic working for the Rider team now?"

"It's a paycheck."

"If you agree to this, when this is over," Mica interjected, leaning forward and making unwavering eye contact with Lucius, "we're done. We don't take jobs that cross each other's paths."

"'*The enemy of my enemy is my friend*'... but only temporarily."

"A temporary working relationship. A permanent truce."

He smiled, another cold, slithering thing. "Won't be a problem."

AFTER MICA HAD confirmation Lucius agreed to "help" Rider take down Shoup, she spent the next day without Lucius and with her core team—Rafe, Dia, Jackson, Claire, her husband Drake, Maxine, and Vladimir—working out the final details of this project and planning the next steps involving Lucius and Shoup. Currently, everyone but her and Jackson were off to Chicago. She had moved Dorian to the protection detail of the Sizani family.

Now, the snake—er, man—sat before her once again in her conference room as they discussed his upcoming meeting with Shoup for which Lucius would soon be flying to Chicago. Hoyle stood in the corner like a brooding mountain man.

Jackson leaned on a wall off to one side, playing calmly disinterested. He was playing the role of bored employee surprisingly well. She would keep his acting skills in mind for other jobs.

"I need your shoe," Mica said to Lucius. She was on edge but kept her composure.

The escaped convict didn't need to know how frayed her nerves were, because a predator like him was always on the prowl for prey. The weak shed fear whereas other predators did not.

"My shoe?" Lucius arched an eyebrow at her.

"I'm not sending you in to have a private conversation with my enemy and allow you to plot against me. I want a bug in your shoe. If Shoup looks for a wire, he won't find one."

"I thought Jackson here was your eyes and ears."

"And I'm not taking the chance he'll be excluded from your conversation with Shoup, rendering me blind and deaf to what's happening. So, your shoe."

With a shrug, Lucius gestured to his right leg. Jackson pushed off the wall, bent over, and removed the loafer before he set to work, laying it on the table, peeling back the sole, and planting the bug.

"Hit me with the recap," Mica said to Lucius.

"I beg your pardon?"

"We just spent forty-five minutes reviewing the plan. Give me the five-minute recap."

"What is this? Junior varsity football?" Lucius glared at her. "I've got the plan."

"Then you won't mind running through it. There's a lot more at stake here than prom date bragging rights."

"Fine. I'm flying to Chicago today to meet with Shoup tomorrow. Thanks to Claire—whom you haven't let me see yet—is she still upset about the kidnapping thing?" He wriggled his eyebrows then shrugged when Mica didn't answer. "I have an alias, fake ID, and a plane ticket. I convince Shoup to join forces with me against Rider SI. If he agrees, we scheme." He smirked at Mica. "He won't agree right away. He'll need a few days to think it over."

Jackson handed Lucius' shoe back to him. Instead of taking it, Lucius gestured that he should put it back on for him. Jackson rolled his eyes but slipped it onto his foot.

"Not a problem." Mica felt a brief wave of relief when Jackson eased back into his chair.

As Lucius had talked, Jackson had not only finished installing the bug in the shoe but planted a second bug in Lucius' wheelchair at an angle unseen by Hoyle. Because the chair appeared custom made, they took a chance he wouldn't travel without it and would therefore be the best place to plant a listening device.

Lucius continued his summary, "Once I'm in Peter Shoup's good graces, we plan the best opportunity to steal his files."

"Precisely." Mica leaned back in her chair. She and Claire were already making plans which didn't include Lucius, and Lucius would certainly be making his own plans without the Rider team. In the end, they would see whose strategy succeeded.

DIA AND RAFE landed in Chicago and took a rideshare to their hotel. An hour later, she went to the hotel bar to meet him for drinks. They had the evening off but would soon be infiltrating Shoup's office or home, depending on how Lucius' meeting with Shoup progressed. Mica had reviewed multiple scenarios with them.

Dia had been wary when Rafe asked her to join him for a drink. Did he know the implications of that invitation? The last time they'd had a drink at a hotel bar together, it had ended in an incredible tumble between the sheets. Perhaps he hoped for a repeat performance.

Perhaps she wanted that also.

She spotted him sitting at the end of the bar, wearing jeans and a t-shirt that read 'TACOS FOR LIFE'. His hair was in a ponytail, but his distant expression as he stared into his drink held a melancholy edge. Bourbon, she guessed. He'd picked a location with some privacy, though overall the small bar only had a few patrons.

"This seat taken?" she asked.

His face lit with a delighted smile, and thrill ran through her, knowing she could lift his mood so instantly by simply arriving.

"It is now."

"Thanks." She slid into the seat and ordered a mojito.

"Have you ever done an assignment like this before?" Rafe asked.

She chuckled. "My work with the Rider team is a whole lot of firsts for me. I specialize in software, not cover fire and covert operations."

"Do you think you'll ever do more covert work? More like your father?"

She rolled her shoulders as her drink arrived. "I considered it, but I didn't want to be a spook, dealing with liars and thieves. I like my work in the tech world."

"You're cool under pressure. I'm sure you're amazing at anything you want to do."

"Thanks."

"You never hesitate pulling the trigger."

She sipped her drink, savoring the sweet mint flavor. "I've had many training hours with numerous types of weapons. Cusco was the first time I killed anyone. It still haunts me. I did the right thing, protecting you and my father. All the same, I prefer my desk work."

He let the silence linger, and Dia sensed he was trying to decide if he believed her. The thought he didn't trust her stung, though she deserved it. And she would shatter any tenuous trust she might build if she ever told him she was also MI6.

At last, he broke the silence. "I like being on the go—the travel, the action. Besides, when I'm home alone, I miss my twin."

The sentiment touched her deeply. She had no siblings, but she understood loneliness and an empty home. She took a bigger gulp of her drink, feeling the growing urge to be physically closer to Rafe.

"Tell me something quirky about Dia," he said, eyes lighting. "What's a fun fact no one else knows? Or only your closest friends."

Her mouth curved as she debated telling him a weirdness she'd told no one. "Do you know the game Mario Brothers?"

"Of course, Santino and I have played that game many times."

"I did a lot of gaming as girl. Mario Brothers, Destiny, Mine Craft, Pokémon. Hours and hours."

He grinned, "That's not weird. That's our generation."

She shook her head, blushing now. "The weird part is now as an adult, I think of my enemy targets as computer game characters."

Rafe cocked his head to one side. "How so?"

"The gunman at Cadillac ranch I took down was a Goomba."

"Goomba? The little mushroom guys from Mario Brothers?"

"They are the master villains' foot soldiers."

"Okay, I can see that."

"At the mines, you and my father were surrounding by Piranha Plants."

"Oh, yeah. Those carnivorous things that popped out of pipes. Those were so annoying. I lost so many lives trying to time Mario's jumps just right."

She shrugged one shoulder. "Probably juvenile, turning life into a video game."

Rafe gave her an empathetic look as he laid a hand over hers where it rested on her knee. "What you do is protect people. When that means hurting those who would hurt the innocent or your asset or people you care about, I think creating a coping mechanism is acceptable. I'm sure thinking of them as evil cartoon characters also helps you alleviate some of the fear when facing your opponent." He squeezed her hand gently. "Maybe I should try that sometime."

His soft touch, gentle words, and bottomless understanding had a lump forming in her throat. Gooseflesh rose up her arms.

"Do you want to continue this conversation upstairs?" she asked, giving him the same invitation she had in Cusco.

He smiled. "I'd like that."

13

*D*ia and Rafe both downed the last of their drinks and settled the bill. They rode the elevator up to her floor, and he followed her down the hall. The mojito had given her a light buzz, and her body zinged with the anticipation of having Rafe's hands on her. She'd wanted to indulge in the feel of him ever since their night in Cusco.

When they stepped inside her room and let the door close, Rafe reached up and stroked a hand along her cheek and down her neck.

She closed her eyes. "I want you."

Their lips met as they pressed their bodies together, and Rafe backed her into the wall, the kiss deep and passionate, shattering her and building her up all at once.

She felt both invincible and as wispy and airborne as a feather. She wanted this, wanted him. More than she should, and more than was safe.

Just one night, she told herself. She would allow herself to be with him one more time. She wouldn't submit to the pull for more, because the urge to lose herself to him was frighteningly strong.

His kisses, his touch, set her on fire. She needed to feel his hands on her skin, his body against hers, moving together.

Just one night, she thought again. If she did this, she could get him out of her system and return her focus on her work, her career.

She reached to pull her shirt up, saying, "This isn't serious. We'll keep it casual."

Rafe stopped her hands before she could tug her shirt up and off. As the temperature in the room plummeted, Dia pulled the fabric back down and crossed her arms. His gaze had turned from heated to frustrated.

He took a step back from her. "I know we have real chemistry, Dia. Genuine feelings. I won't let you brush that aside. Our first night together in Cusco was amazing. Maybe to you it was casual sex, but I couldn't help thinking how I wanted it again. I wanted to find you and re-create that night—conversation and sex. A hundred times over. I think you feel the potential for what's between us as well. I won't let you minimize what we have or could have."

She gaped at him, speechless.

"This—" with rising frustration, he gestured between them "—is not just sex. When you're ready to acknowledge that, you know where to find me." As if to soften the blow from his blunt words, he leaned forward and placed a chaste kiss on her lips before leaving the room.

Dia stood alone, hugging herself as her head spun and emotions tumbled. Rafe had rejected her, which came as a complete shock. The rational part of her brain knew he hadn't rejected *her* so much as her approach to their relationship—or attempt not to acknowledge one.

He clearly had feeling for her and wanted them to be in agreement with their expectations before they were intimate again. She tried to balance the sting of rejection with feeling flattered that he wanted to share much more with her than another one-night stand.

Oh, how she wanted what he offered, which made it all the more terrifying. But she worried that if she fully gave her heart over to him, she risked giving into anything with him. Giving up everything for him. That didn't seem like a healthy, happy relationship. She loved her career. She had a one, five- and ten-year career plan rising in the ranks of MI6, and it didn't include relationship complications.

As she let the heat settle and blew out a breath, she considered the experiences of her parents. Her mother and father had had an incredible week together in a whirlwind romance. That wasn't enough to make him stay. He went back to the spy world, and her mom was left being a single parent.

In fairness to her dad, he hadn't known he'd had a daughter. He eventually tracked her mother, Katie, back down because he'd felt they'd had something special. But her mother had spent the first six years of Dia's life alone, with only the memories of a fleeting romance to keep her warm at night.

Dia feared if she committed to a relationship, she'd either have to give up the career she loved or subject the man she loved to her continual absence. She knew how devoted Rafe was to the Rider team, and she wouldn't, couldn't, ask him to give that up.

Impossible relationships.

She silently fumed. Why couldn't the man have accepted her offer for a one-night stand? Now she was both sexually and emotionally frustrated, and with work to be done.

* * *

Jackson blinked as Rafe entered the hotel room. Irritably, Rafe kicked off his shoes. Was he the biggest idiot of all time for turning down Dia's offer? Probably.

Clicking the television off, Jackson said, "I thought having drinks with Dia meant I'd be the one sleeping alone tonight."

"Me too."

"Well, you tried. She doesn't know what she's missing. Except, you've already slept together, so I guess she does." Jackson scratched his chin.

"I turned her down." Rafe plopped into the chair across from where Jackson lay propped up on his queen bed.

"I'm not following," Jackson said.

Rafe tugged out his rubber band and ran a hand through his hair. "We made it to her room, kissing. She was about to take her shirt off when she added stipulations."

"Stipulations?"

"She said we'd keep it casual."

"You turned down casual sex?" Jackson's eyebrows lifted. "From a beautiful woman who is also a badass?"

"It didn't feel right. Her no-strings-attached offer had the opposite effect on my libido."

"Um…"

"Weird, right? I don't want a fling or a one-night stand with Dia. I want something more."

"What something?"

Rafe tossed his hands in the air. "Hell if I know." Scrubbing hands over his face, he added, "Substance. Something of substance."

"Word of the day. Prudence. Caution or discretion, often in risk-avoidance."

Rafe kicked his shoes off.

"But who is she, really?" Jackson asked after several beats.

"What do you mean?"

Jackson shifted his weight. "What do you know about Interpol?"

"Just what I've seen on TV, so probably nothing. They're an international police force, right?"

"Yes, but they don't carry weapons. They have no authority to shoot anyone. And yet, your woman knows how to use a rifle and has shot how many people in how many countries? That you know of?" The former FBI agent spoke with a measure of care, as though explaining out of concern for Rafe.

Not my woman, Rafe thought, though he liked the idea of Dia being his. And where had that bit of possessiveness come from?

"You think Interpol is her cover," Rafe deduced.

Jackson raised his hands next to his head as if to convey he was a neutral observer and not intending any offense. Valuing his friend's insight, Rafe took none.

"I'm merely suggesting she's more than meets the eye." Jackson walked to the sliding doors and stepped onto the platform.

"Heard that," Rafe agreed.

Not Interpol. Or not only Interpol.

Jackson had given him scenarios to consider.

Prudence dictated Rafe used patience is seeing how events unfolded with Dia.

<hr>

NICK FRISKED the guy in the wheelchair for a wire. He'd first tried his handheld radio frequency bug detector, but Lucius' wheelchair must have had magnetic parts because the small machine wouldn't stop beeping relentlessly at some interference. Nick had to turn it off and search manually.

Shoup been more than a little intrigued when the infamous Lucius Titan reached out to him for a meeting, wanting to discuss their mutual adversary.

Shoup didn't need Lucius' help to burn the Rider team to the ground, but he was curious to see how the mighty had fallen. Shoup had risen to the top in the security industry partially because of the void Lucius' incarceration had created.

Outside his office, Lucius' known accomplice, Hoyle, sat and waited. Beside Hoyle stood a man Shoup knew only from the list of Rider employees. Shoup had made it his business to know all of them. This tall suit was Jackson Hart, a former FBI agent and newer higher. For someone accompanying Lucius to keep an eye on him, he hadn't taken too much convincing to wait in the lobby. Judging by his scowl, he wasn't happy about it, though.

Left shoe, Lucius mouthed.

Nick did a double take before looking to Shoup.

Shoup nodded, and Nick took off the shoe, peeled back the sole, and withdrew an electronic bug. He dropped it into a cup of water.

"Any other bugs?" Shoup asked, cocking his head to one side.

"No," Lucius replied.

Shoup dismissed Nick and took a seat behind his desk. "I confess my confusion. You request an audience with me under the guise you want an alliance, but you were bugged and yet revealed it. And you show up with a Rider employee."

"Mica Rider sprang me from prison. Following this, she begged me to team up with Rider SI to take you down. The tagalong is Mica's doing. He won't be a problem."

Shoup grunted. The little Rider ragtag team ought to realize they were out-manned. Pitting one security giant against a former formidable one made sense.

Lucius continued. "I agreed to their demands, but obviously I can't help the very team I despise. I have standards. So, I give you all the inside details of their plans in exchange for you killing them all."

"What keeps them from having you thrown back into prison?"

"Me telling the FBI the Rider team are the ones who helped me escape. They forged fake IDs for me. They can't turn me back in without going to jail themselves, and they can't take you on without me pretending to be their inside man."

Shoup considered the plan, trying to find the weakness, the double cross. Lucius obviously no longer had the resources to retaliate against Rider SI as he desired. Shoup could use his insight. And if any of Lucius' words turned out to be lies and deception, the wheelchair bound remnant of a man wouldn't be difficult to dispose of.

⁂

Rafe sat beside Dia in the hotel conference room as they watched the live stream of the web meeting. Behind Mica on the screen was the familiar conference room of the third floor of the Rider SI headquarters. Lucius and Jackson were elsewhere, probably still rubbing elbows with Shoup.

Dia looked sleek in black slacks and a white button-down shirt. Rafe's eyes strayed to those full, kissable lips, reminding him what he'd missed out on. She hadn't mentioned the post-bar incident, so he remained cordial. She didn't seem bitter toward him, which meant perhaps he could turn up the charm and convince her to take a chance on him when the mission was over.

"This is Shoup's five-million-dollar house in Chicago. Not to be confused with his ten-million-dollar office building with its square, modern appeal and abundance of windows," Claire explained as the video conference showed a view of Shoup's house.

"Men in glass houses," Dia said.

"Except, you don't have to worry about people throwing stones when you have a dozen armed security guards and a state-of-the-art system."

"But you're Claire, so it's not a problem for you," Rafe said. So far, he'd seen nothing in the tech world stand in Claire's way. Time and keystrokes were all she seemed to need.

"The office building isn't the problem. If we get inside the building, we still have his personal office security to bypass, which includes thumbprint, facial recognition, and a badge key card. Jackson is working on the badge. You and Dia are on thumb and face. This will require infiltrating his home, where he keeps a laptop. I won't need to bypass his home security system or figure out how to sneak you past his guards because you'll be waltzing right through the front door."

"Internet repair crew? Gas leak? HAZMAT? Animal Control?" Rafe enjoyed it when Rider's stellar plan had them walking through the front door like they belonged there, only to plant listening devices or steal confidential information for their clients' safety.

"Operative word being waltz," Mica said. "Shoup is hosting a party at his house tonight. His fiftieth. Thanks to Lucius, we have a few invitations."

Interest piqued further, Rafe asked. "Will there be actual dancing involved?"

With a hesitant expression, Mica looked back and forth between Dia and Rafe. "I suppose that's possible. The objective is for you two to blend into the party as a couple until you can sneak upstairs."

He glanced in Dia's direction, but she kept a good poker face, so he couldn't gauge her feelings on the assignment. They would be infiltrating as a couple? Mica had never assigned such a role to him. Then again, there weren't many women in Rider SI. Billy was overseeing Ethan Storm's protection team, and Mica, as the boss, limited her field work. Dia's willingness to participate gave the team an opening they might not otherwise have had.

Claire continued speaking, explaining where Shoup's home office was located and how they would infiltrate it during the party to steal information off his hard drive.

"Question?" Rafe lifted a finger.

Claire nodded. "Yeah?"

"Lucius knows our plan, right, since he got us the invitations?"

"Yes."

"So, how do we know Dia and I are aren't walking into a trap?"

"Because of our eavesdropping on Lucius," Claire replied.

Mica clarified, "Lucius knows our intentions are to steal information off Shoup's laptop, and he's divulged as much to Shoup, who initially planned to set a trap. Lucius talked him into instead letting us in and countering with malware to hack our system once we opened it."

"Our big mission is to steal malware?" Dia asked.

"You will complete two additional objectives. First, when you attach the USB drive to steal his files, Claire has a program that will download into his laptop. This is designed to capture a five second video of Shoup's face the next time he uses his laptop and send the mp4 to Claire. We need this to create a 3D face that we can use to bypass his office facial recognition software. Secondly, we need you to collect his thumbprint from his home office."

Rafe nodded in appreciation of the plan. "We're a decoy to the real intended information heist to take place in the future at his office building, but also we get what you need to make that future theft."

"Exactly."

Rafe liked the plan and especially liked the idea of concentrated time with Dia. His mind churned. Did Mica devise it that way when other options existed? Maybe other options didn't exist. Most of the men were nearing forty, which would be a little old to pair with Dia, who wasn't thirty yet. That left him and Jackson, and Jackson had already been introduced to Shoup as one of Mica's men set to watch Lucius.

Luck and circumstance had him by Dia's side for this assignment. He planned to ensure there was actual waltzing involved—or at least some form of couples' dancing.

He'd shrugged off his chagrin from the other night when Dia offered to reduce them to casual sex. After calming his burning frustration, he'd decided he would work to convince her to take a chance on him. To do so, he needed to enact some proper wooing. Since he couldn't take her on an actual date with the active job underway, he would need to be creative in other ways to let his interest be known during their working activities. A party might serve his purpose nicely.

A dangerous party with dangerous men.

He felt an odd protective flare toward Dia. She could certainly handle herself in a fight, so why worry? She didn't need a knight in shining armor—which he was most certainly not—and she would probably take offense if he acted as such.

They were equals on this mission, and he would treat her with the same respect he would give any of his colleagues.

⁂

SHOUP EMERGED from yet another meeting with Lucius. The man was a fount of knowledge on the Rider team and their weak spots. He was proving to be a valuable ally, though Shoup would wait before affording him any real trust.

He left Lucius and went to the men's restroom. After finishing, Jackson emerged from a stall to wash his hands. The former FBI agent had once again not been allowed to join in Shoup and Lucius' meeting.

"Lucius claims you're unhappy with Rider SI. Looking for a way out."

Jackson grunted as he lathered his hands. "Lucius told you I work for Rider? He wasn't supposed to do that."

"I do background on anyone stepping foot in my territory. How'd you go from the FBI to the Rider team?"

"Looking for something better." He shrugged even as his jaw ticked. "The FBI is too slow. They're burdened by tiptoeing around to avoid upsetting politicians and the public."

"And anyone who fails to maneuver those delicate boundaries is looked upon unfavorably," Shoup added as he dried his hands, enjoying Jackson's discomfort with the topic. The FBI was known for putting their reputation before the welfare of their agents.

"That's right."

Perhaps this man wanted to leave Rider SI and work for Lucius, and perhaps he lied as a ploy. But despite his orders to stay by Lucius' side, Jackson had been willing to turn a blind eye to let Lucius and Shoup discuss matters alone.

Shoup would see how things played out with Jackson. He was too new to Rider to know much about the organization so torturing information out of him was unlikely to be a fruitful endeavor. Perhaps he could be turned to Shoup's side and had valuable FBI contacts.

His men reported Jackson driven his SUV into one of Shoup's helicopters. Reckless or skilled? Shoup liked men with a bit of both.

"Let's talk sometime when you're done being Mica's patsy."

14

Rafe, hands tucked in his tuxedo pant pockets, waited in the hotel lobby for Dia to join him. He wished he had his harmonica to toy with and calm his nerves.

Dia arrived, wearing a shimmering champagne dress and looking good enough to drink. The silky material draped lovingly over her curves. With an elegant plunging v-neck and simple should straps, it revealed copious amounts of her mouth, dark honey skin. He wanted to run his lips along every exposed surface of her body. She wore light make up accentuating her cheekbones, eyes and long lashes. Parts of his body chastised him for not seizing her offer to sleep together, but he'd meant what he said about casual not being an option.

Jackson, playing the role of chauffeur and back-up, waited outside in their rented car for the evening.

Rafe held out an elbow for her. "You are exquisite."

"And you're quite handsome in that tux." She slipped her arm through and walked with him.

He'd thought she had liked it by the way her eyes had widened when she'd seen him, but the compliment was nice to hear. When they arrived at the car, Rafe held open the door for Dia.

"A Cadillac? Seriously?" he said to Jackson.

The man grinned. "I thought it poetic. Dia, you look lovely."

"Thank you."

Rafe sat in the back beside Dia. He pulled out the discrete earpieces they would use for communication for tonight from their respective cases and pocketed them. Although small, trained guards might spot them, so they needed to wait to don the communication devices until they were through Shoup's security. And surely a man in his position, catering to so many unscrupulous clients, would have security for a house party.

Dia adjusted her dress strap with a slight annoyance to her demeanor. "I understand the attire, but I don't like wearing dresses on missions."

"Why is that?" Rafe asked, unable to see a downside when she looked so stunning.

"There's no place to put my nunchaku. If something goes awry, all I have is a small, weighted, ceramic knife. It'll pass metal detectors, but it's not much of a weapon."

Rafe's mouth dropped open. "You use nunchucks?"

"They are extremely useful in a fight. You'd be surprised how difficult it is for even seasoned fighters to anticipate a blow from the wooden ends because you can swing it so fast."

Nunchucks. *Well, damn,* that was a sight he wanted to see. Dia wielding nunchucks. He might have just found true love.

Jackson drove them to Shoup's house, where he dropped them off in front of the mansion in East Winnetka along an enormous circle drive. The exterior was tan brick and limestone with a slate roof, giving it a timeless look. The front lawn was painstakingly mani-cured, including a dozen perfectly rounded holly shrubs in front of the house.

Rafe had memorized the interior layout—six bedrooms, six and a half baths, three fireplaces. The spectacular kitchen had top of the line appliances, including two Sub-Zero refrigerators, a luxury Wolf range, and an espresso/cappuccino machine. The finished lower level included an entertainment room with fireplace and TV, refrigerated wine cellar, full size wet bar, and media room with state-of-the-art technology, surround sound, and leather reclining chairs. And because Shoup liked the latest in all things electronic, he had a high-end security system, central vacuum, back-up generator, and Smart home wiring where all things electronic could be operated through his phone.

Escorting Dia up the stairs, Rafe presented his phone with the invitation, courtesy of Lucius Titan, which one guard promptly scanned and nodded their admittance. The next guard waved a wand over Rafe and Dia, making him thankful Claire had advised against carrying any guns. Shoup's security team, however, were armed and not disguising the holstered guns under their black blazers.

Inside, the opulence was stunning. The foyer had a golden chandelier dripping with sparkling crystals. A large staircase led to the upstairs bedrooms and office. With Dia on his arm, Rafe perused the main level. The wall between the huge living-room and dining-room areas had slid open to create an enormous dance floor, where a live band played. Waiters circled the area, carrying trays of champagne and hors d'oeuvres.

Rafe and Dia discreetly slipped in their earpieces.

"Com check," Rafe said into his.

"Check," Jackson said.

"Check, check," came Claire's reply.

Claire hid in a van nearby somewhere with her husband Drake, who had posed as a caterer earlier to access the property and plant a device to tap into Shoup's home security feed. They would monitor the same cameras during the party that Shoup's men were watching. Claire was also transmitting her live feed to Atlanta so Mica could watch.

Rafe and Dia milled around for a few minutes, gauging the crowd and its level of distracted conversation and alcohol consumption.

"Could you ever see yourself in a house like this?" Rafe asked.

Dia shook her head. "Heavens no. Too big. Too much maintenance. This thing has to be a money pit. No, I'd take something small and secluded and save my quid to visit opulent places someone else maintains. What about you?"

"Too big," he agreed. "I like small and secluded. Some of my happiest childhood memories were the three of us in a remote shack somewhere, living off what we hunted and grew."

"I've never had to hunt for my food. There has always been a corner grocery store."

"You're exceedingly capable. You could if you had to."

"If there's an apocalypse?" She grinned.

"If I sweep you away to an exotic escape away from civilization."

Her cheeks flushed adorably.

"We need to dance," Rafe extended a hand. "Otherwise we'll look suspicious standing around, talking to only ourselves." He left out how he needed to have her in his arms.

"Okay."

When she took his hand, he led her to the dance floor, eyes scanning the surroundings and seeing no threats. He flicked her into a twirl before pulling her into his arms to sway.

She let out a gasp of surprise as their bodies pressed together but soon melted into him. "Did the Rider team teach you about blending-in?"

"A little. Mostly, I learned from my father. He would never have thought to prepare me for a fancy party, but he was all about blending in as a tool. If he wanted to learn to fly, he made friends with pilots. If he wanted to learn to shoot and survive the jungle, he became a guerrilla fighter. Blend to survive."

"Well, right now, I'm appreciating these dance moves."

"Ah. These I learned for the ladies. My father had two left feet." Rafe shook his hips.

"Lots of ladies?" she teased.

He grinned. "A few. Growing up, we mostly lived around older women—motherly figures. In college, I finally put my dancing skills to good use. No serious relationships," he added.

"No one who tempted you?"

He shrugged. "I never thought I was the type to settle." Perhaps his phrasing wasn't entirely accurate. He thought if he ever shared information about his unconventional upbringing with a woman, she would run screaming. By that logic, he didn't think he would find a woman accepting of him and his past and therefore settle with him.

But Dia, who'd seen him in action, was intrigued by his past.

He spun her away and back again. "Why do you ask? Are you hoping to tempt me?" He moved one hand down to her hip, teasing with his touch as he teased with his words.

Her heated gaze trailed to his lips. What would he do if she said yes? He doubted Dia could settle either, considering the way she livened talking about her work and travel. He enjoyed entertaining the thought of some type of future with Dia—every moment with her made him feel vibrant—but he couldn't define what that future might be.

"I have a plan," she said. "Many plans, actually. Short and long-term career goals."

"Ah. And I'm guessing you have all of those outlined in spread-sheets. Probably color-coded, too."

"How did you—"

"I recognize the traits of a type A personality. Competitive, ambitious, organized. You like symmetry by the way you arrange your utensils and meticulously yet absent-mindedly fold your cocktail napkin during conversation."

She stiffened. "There's nothing wrong with being organized."

"On the contrary, it's admirable. You're hard-working and goal-oriented. You'll reach those goals."

When she relaxed slightly at his compliment, he took the opportunity to spin her away then back again.

Rafe treasured these precious moments with Dia in his arms. If he could draw this out, he could show her what time spent with him could be like. Except, there wouldn't be time together if he kept hinting at idiotic vacations in shacks where you gathered your own food. He'd been thinking the seclusion would be romantic, but when he replayed the conversation in his head as he danced, hunting for their dinner didn't sound so romantic—especially to a woman who'd said she wanted opulent getaways.

Mica's voice in their earpiece broke the spell between them. "If you're done making magic on the dance floor, please get busy making magic in Shoup's office. Wait, that didn't come out right. Ugh—start moving toward the staircase. The guard is about to move out of view."

Dia smiled, all radiant beauty as she took his hand and led him off the dance floor. When they reached the foyer and bottom of the staircase, they hesitated a moment as a couple passed by. Rafe and Dia glance around, ensuring they were unseen, then, together, they stepped over the velvet rope.

Giggling like she'd had too much champagne, Dia scrambled up the stairs, tugging Rafe right behind her, who obediently followed like a lovesick puppy dog.

"Okay, this is where I don't have any cameras," Claire said. "I can let you know if someone comes upstairs, but I won't know if anyone's already hiding up here, so watch your back."

They made their way to the far end of the north wing, where Claire's schematics had suggested Shoup's office was.

They tried the door.

"Locked," Dia said.

"Not a problem." Rafe produced a small kit from inside his tuxedo.

"Lock picking, too?"

"Of course. When the apocalypse strikes, there will be many doors to unlock." This wasn't his standard metal kit, which would have a set off the security wands, but a polycarbonate Claire had given him. The stiff, plastic, 3D-printed lock picks would still do the job.

He set to work on the cam lock, using a tension wrench to apply torque and hold the picked pins in place while using the half-diamond pick to move the pins. He had it open in sixty seconds.

They slinked inside the room, closing the door behind them. Rafe took in a large office space with a robust walnut desk of a size that must have been assembled inside the room. On top of the sleek wood sat two large monitors connected by wires to a laptop. The dark auburn walls seemed a sad, missed opportunity for a classic spread of wall-to-wall bookshelves. Instead, the room was adorned with taxidermy—swordfish, bass, angelfish, bucks, bears, moose, and more. The array left little doubt for the man's passion and pastime.

Dia withdrew a thumb drive from the Velcro garter on her thigh, hidden snuggly under her dress. She plugged it into Shoup's desktop so Claire could use her spyware to hack it. "You're in, Claire."

"Copy that." Her chipper voice chimed in stark contrast to the danger of their current situation. "Working like a charm. Three more minutes."

Rafe set to work with the fingerprint dust—white for dark surfaces and dark for light surfaces—on the laptop, desk, lamp, and chair. He wasn't sure which ones were fingers and which were thumbs so he took pictures for Claire to analyze of everything that showed up. When he had a dozen photos, he pulled out the handkerchief in his breast pocket and wiped away the black and white dust.

"Armed guard, making his way up the stairs," Mica said.

"Time to intercept?" Rafe asked.

"If he makes a beeline straight for the office, at his pace, two minutes."

If Shoup's men caught them, there'd be hell to pay. Maybe. In this tangled web of deceit, Shoup knew he would be infiltrated, but not by which Rider team members so Rafe and Dia had hoped to go unnoticed. In Shoup and Lucius' conversation, Lucius had suggested Shoup let Rider think they were stealing information. But if Shoup's men caught them in the act of stealing, would Shoup actually let them go?

What if they didn't know the full spectrum of Shoup's plan? After all, they only knew what Shoup chose to tell Lucius. Would he only feed them false information, or would he trap them and kill them?

Rafe didn't want to find out by being pitted against Shoup's security team of former military men. He and Dia could get past a guard or two, but not all twenty if someone alerted the rest to intruders.

15

*R*afe took shallow breaths, as if they could be overheard by the man heading in their direction. Dia's hand hovered over the USB, waiting for the green light from Claire.

"Done," Claire said at last. "Take the USB, and you're good to go."

Dia tugged the thumb drive out and slid it back into her thigh holder, then made her way toward Rafe, who was already opening the door and exiting. He grabbed her hand and led her out, closing the locked door behind them.

They shuffled down the hallway toward the stairs, when Rafe glimpsed the guard Claire warned about reaching the hallway. Rafe's heart thudded as his mind ran through the list of potential exit points.

He spun Dia into the nearest room with a door open, pulling her body against his. They had entered a bathroom and were crammed against the sink as Rafe's head pivoted in search of an exit route or hiding spot.

Worst case, he could stay and fight while Dia escaped. She was more than capable of handling herself, but he didn't want her captured when they were outnumbered and outgunned. Shoup wasn't the type of man to take prisoners.

Footsteps approached.

Dia hiked one leg up on the counter, pressed her body against Rafe, and grabbed his chin, forcing him to face her. To his surprise, she pressed her lips to his.

Instantly, his shock faded into a surrendering, yielding kiss. When she fisted her hands into his hair, he moved a palm down to cup her butt cheek. He knew she was playing a part, but he could lose himself in this woman for days.

"Hey," a voice snapped. "No guests allowed up here."

Dia broke from the kiss, giggling and looking a little sheepish. "Sorry. I got carried away." She heavily layered her British accent, adding a pouty tone.

Rafe shot the man a grin. "A beautiful woman says 'come with me,' and what's a man to do?"

"Guests loitering on the second floor. I'm escorting them down and outside to leave." He spoke into an earpiece he wore.

Rafe wasn't sure if the guard found their act convincing—which would be odd because that sensual kiss certainly convinced Rafe—or if the man was simply following protocol.

"I'd love another glass of bubbly. Darling, can I have another glass of bubbly?" Dia asked, leaning into Rafe.

"Anything you want. But I intend to complain to our host about being treated rudely when we're fully cooperating."

"We said we're sorry. Didn't we apologize?" she glanced back at the guard behind them on the stairs. "We are sorry." When he said nothing, she turned back around. "I don't think Mr. Grumpy back there believes we're sorry."

"Very well then," Rafe said, relieved they might be able to depart immediately after the theft. "We'll leave, but we'll cancel the security services."

"I think that's harsh for a misunderstanding," Dia complained.

They reached the bottom of the stairs, where they stopped before the velvet rope divider. The guard walked around them, unhooking it and motioning for them to pass.

As Rafe stepped around him, the man held up one hand to the couple and the other to his earpiece.

The guard's demeanor stiffened. "Detained. Copy that."

Detained?

He and Dia sure as hell couldn't allow themselves to be caught now. What if Shoup's guards searched them and found the USB drive? Sure, Lucius had warned Shoup of a theft, but there might be actual hell to pay if they were caught. Rafe knew Shoup would lose little sleep over killing both of them.

Rafe grabbed the stanchion post where the velvet rope had been clipped and jerked it straight up into the man's jaw. With Shoup's security team alerted to their presence, they only had a finite amount of time to escape before his hired guns converged on them.

The guard's head snapped back as he stumbled, falling onto the stairs. Dia reached for his gun and yanked it from his shoulder holster. As soon as she had it in her hand, she spun, and the pair of them raced for the front door.

"Cover's blown. We'll need an extraction. We'll have to make it to the end of the drive with a pickup on the road," Rafe said. "Too many cars at the circle drive."

"Just get moving. We'll track you," Mica said in the earpiece.

"I'll be there," Jackson said.

When they exited the front door, their swift motion caused the two outside guards to turn and regard them. The gun in Dia's hand was a dead giveaway she and Rafe were the disavowed guests their comrade had mentioned on the radio.

Rafe didn't hesitate to charge the one nearest him. He couldn't give the man time to pull his weapon and take aim.

Meanwhile, Dia withdrew her lead weighted ceramic knife from her thigh strap and threw it into the right arm of one guard, a safe play since he probably wore chest armor and a knife in his gun arm would make it hard to shoot.

Rafe plowed into the other guard as he raised his arm to take aim. The gun flew out of sight, and they landed on the hard concrete of the circle drive, the guard's back taking the brunt of the impact.

The man let out a grunt but kept his wherewithal to stay in the fight. He rolled with Rafe, trying to pin him to the ground. Rafe swung a fist into his jaw, stunning the guard long enough to bring a knee into his groin.

As the man rolled off him in agony, Rafe landed a punch to his throat. He would be too busy breathing for the next two minutes to worry about not letting Rafe escape.

Rafe turned back to look at Dia in time to see another guard dive off the porch and crash into her. They disappeared into the bushes.

Why hadn't she used the gun? Perhaps she hadn't wanted the noise to gain further attention, but their skirmish did just that.

The man in whom she'd imbedded her knife took that moment to speak into his mic. Rafe couldn't hear what he said but suspected he was calling for reinforcements.

Rafe attacked the man from behind, landing a solid kick to his kidney. When the guard fell to his knees, Rafe gave him one more blow to the abdomen before reaching down and snatching up his gun. He felt the odd grip.

Hmm. Biosensored.

He believed that meant only its owner's grip print could activate it. That was a pricey feature. And explained why Dia hadn't fired the weapon she'd confiscated. She couldn't, and a cyber weapons expert like her would know that.

Rafe left the man writhing on the ground as he ran to the bushes to help Dia. With a snarl, her attacker stumbled out of the foliage, clutching a bloody nose. She pursued, landing a precision kick to his knee. With a crunching sound, he cried out and fell.

Her tattered champagne dress still mostly covered her, but the holly bush had raked pointed leaves across her skin, leaving dozens of angry red scratches. Panting, she patted at disheveled, unruly hair with one hand while the other was pressed into her lower back. Rafe couldn't tell if she'd been injured more severely, but she was standing.

"Can you run?" he asked her.

She nodded.

"Let's run."

They took off at a sprint, crossing the lawn. Her pace seemed slower than Rafe expected, because he'd seen her run at Cadillac Ranch. He noted a new unevenness in her gait.

Maldición.

Damn. She was injured, and he hoped it wasn't too serious.

WITH EYES WATERING, Dia slid into the car and tugged on her seatbelt. She caught her breath, though each inhalation pulled at the ever-tightening muscles in her back. Something in the tackle had rattled her spine, causing the muscles on either side of her vertebrae to spasm and lock.

She sat as still as possible, riding out the curves and minor bumps in the road.

"We took on a few Goomba's," Rafe said, smiling at her.

"We sure did." She smiled back, adoring the way he used her Mario Brothers' reference.

"What part of that was covert, exactly?" Jackson asked, glancing in the rearview mirror intermittently as if looking for a tail.

If Shoup's men had followed them, they had a back-up plan to reach Lake Michigan and escape by boat. In her condition, she desperately hoped a boat ride wasn't in her immediate future.

"The part where we got what we came for," Rafe said.

He set the gun he'd confiscated down on the seat between them. "Biosensored."

She nodded. "Smart guns. These aren't even released for public use yet. It requires a combination of a fingerprint and radio-frequency identification."

"How does that work?" Rafe asked.

Jackson made a right turn at a light. "RFID uses electromagnetic fields to automatically identify a tag attached to an object."

"Like a ring or bracelet," Dia added.

"So only the person who has both the matching fingerprint and is wearing the radio-frequency device can unlock and use the gun?" Rafe asked.

"Exactly. The man likes his fancy toys." She turned her head to face the window, so Rafe couldn't see her pain.

Any minute, the tightness would subside and the tension in the muscles ease. A cold sweat trickled down her neck. Maybe if she focused on something else, she could get her mind off the discomfort.

When the car hit a bump in the road, a finger brushed hers. She glanced down to see Rafe had rested his hand beside hers on the middle seat as he gazed out the window.

She thought of dancing with him, bodies pressed close as they moved to the rhythm. For the first time in her life, she hadn't minded being led. She could give control over to him for fun, for pleasure. Oh, and kissing him again had been pure pleasure.

I think you feel the potential for what's between us as well. I won't let you minimize what we have or could have.

His words were still seeping through her, permeating like a warm elixir and infusing her mind with possibilities. What could they have? What did that relationship look like? She couldn't envision it, which scared her. What if she gave too much of herself over and lost everything she'd worked so hard to become? What if she lost Rafe because she held back and didn't give enough of herself to the relationship?

Ugh. Her mind was stuck in an impossible loop. If she didn't act on her feelings, her attraction, then the loop couldn't morph into a tornado and spiral out of control. Right?

⁂

JACKSON DROVE them to the hotel. "Chauffeur service complete," he announced with a grin at Rafe and Dia in the rearview mirror.

Rafe reached for the door handle when Dia crushed his hand in hers.

"I'll need help," she said, voice strained and breathless, her grip vice-like.

Rafe went on instant, high alert. "What's wrong?"

She sat very still and faced forward, one hand on his and the other a white-knuckled grip on the door handle. "I think I strained something when Shoup's man tackled me. I don't think... I don't think it's a slipped disc or I wouldn't have been able to run at all. Maybe a pulled muscle or more than one? I can't move without pain."

"Where does it hurt?"

"My lower back. Hurts if I move or take a deep breath."

"We'll take you to the hospital." He signaled Jackson to drive.

"No." She shook her head. "Like I said, if the injury was serious, I don't think I would've been running. I only need time and a shit-ton of anti-inflammatories. But for now, I need help to get to my room."

"Okay. Let me come around to the other side." He exited the car, walked around, and opened her side door.

Jackson cut the engine and came around to help.

"I'll carry you," Rafe told Dia as he bent down.

She shook her head, one eye twitching. "No, I think the weight distribution of that will hurt. Sitting is okay. I think I can walk maybe with help."

Rafe straightened and thought for a moment. They needed a wheelchair, but that wasn't something to which he had ready access. He glanced to the lobby of the hotel. What about a chair and wheels?

"Don't go anywhere," he told her as he turned to go inside the hotel. His tease was rewarded by her scoffing noise.

He walked through the sliding glass doors into the lobby.

Chair and wheels.

We can make this work.

He picked up one cushioned chair from an array in the lobby and walked toward the bell hop. Apparently, his tuxedo lent him credibility, because the young man merely gave him an inquisitive look rather than accusatory like he might be stealing the furniture.

Rafe explained what he had in mind and the situation. The bell boy obliged his request. When Rafe returned to the vehicle, he had a wheeled luggage cart and a chair.

He smiled at Dia. "I brought you a wheelchair."

She started to chuckle but clamped it down when it caused obvious discomfort. He hated to see her in pain.

He arranged the chair on the ground outside her door. "I'll get in the car and straddle you. I'll lift you up enough and pivot us as one in order for Jackson to get his arms around you. Then, we'll turn you ever so slow, slow, slowly, back, facing outward, your back to him with your legs and knees toward me as we ease you onto the chair."

"Okay." She gave him a tight-lipped nod. "This is mortifying."

"We got you." Rafe crawled into the vehicle, careful not to bump Dia, and squatted low so he would use mostly his quadriceps and glutes for this maneuver. Bending over her, he reached around under her arms.

"Try to control yourself," he said lightly. "This isn't the time to get frisky."

"I am so not feeling frisky right now."

"*Oh, mi corazón,*" he said in mocked affront.

Gingerly and attuned to her every discomfort, they maneuvered through extricating her from the vehicle and onto the chair. When she was situated there, she gripped the wooden armrests as Jackson and Rafe lifted her with the chair onto the luggage cart. Her head came barely under the overarching bar on top. Slowly, Rafe rolled her to the elevator, Jackson following.

A few minutes later, they entered her room, where Rafe and Jackson eased her onto the bed.

"I'll fetch some water and ibuprofen," Jackson said.

Rafe used the time Jackson was gone to adjust Dia's pillows to her liking.

Her complexion was less pale and peaked by the time Jackson returned. He handed her the medication and glass to rinse it down.

"Food?" Rafe offered, taking the water bottle back and setting it on the nightstand.

Swallowing the pills, Dia shook her head. "No, thanks."

"You need anything else from me?" Jackson asked. "I'll go park the car and head back to the room."

"No," Dia said. "But take the USB. You can get it to Claire." When she moved her to hand down to access her thigh belt, she grimaced.

"I'll get it," Rafe offered.

Fingers grazing her thigh, he felt the strap and tugged the jump drive out of one of its pockets, handing it to Jackson who'd been gentleman enough to look away. "We're good. I'll call you if we need anything."

"I'll get it to Claire." With that, Jackson slipped away, the hotel door closing behind him.

Rafe turned back to Dia and frowned. "We set you up on top of the covers. Probably not the best move. I can fold them in half over top of you so you don't get cold. Do you want to get out of that dress? It's covered in dirt and leaves like you tangled with a black bear."

"I feel like I tangled with a black bear. I need a few minutes to let the ibuprofen kick in before I try to move. You can go. I don't need you to babysit me."

"This is taking care of a partner, not babysitting. I'll be right here if you need anything."

Taking off his tuxedo jacket and shirt, he left on his undershirt, then eased into the empty space on the queen bed beside her, keeping his distance and careful not to cause movement of the mattress that might jostle her back.

"I'll lie here because the stiff polyester chair looks uncomfortable, but try to keep your hands off me."

She rolled her eyes, but the grin she couldn't quite suppress betrayed her amusement and perhaps how touched she was that he'd stayed.

16

___

The next morning, Dia woke sore and stiff to an empty bed. Good. She didn't need an audience when she hobbled around like a ninety-year-old. She'd appreciated that Rafe and Jackson had followed her request to go to her room and sleep it off and hadn't tied to over protectively manhandle her and demand she get medical care.

First order of business was ibuprofen, and—oh—three tablets rested beside a bottle of water on the nightstand.

Bless that thoughtful man.

She pushed herself up slowly, gingerly, as the taut, tense muscles of her back protested, like the stretching of a string on a bow. She managed to sit upright, pop the pills, and wash them down with a slug of water.

After carefully standing, she walked over to her suitcase. She craved a hot shower, and thinking about the bathroom arrangement, hoped she could step over the side of the tub to get into the shower. No, the real challenge would be bending over to turn on the faucet.

She looked between the bed and the open bathroom door. Rest waited in one direction and pain in the other, but lying around all day wasn't an option. She thought about Rafe calling her out for being type A. Part of that personality trait was disliking wasting time, even for an injury.

Leaning down, she intended to pick out an outfit for the day when her spinal muscles spasmed in protest. Gasping as the pain radiated outward, she shot out one hand against the wall to brace herself and take the weight off her back muscles.

She was still holding that position when the electronic click of the door sounded and it opened. She glimpsed Rafe from her peripheral vision but didn't risk twisting her neck to fully look at him and torque any more muscles.

"Are you holding up the wall or is the wall holding up you?" he asked.

"It appears I'm not yet physically able to go through the motions of taking a shower. This is as far as I managed."

"Not alone, anyway." He sauntered into the room, letting the door close behind him as he carried a bag and two steaming cups. She hoped at least one of those contained hot tea.

At her slit-eyed gaze, he said, "Relax. As much as I would love to take a shower with you, I was referring to starting and adjusting the water. I'd be happy to jump in there and help you wash, though."

Despite her pain, her traitorous body tingled at the imagery.

He set everything down on the dresser beside the TV, pulling out some wrapped goods she suspected were bagels and other objects she couldn't identify from the distance and the angle of her vision.

When her muscle tantrum subsided, she slowly straightened and let go of the wall. "What all did you pick up?"

"Hot tea—Earl gray. Bagel—lox and cream cheese. I took a guess there. And I wasn't sure if you'd want heat therapy or ice therapy. So we got heat packs and ice packs." He lifted them up, one in each hand, and wriggled them in the air.

Everything looked wonderful. "Are you trying to make me fall in love with you? It's working."

He handed her the tea, but she avoided eye contact, not wanting to know how he'd interpreted what she'd inadvertently blurted. When she took a sip, the warm liquid instantly soothed the ache in her throat from when she tensed and gasped in pain. Next, she eagerly ate the bagel sandwich.

"You guessed right," she said with a moan of gratefulness at the delicious food. "And I think I'll start with the heat therapy to loosen things up enough to take a shower, and then we'll cool down the inflammation."

She took another sip of tea. "What does Mica have planned for us for the day?"

"Rest. She knows about your setback, and there's not a lot to do today, anyway." He took a bite of his bagel, which looked to be pumpernickel with a veggie cream cheese spread. "They'll send Lucius in to gauge Shoup's reaction to the theft and see what type of retaliation he's scheming."

He drank his beverage, coffee, she suspected by the scent. Gesturing, he said, "This TV is fully equipped with all the major retailers—HBO, Hulu, Disney Plus, Netflix, and Prime. We'll have a marathon while you're on bedrest."

Dia frowned, trying to recall the last time she laid in bed all day and watched TV. High school maybe? Even then, she was more likely to waste a day playing video games. With her current condition, she wasn't likely to achieve much else.

She set her bagel down, half-eaten, and washed down the bite in her mouth with tea.

Rafe picked up the heat pack and snapped the device within that activated the bag. "*Vamos.* On your stomach. Heat and a massage should do the trick to get you loosened enough for the shower."

She crawled onto the bed on her stomach, but paused to turn around and blink at him. "Massage?"

Rafe shrugged. "Well, it's no hot stone massage and five-star spa, but these hands have been known to work a little magic." He made a show of stretching his fingers in the air.

"You're giving me a back massage?"

"You ask that like you've never had a massage before."

"Not from a—" *dang, what the heck is he?* A love interest? A man she'd seriously considered sleeping with again after that dance last night. "Not from someone I've been intimate with," she finished, settling down on her stomach and relaxing into the bed. She moved the pillow out of the way because it caused too much of an arch in her back and too much tension.

Rafe placed two heating bags on either side of her spine, and the warmth instantly softened the sinewy tissue.

"You've never had a boyfriend give you a massage?"

"No. Is that something expected?"

"Given my upbringing, I'm obviously no expert on what's normal. In my opinion, the man ought to like and appreciate the woman's body enough to find reasons to get his hands on it. If he's a true gentleman, he'll give a massage expecting nothing in return."

"So, he's giving a massage without an ulterior motive?"

"Not entirely. He may have many motives, like to make you feel good, hoping the soothing touch leads to sex, but even without it, he should feel an intrinsic reward for making you feel good. To be clear, in your current condition, I'm not after sex. At least not today, anyway. Another day, perhaps you can beg me to bed you."

She laughed, then winced at the pain laughing caused. Fortunately, the warmth of the heat packs continued to ease her muscles.

After a moment of shuffling about the room, Rafe said, "This will feel better if I'm not rubbing through your dress."

"Okay." She found she trusted him fully.

The packs lifted, and the teeth of the zipper on the back of her dress buzzed, followed by the sensation of the fabric falling away.

He tucked the dress respectfully around her so only her back was exposed. Next, she felt the coarse texture of a small towel on the lower half of her back and the heat of the pads placed over it. Warm hands began massaging the upper half of her back with creamy smoothness. Lotion, she realized. She pulled the pillow over her head and groaned her relief into it.

"Don't get any ideas about seducing me," Rafe said. "This is strictly a therapeutic massage."

"It feels so damn good. And I'm not thinking about sex in my current condition."

"Liar."

She chuckled into the pillow, and this time her back didn't spasm in pain.

He spent a solid fifteen minutes on her upper back, seeming to find all the tight knots and patiently working them loose. Before moving lower, he shifted the towel and heating pads to her upper back. His method seemed to ensure the muscles were pliable and warm before he worked on them and stayed loose and relaxed when he was done. Shifting the heat around also meant she didn't get cold with her back exposed in the hotel room, although she suspected she couldn't get cold with this man running his hands over her bare skin.

He was right. She couldn't help but think about sex. How could she not when they were alone together in a hotel room and she already knew how incredible intimacy was with Rafe?

After another fifteen minutes, he stopped. "Feel better?"

"Yes. That was wonderful."

"Do you want to rest awhile or take that shower?"

"Oh, definitely shower."

His weight lifted from the bed. "I'll get the water started and stay out here in the room in case you need anything."

AFTER HER SHOWER, she dressed in clean exercise clothes and exited the bathroom to find Rafe relaxed on the bed, flipping through channels on the television like he owned the place. Surprisingly, she liked this man in her space.

"Jackson dropped off a medical kit," Rafe said, gesturing to a blue bag on the TV stand. "He thought you might want the Neosporin in there for your cuts and scrapes."

"Damn holly bushes." They had stung under the soap and water of the shower. She walked over and rummaged through the bag. Surprisingly, the medical kit was packed with goodies. "There's muscle relaxant cream in here." She pulled it out and set it aside next to the Neosporin. "Burn cream. Every shape and size of bandages. Sutures. Lidocaine. Sleep aids. Epi pen?"

"Never know when a client has a peanut allergy. The Rider team has a locker of weapons and medical aid kits in all the major cities we fly into. There are three spouses who are physicians—David, Jenna, and Jessica. I think they designed these, so they're not your standard over-the-counter first aid kit."

"I'll say." She carried an antiseptic cream over to the bed and sat beside Rafe.

"I found *Chuck* reruns."

Wriggling into her pillows, she said, "Let's do this."

⁎

SHOUP NURSED the hangover from his birthday celebration as he stared out the window of his Chicago office building. The party had been a success, accounting for satisfied guests, most of whom were customers or were at some point and could be again.

The Rider SI infiltration was anticipated, and they'd only succeeded in stealing what he'd allowed them to steal, but their very presence on his property irked him. No, he was irked they'd escaped unscathed. He'd hoped his men could have at least inflicted as much physical damage on the duo as they'd done on them, even though the spineless Lucius Titan had suggested simply letting them sneak in and out, thinking they'd been undetected. Instead of pulverizing the Rider thieves, Shoup watched the video of them dashing away across his lawn.

"Who was the woman?" he asked his audience.

Nick stood looking out the window as Lucius and his redheaded Pitbull Hoyle sat across from Shoup's desk.

"I don't know that one," Lucius said. "Could be a new hire."

"I want to kill every last Rider," Shoup grumbled.

Lucius steepled his fingers. "Targeting any one of them will incur the wrath of the rest. I can assure you, you don't want that type of trouble. I tried a well-orchestrated attack on multiple team members, and it landed me in both a wheelchair and in prison. Consider alternatives. You have to first discredit their organization. We find and kill the Sizani family—there's no press announcement of their death, so they clearly survived the crash you mentioned. We pin the leak of their location on Jackson, whose loyalty has been questionable at best. This failure will affect their ability to get clients. Slowly, we chip away at other clients, targeting them. Once the organization is completely crippled, we can start eliminating them one by one in way that won't link back to us."

Us? Shoup wasn't sure an *'us'* existed in any scenario. Lucius' proposal sounded slow, tedious, and tiresome. Months to years could be involved to completely dismantle Rider SI. He had no intention of spending the time and resources Lucius suggested.

Defacing Mica's security company by killing the Sizani family had its appeal, though. He'd failed twice to kidnap them and already the man who'd hired his company was threatening not to pay the second half on delivery due to the time delay. The coup was likely to fail anyway. If his team found the Sizani family and killed them, Shoup could claim an accident in the attempted kidnapping. If the man didn't pay, Shoup still would have succeeded in damaging Rider's reputation.

First, they had to find where the Sizani's were being hidden. For that, he needed Lucius.

"We'll start with the Sizani's and discuss how to further undermine Rider when that issue is settled."

17

"What's the word?" Mica asked Claire as she strolled into their refurbished car garage command center.

Claire had flown back from Chicago last night with whatever Dia and Rafe had downloaded from Shoup's home computer. A jumbo-sized coffee sat on her desk.

Before Claire could answer, Mica added, "We need a name for this place. We're like mission control here." She liked having a clandestine workspace away from the Rider offices, which were open to the public.

"The Bat Cave?" Claire suggested.

Mica countered. "Ooh. The Justice League Watchtower? That was a space station, though."

"*Themyscira*—Wonder Woman's secret invisible island?"

"As fun as those sound, I think it needs to be something more discrete. Something no one would decipher if we were overheard."

Claire spun in her chair to face Mica, eyes lit with excitement. "Like—are they talking about a person, a place, or a pizzeria?"

"Exactly."

Food, Mica thought. She considered the whitewashed walls on the exterior of the renovated garage and the steak restaurant off Piedmont Road where she and David liked to go once a year for their anniversary. "Bones."

Claire tilted her head to one side. "Drake took me there once. Nice place. Okay. Bones. Not as mysterious sounding as *Themyscira,* but it'll work."

If she and Claire planned to be spending more time in the garage, Mica would need to hire someone at the main office for public appearance and walk-ins when she and Claire were here.

Claire turned her ergonomically and outrageously expensive chair back around to face her five-screen monitor consul as she rolled her shoulders. "Back to the word. The word is *malware.*"

Mica nodded. "As suspected. A tiger and his stripes. We knew Lucius would betray us. Now we have the proof."

Claire snorted. "The proof is in the transcripts."

"True. But we can't call out Lucius to his face using those because we don't want him knowing there's a bug in his wheelchair."

"Well, we have proof. And Shoup completely destroyed my laptop," Claire said. "Also, for the record, I haven't had a decent night sleep since Maxine broke Lucius out of prison."

Mica grimaced. "I'm sorry."

Claire had been kidnapped with intentions of torture by Lucius men. Fortunately, Drake had rescued her. Mica hadn't intended for Lucius' release to wreak havoc on Claire's nerves. Hopefully, in a few days they would get him arrested again and back in prison.

"What about your laptop?" Mica asked.

Claire gestured to a laptop on her computer table. "I sure as hell wouldn't plug that thumb drive into my master mainframe to test it. I took my laptop offline and plugged in the thumb drive from Shoup's house. The virus wiped out my computer."

"That's it? He gave us a computer destroying USB drive?"

Claire nodded. "I'll go back and dig in a bit, but my suspicion is that it was designed to send our data to him via the Internet and then self-destruct. But I didn't have the laptop connected to Wi-Fi so it couldn't transmit."

"We'll let a little time pass, and then I'll harass Lucius for his entirely expected double-cross. Since he's all about favors, I'll turn this into a *you-owe-me* conversation."

She meandered over to Claire's other workstation where gadgets tangled in mid assembly on a long rectangular table against one wall. "What are you working on?"

"Little concoction just for Shoup." A mischievous grin spread across Claire's lips. "He's got to have the latest and greatest, right? Including biosensored weapons for his team, one of which Jackson gave me when he handed over the USB drive. Shoup's high-tech guns aren't even on the market yet."

"Why the switch? He didn't have those a year ago."

Claire raised a finger in the air. "I believe he made this transition after our showdown at Poindexter Pharmaceuticals. If you recall, Reece, who had been unarmed and facing execution, took out a half a dozen of his men using their own weapons, during which Shoup nearly died himself. I'm guessing the man's thinking he needs an extra layer of protection against badass Army Rangers and Marines."

"So where do these come into play?" Mica picked up the two halves of Claire's work in progress.

Claire wriggled her eyebrows. "I'm creating small EMP devices. Short range. If we go head-to-head with Shoup—"

"*When* we go head-to-head," Mica corrected.

"*When* we go head-to-head with Shoup, these little babies will fry their handguns and nobody can use them."

"Fry?"

"Okay, so, technically, they won't be sizzling with smoke, but the electromagnetic pulse will destroy the radio frequency device that reads the armband and allows the gun to be activated and the trigger to be pulled by the user."

"Hmm. Color me impressed. But Shoup must know there's a

vulnerability to using these types of guns, right? Why would he risk they might be deactivated?"

"He's clever, but he's also an arrogant son of a bitch, am I right? He knows no hand-held EMP device exists on the market. Would he believe somebody could create a handheld EMP to use against him? I think not."

"You're amazing, Claire."

"Thanks." She blew against her fingernails and dusted them off on her t-shirt with an air of playful self-importance. "Still," she frowned as she cautioned, "they could have standard handguns as backup."

Claire rolled her chair over to her gadget workstation. After adjusting her rubber gloves, she leaned over and began tinkering. She never handled anything involving sterile substances, so Mica guessed the gloves were to avoid something caustic on her hands or prevent shocks. Based on the wiring on the table, Mica suspected the latter.

"Is that a disposable camera?" Mica asked.

"Yes, smallest one I could find. I pried open the chassis to get to the circuit board and electrolytic capacitor." She gestured to a black cylindrical-looking component with two leads. "Then I discharged the flash and confirmed the discharge with my voltmeter. Next, I removed the printed circuit board and replaced the charge switch."

Mica leaned over her shoulder. "This is your mini-EMP." Amazed, she leaned closer. "You added these insulated copper cables onto the capacitor's two terminals and connected one end to this switch."

Claire had wrapped the enamel-coated wire a dozen times around a circular object about two inches in diameter, with the wire lined up precisely without crease or overlap. She pulled out the two-inch PVC pipe, leaving the thick loop with protruding ends that she connected to the terminals.

She added a small iron rod, explaining, "This will intensify the generated magnetic field."

"Cool. What's the radius?" Mica asked.

"I'm expecting something like fifty feet. I'll test it, but I still need to sandpaper the enamel coating off the tips—" she gestured to the two wire leads protruding from the coil, "—before attaching one to the other terminal of the capacitor, followed by attaching the remaining lead to the 'on' side of the switch, then put the battery back in and make a case with our 3D printer to contain everything."

Claire had spoken so quickly, Mica had lost the sequence of next steps.

"Okay then. I'll leave you to it."

***

THE NEXT MORNING after their *Chuck* marathon, Dia stretched in bed, feeling her back muscles had substantially loosened since yesterday. Rafe had worked some serious magic, followed by hours of relaxation and a camaraderie she hadn't enjoyed since friends in college.

She felt at ease in his company, and despite wanting much more from her, he didn't push.

"How are you feeling?" he asked.

She blinked her eyes open to see a handsome man on her bed. He was propped up on one elbow, mouth curving in an appreciative grin as if he'd enjoyed watching her stretch. They were both still fully clothed, which she was grateful for because the intimacy of pajamas might have tempted her to make a move, and sex was something neither her body nor her emotions were ready for.

"Much better, thanks to you. I think today will be a good day for some movement. Some light walking."

"You need to stretch more than that."

"I will." But she knew her defensive tone betrayed that she hadn't considered she needed to stretch more.

He arched an eyebrow at her. "Didn't your martial arts teacher educate you on the importance of stretching?"

"I'm sure we covered the topic."

Rafe rolled off the bed and walked around to her side. "I'll help you. Stretching is more effective when someone helps you elongate those muscles even more than you can do easily on your own."

"Okay." She was open to any suggestions that would have her on a faster road to recovery, and he seemed to know what he was talking about.

Rafe pushed furniture around the room to make a space on the floor. When he had her lie down on her back, she tensed. They were close, with his hands on her body.

"Relax," he told her. "I won't make a move on a hotel room floor. I do have standards."

She did relax after that. They cycled through a series of stretches and twists involving her torso, legs, and arms. By the end, her muscles were positively grateful for the stretching, but her core had an entirely different reaction to his fingers deftly moving over her shoulders and thighs as he extended different muscles to elongate them.

When he finished tantalizing her body with his therapeutic hands, he helped her stand. She felt oddly breathless, though she hadn't expended any physical energy.

"Good?" His body hovered close to hers.

"Yes," was the only word she could manage without betraying her arousal.

His gaze trailed from her eyes down to her lips, and his dilated pupils betrayed his own sexual desires.

He took a step back. "I'll touch base with Mica. Why don't you finish loosening those muscles in the shower, maybe top it off with the muscle relaxant cream from the first aid kit. I'll meet you downstairs at the hotel buffet for breakfast in an hour."

Dia swallowed and nodded, unable to do anything but watch him walk away and leave her hotel room.

⁂

An hour later, Rafe sat in the hotel restaurant trying to shake the sensation of Dia's body in his hands. The dance, the kiss, the massage, and the stretching were taxing his limits of self-control. His restraint was either the mark of a saint or an idiot, he wasn't sure yet.

Yesterday, though, had strengthened his desire for a relationship. They had relaxed, watching TV and laughing at the comedic moments. He'd liked seeing her unwind and enjoy life.

Dia approached and took a seat. Her short brown hair was neatly combed to one side, and her honey skin had a healthy glow. She moved with greater ease this morning, he noted. Although she sat with impeccable posture, it wasn't the ramrod straight it had been in the car.

"Feeling better?" he asked.

"Yes. Thanks to you, I'm much more mobile. You ordered me tea." She opened the pouch for Earl Grey, placed the tea bag in her cup, and added hot water from the ceramic teapot.

"I haven't been here long. It's still warm."

They made pleasant small talk about the weather until their order arrived and plates of bacon, eggs, and fruit spread before them.

"Thank you for yesterday. I haven't laughed out loud that much in years."

"It was fun. I think neither of us have enough of these light moments in our lives."

She munched on a piece of bacon. "My excuse is too much work."

"Don't forget the planning. Too many spreadsheets and goals."

She narrowed her eyes at him. "I like my spreadsheets. Anyway, what's your excuse?"

"I suppose it's always waiting for the other shoe to drop. That's the phrase, right? Growing up, the only certainty was change. I'd start to like a place, make friends, and suddenly Dad's uprooting us to a new country. Soon, I was slower to form attachments. I started to live in a constant state of unease. When was the next life-altering event going to strike? Turns out, it wasn't the apocalypse, but my Dad's death was a huge shock. It took years to unravel that lifestyle he'd taught us."

"And now?" she asked, voice intrigued and devoid of judgment.

"I'm getting better. Building friendships. The Rider team gives me stability. Roots I've never had." He shook his head. "That was heavy conversation for breakfast."

"I appreciate you sharing it with me."

He swallowed at the raw emotions stuck in his throat. He'd never opened up like this to a woman. He considered his top three reasons for never thinking he'd have a long-term relationship: not feeling worthy given his background, his actual background, and his angst about the ever-shifting future. Dorian had boosted Rafe's self-worth, Dia had shown him how his background made him the exceptional man he was today, and time spent with her made him feeling like taking a chance of having a future together.

Clearing his throat, he said, "We have our new assignment."

"Let's hear it. I'm here to help with anything that contributes to the safety of the Sizani family."

He was grateful she didn't press him to divulge more of his past. Although she held no judgment, sharing took an emotional toll him him.

"Then this is right up your alley. You and I are to join the protection detail for Hiba and the kids. Reece, Ryan, and your father are guarding them right now. We have two days to get to Atlanta and then to the safe house." He took a bite of his omelet and washed it down with coffee.

"Two days. Okay." She speared a piece of pineapple. "Anything I'm responsible for before then?"

"No. Why? You have a hot date?" he teased, though suspected her question had been more related to giving herself a little more time to recover from her back injury.

"No." She chuckled before eating the piece of fruit. "I'd like another day or two recovery time."

Rafe looked down at his empty plate and over at his empty coffee mug. They were both flying back to Atlanta today, but not on the same flight. Claire had booked him through the Rider company, and Dia had booked her own.

He should say something witty, and maybe romantic. Something to make her miss him while they were briefly apart, but nothing came to mind. He would see her again soon, he assured himself. This was a short-term goodbye. Nevertheless, he lingered at the table until she finished eating, then signed the form to send the dining bill to the room.

Side by side, they walked to the elevator.

As they rode up, he turned to her. "Farewell kiss to hold me over till I see you again?" He gave her his most playful smile.

"Sure," she said, narrowing her eyes at him before presenting her cheek.

The elevator dinged, and the door slid open. Rafe blocked it open with one foot as he leaned over, cupping her chin gently and turning her lips toward his. When she didn't resist, he kissed her.

He didn't stop at something sweet and simple as he'd intended. With his lips and tongue, he pushed more firmly and coaxed her lips open, diving deeper with his tongue and exploring as she moaned her approval.

Feeling her hungry mouth against his was enough to drive him mad. He had visions of backing her against the elevator wall and hoisting her up so he could grind against her. But this was Dia, the woman with whom he wanted a future. He would bring her endless hours of pleasure, but only after she accepted he wasn't a fleeting fling. Groping in an elevator wasn't the message he wanted to send.

When the elevator beeped in angry protest at being kept open, Rafe forced himself to separate and slide back. The look in her eyes before the contraption swept her up to her floor was one of shock mixed with arousal.

He couldn't wait to kiss her again like that. But their next assignment had them back protecting the Sizani family, and all under one roof with her father. He had permission from him to date Dia, but intimacy under the same roof wasn't something either man was prepared for.

Rafe would have to keep his hands to himself if he wanted to keep them attached to his body.

18

Dia packed despite her spinning head after Rafe's kiss. Meticulously, she separated clothes in different compartments from each other and from toiletries. She wondered what Rafe—who noted her neatness—would say about her luggage orientation.

She squeezed her hands around the nunchaku she never had an opportunity to use on this trip before tossing them on the bed next to her suitcase.

The man was relentless—the dance, the attentiveness, the kiss. She wanted more, and he knew it. Reveled in it.

Stay strong, Dia.

A knock sounded. "It's Rafe. I've come to say goodbye."

Rafe.

Hadn't he already said goodbye? Was he planning on kissing and teasing her again into a frenzy.

Scolding her ridiculous heart as it kicked up a notch at the sound of his voice, she walked to the door. She didn't have time for infatuations and distractions. She had a tremendous amount of work to do between updating her boss and preparing for the next part of protecting the Sizani family. Not to mention a hundred emails she'd let slide yesterday in favor of a television series marathon. While this assignment was her most active, most pressing, she still researched and prepared for other assignments—had the spreadsheets to prove it. Other countries were in need of her expertise to either get their enhanced digital security in place or troubleshoot their challenges.

Just goodbye, she assured herself. He'd already given her a doozy of a kiss, and he'd sworn he wouldn't do more unless she accepted a relationship.

This was a brief farewell.

She opened the door to see him standing in his Rider bullet-resistant suit. His destination was the airport and not an assignment, but, as one who traveled a great deal, she understood wearing the suit was often easier than packing it.

With a quirk on his lips and glint of desire in his eyes, no one would know he was a deadly shot, but they might guess he was amazing in bed.

This man is too much to handle.

He eased inside her room, rolling his luggage behind him. "My flight's in two hours. Claire will text you with everything you need to meet up with me in Atlanta in two days. From there, we'll drive to the safe house." He looked around the room as if sizing up what she had packed and what remained. His eyes lingered briefly on the nunchaku.

"Okay." She turned and let the door close.

Apparently, they were on terms such that he could waltz into her room without an invitation. To be honest, they were. Her irritation stemmed more from her body's warm reaction to seeing him again so soon.

When she turned back around, Rafe had moved close to her, snaking an arm around her waist. How had he been so quiet?

"You already had your goodbye kiss," she said, voice raspy.

"I'm greedy. I came back for another one."

He pressed his lips to her, causing her body to erupt in flame. What was wrong with her? Couldn't she play a little hard to get?

Not with him.

Her body knew what it wanted, and Rafe was the man her body wanted it from. She kissed him back even as she drowned in the intoxicating feel of him.

He maneuvered her toward the bed, and she didn't resist when he stepped back to slide her shirt over her head.

"You said—"

He cut off her words with another kiss, this one began on her lips and trailed down her neck, then collar bone, to her bra strap. Helplessly lost to him, she moaned.

"I know what I said." A playful tone lit his voice as his fingers slid over her skin and under the waist of her pants.

He slid them down so she wore only her bra and panties. The sight of his hungry gaze had her swooning.

No way.

She was MI6. She did not swoon.

When he eased her onto the bed, he loomed over her like a hungry predator intent on devouring her. "You are so beautiful." His throat bobbed in a swallow.

Lowering himself, he kissed his way down her neck again, this time not stopping at her clavicle but moving down her chest.

When he nipped at her breasts, she sucked in a breath. Warm fingers trailed up her thigh, ducked under her panties, and moved into and within her. He took his time, working her into a panting frenzy until his lips worked lower, over her abdomen, down one hip, and to her thigh.

She was writhing now, lost to him. When the warmth of his tongue settled in the perfect spot, she sank fingers into his hair and lost herself to the pleasure of his touch.

After leaving Dia sated, Rafe walked through the hotel lobby toward the front entrance. He could still taste her and hear the echoes of her moans. He took a drink cold water from the bottle he'd packed, cooling his internal heat. He had a plane to catch.

Walking away from her when he wanted nothing more than to sink himself inside her and take what she'd offered him had required all of his willpower. He had to continually remind himself he'd meant what he said about wanting a relationship—even if it meant his physical desires and needs would go temporarily unfulfilled.

He sent a quick text to Dia, and once outside, he realized in his distracted state, he hadn't used his phone app to summon a rideshare. After checking his watch, he decided he would take a taxi instead, knowing it would be more expensive. He spotted one already at the curb, probably waiting for hotel guests. He needed to first take the medical kit he carried back to the Rider locker, then head to the airport. After Jackson had left the supply bag with them, he'd returned to his assignment by Lucius' side.

Jackson. Rafe worried about his colleague's safety, working so close to a scoundrel like Lucius. Drake, Maxine, and Vladimir were in Chicago, too, so he wasn't without immediate assistance should he need it.

When summoned, the the driver popped open the trunk and hoped out.

"I've got the luggage," Rafe told him. He hoisted his luggage up and set it inside, then slid into the rear passenger seat, one hand still on the door.

Before he could close it, a boot lashed out, striking his forearm. The pain lanced through his elbow and radiated down to his wrist.

The taxi driver cried out, and Rafe caught movement in his peripheral vision, suspecting someone was wrenching the driver out of his seat.

The man who'd kicked Rafe tried to join him in the backseat, but Rafe pivoted on his butt on the smooth fake leather seat and lashed out his own leg, connecting solidly with the man's hip.

The force caused Rafe to slide back at an angle, bumping into the backside of the driver's seat. He was about to push off and go after his attacker, when something sharp dug into the side of his neck.

Rafe tried to scramble away but found his limbs heavy and clumsy. *Drugged,* he realized dimly. The intramuscular sedative worked fast, as only seconds passed before Rafe's vision grew blurry and cobwebs formed in his head.

The man who'd first kicked him, chucked Rafe's legs aside and sat beside him. The person—a blonde-haired woman Rafe now saw— who'd injected him slid behind the wheel.

Ambushed like an amateur, he scolded himself. They had been ready to pounce outside the hotel as soon as they identified his transport vehicle.

Using all of his strength and willpower, he turned his head to face his attacker. "Wait a damn—"

The butt of a man's gun came down hard against Rafe's cheek, and he slumped over, his back half on the seat and his front half propped up on the driver's seat.

He felt as though someone had stuffed ten cotton balls in his mouth as his muscles went lax. Completely helpless, he felt the vehicle lurch into traffic.

The woman driver fidgeted with the radio. "Toss his phone in case his whereabouts are being monitored."

Alanis Morissette's *You Oughta Know* blared through the speakers.

Rafe was still hunched over, body limp as a noodle, with pain throbbing in his right cheekbone and right forearm. He thought nothing was broken. He wasn't dead yet, so they hadn't poisoned him. At least nothing fast-acting. The injection seemed to be a sedative, as he'd initially surmised.

"Lola, can you change the damn music? This is like nails on a chalkboard," the man complained.

"Driver picks the music," the woman retorted. "Besides, I like Alanis—you know, before she went soft. Her music puts me in the mood to kick ass. And we are so going to kick this guy's ass."

The glee in her voice had Rafe inwardly cringing. He believed she would enjoy hurting him.

"You'll get off torturing him, won't you?" her companion asked.

"Hell yeah, Cap. I'm not like the rest of Shoup's mindless meat heads. I've got skills. This joker will sing like a canary. I hope he resists, though. It's more fun when they resist."

"Psycho bitch," the man murmured.

The woman seemed not to hear him over the music.

After a series of quick turns, the car stopped, and the blonde killed the engine. When she yanked open the passenger door Rafe had been partially leaning on, momentum had him falling on concrete. With sluggish reflexes, he tried to catch himself, but he ungraciously only avoided hitting his head as he tumbled.

The man, Cap, pulled his wrists forward and slapped a pair of cuffs on him. He frisked Rafe thoroughly, patting his pockets, torso, back, hips, and ankles. "No weapons. Grab his legs," the man said, grunting as he hoisted arms under Rafe's and lifted his torso.

Rafe spotted another vehicle. They intended to move him from the stolen taxi, which could be traced, to a black sedan. And then where?

Roughly, they tossed him in the car's trunk. His back was to them now, but he could hear zippers and ruffling. Checking his bags, he suspected, for weapons or back-up phones. He had neither. He was a Latino man with a juvenile record; no way he would travel with weapons even in his checked baggage. Mica and Claire always arranged for his weapons to be delivered for each job and stored between jobs.

In a few minutes, they were back on the road, his battered body feeling all the bumps and turns, especially as he jostled against his own luggage.

If they weren't killing him right away, where were they taking him? Somewhere to torture information out of him, that much was apparent.

More importantly, how will I escape alive?

He was in no shape to defend himself, and he didn't know how long the sedative would last. These weren't amateurs. They either had more drug or knew he would be sedated long enough to reach their destination and properly restrain him. In order to counteract medication, he would need an antidote, or a big shot of adrenaline.

Adrenaline.

He thought of the medical kit in his luggage. Blindly fighting through the fog, he felt around inside his carryon for the medical bag. After he found the nylon material, he identified the metal zipper and slid it open. Fumbling his fingers within it, he searched for the long, slender container.

First aid training had been a large part of his survivalist skills. The EpiPen had a spring-loaded needle. When pressed firmly against the thigh, it would release the medication. He couldn't press it against his thigh because he was wearing his bullet resistant suit. He would have to press it against the exposed skin on his neck and hold it there for the standard ten seconds.

He could get more of an adrenaline boost if he got the epinephrine directly in his bloodstream—through a vein instead of through his muscle. Most EpiPen needles were one to one and a half inches long, so perhaps, with a little aiming, he could hit his jugular vein. Anatomy had been another lesson his father had harped on— one needed to know anatomy to know which injuries were debilitating and which were lethal.

Rafe would need to time the injection as soon as the car came to a halt, and hopefully they'd be stopping to take him out and not stopping to refill the gas tank.

First, these cuffs had to go. Placing the unopened EpiPen between his teeth so he wouldn't lose it in the dark, he hunted for his lock pick kit inside his suitcase. The simple black case, when closed, would have looked like a nail grooming kit to a quick observer.

With kit found, he set to work. He'd never attempted to pick handcuffs in the dark while under the influence of sedatives and jostling in the trunk of a car.

This would be an arduous undertaking.

19

____

*D*ia had four hours until her flight to Atlanta. After incredible oral sex, Rafe had left her in a boneless heap on the bed, simultaneously satiated and wanting more. Part of her had wanted to beg him to stay, but she wasn't ready for the commitment he wanted.

Impossible relationship.

"Thank you," he'd said before he left.

What man had ever given something so selflessly only to *thank* her? No, not selflessly. Connivingly. He had planned on giving her that delicious orgasm—a clever and heart stopping ploy to show her what she could have with him. A tantalizing preview of what could be hers. Of how he could give her more.

And damn if it isn't working.

Her phone buzzed with a text message from Rafe, *Travel safe.*

The simple words had a comforting warmth spreading through

her. What was it about this man that she craved? She prided herself on her independence—on not needing anyone. So why, now, did she suddenly want to talk to Rafe every day? She looked forward to seeing him despite only recently having gone their separate ways.

Impossible, she thought again.

She refused to succumb to the urge to text back. This wasn't passing notes in high school. She was a grown woman with a career. And the career came first. No distractions.

Her phone rang. "Midnight."

"Check in," Sweeney's brisk voice snapped.

"I'm headed to Atlanta today. After that, I'll be part of the Sizani protection detail with my father."

"They'll be in good hands, then."

"The man after them has given no indication he knows they're still alive, but he might suspect or at least begin to in the next few days. There's no media mention of another country's first lady and children dying on US soil. The Rider team is working to incriminate him. They're up to speed on events as well. Where do things stand in Comoros?"

"Passable hasn't budged. There is some concern he's stalling and stealing palladium so he can disappear a rich man."

Dia snorted. "If he thinks he'll disappear with millions of dollars' worth of palladium in a few short days, he'll be disappointed. I've seen the Comoro mine operation."

"What do you mean?"

"Their engineer gave me the tour. First, they use fill mining, meaning they drill a bit, haul out the ore, and then backfill the walls with squander rock and sand to keep the mine stable. They don't yet have a lot of mining machines, so this is laborious work, nine feet at a time. The extracted ore isn't simply freely ready-to-use palladium. It's mixed and bonded with platinum, nickel, and other metals. The conglomeration has to be soaked in a solution of hydrochloric and nitric acids to separate all the metals. Palladium is first converted to palladium chloride and then purified as pure palladium."

"What about the palladium the Comoros have already processed?"

"It's not much so far, and they sent most in a suitcase for their liaison to travel to tech companies and start getting quotes. Palladium for Comoros will be a huge economic boost—but not overnight. It's not a get-rich-quick scheme for anyone involved. When General Passable realizes this, combined with facing the wrath of the UN, he'll want to cut and run. Forget the palladium. He'll clean out the treasury."

"The UN has frozen the government assets of Comoro."

"Good. His surrender or fleeing should just be a matter of time, then."

THE CAR WOBBLED and crunched on what Rafe suspected was a part-gravel, part-paved, pothole-ridden surface.

He was free of the cuffs.

When the vehicle came to a stop, he depressed the EpiPen, and the quick sting of the needle bit into him. He counted to ten before dropping it and fisting his hands around his lock-picking tool—the only weapons he had.

His heart quickened as his vision sharpened, muscles tensing on command. The adrenaline was working. Now he had to hope he could instantly mobilize every part of him after riding in the back of a trunk for forty-five minutes.

He lay still, needing to attack them when they leaned in to the open trunk so they wouldn't have time to draw weapons they were likely carrying. When the trunk opened, a hand roughly landed on his arm and jerked to roll him over. He rolled and rose with his lock picks in his hands, plunging them into the eyes of his assailant.

The woman—Lola—stumbled back and unleashed an ear-piercing scream. She drew her gun even as she dropped to the ground, writhing in pain.

Blinking, his eyes adjusted to the sunlight. Rafe didn't have time to see the damage he'd done—didn't want to—as he half-stumbled, half-fell out of the trunk. He had one more person to disable, at least. There could be more people at this place where they'd taken him—a dilapidated, abandoned house, judging by the peeling paint and over foot-high grass.

The man—Cap—had backed away as he drew his weapon. Rafe wouldn't be able to reach him before he could shoot. When the woman fired a random wild shot, both men ducked, Rafe behind the car.

"Stop shooting you crazy bitch," Cap snapped. "He's unarmed. Let me kill him, and I'll take you to the hospital."

Keeping low, Rafe racked his brain to come up with his next move. Behind him stretched a long driveway with overgrown grass on either side. Nowhere to outrun bullets or take cover. Gravel crunched as the man approached.

Rafe crouched at the front of the car now, with Cap creeping around to his left and Lola struggling blindly to stand to his right. Rafe scooped up a handful of gravel and chucked it at her as he ran in her direction, giving her a wide berth.

Although she couldn't see the gravel, feeling it would cause panic as she sensed how close her attacker was. She snarled and fired again, this time hitting the car and shattering the glass of the rear window.

Cap dropped to the ground. "Dammit! Stop shooting, or you'll hit me!"

Rafe plowed into her, reaching for her gun. They hit the ground hard, her on the bottom. She swore in surprise and pain even as she brought a knee up into his rib cage. He let out a grunt of pain but kept her pinned down.

Pushing up, he held her gun hand immobile. With his other hand, he landed a solid punch to her jaw. She went lax long enough for him to roll off of her while grabbing the gun. He kept rolling, suspecting Cap was taking aim at that very second.

A shot rang out. Rafe didn't know where it landed, but not into him. His bullet-resistant suit would keep projectiles from embedding in him, but he would still feel the punch. He rolled to his feet and sprinted toward the house. With no other vehicles in sight, he hoped these two lunatics posed his only threat.

He took cover beside a four by four supporting the carport before hazarding a glance back to the car. His head pounded in pain with every thump of his heart which raced like a jackrabbit in his chest thanks to the epinephrine. Fortunately, the gun was a standard Glock and not one of Shoup's biosensored toys. In his shaking hand the weapon was slick with Rafe's sweat, but he would steady it when the moment called for calm composure.

He was, after all, a trained survivalist.

Cap held his weapon, pointing in the house's direction, but he focused on frisking the pockets of his partner. Lola lay on the ground, now looking unnaturally still. Cap retrieved the car keys before hastily making his way toward the driver's side. Climbing in, he started the engine.

Oh, no, no lo haces. No you don't.

Rafe jetted down the drive after him. If he let him leave, Shoup's man would tell others where he was. Rafe would stick out like a sore thumb—a Latino man dressed in a suit in the Midwest countryside. He had no phone to call for an evac.

He passed the dead woman, avoiding looking at what he'd done to her eyes. She'd been shot by her own partner. For someone who liked Alanis Morissette, her death was morbidly *ironic*. Rafe couldn't be sure by the timing of the bullets with his fuzz-laden brain if the man shot at Rafe and missed or shot the woman intentionally.

He took aim at the moving vehicle and fired.

Unos, dos, tres.

The third shot found the driver's side rear tire. With his foot floored on the gas, probably at the sound of gunfire, Cap lost control. The car fishtailed before dipping off the road into a ditch entirely.

"*Tonterías*," Rafe swore.

A flat tire he could fix. A car half-way in a ditch was useless.

Ignoring the twinges of pain in his muscles and pushing through the lead weight he had for legs, he sprinted down the drive. He couldn't give the man time to phone for help. With any luck, maybe

Cap had hit his head when the car swerved and he would be dazed when Rafe arrived.

The car door swung open. Even from the distance, the man's angry, beet-red face shone like—like a Super Mario Brothers' Piranha Plant. Rafe nearly chuckled at the imagery, courtesy of Dia, and the warm memory steadied his focus.

Still sitting in the driver's seat, Cap raised his gun to take aim. On this strip of road, Rafe had nowhere to take cover. He raised his arm to protect as much of his head as he could and kept running toward the car.

They both fired.

Cap had the advantage of holding his aim steady, and Rafe had the advantage of a sitting target.

Gunshots rang out.

He felt the brutal impact of bullets to his leg and arm. He stumbled but didn't fall, didn't slow. And didn't stop firing.

Five shots later, Rafe finally landed one into his attacker—right shoulder. Cap's gun hand went limp and useless.

Panting, Rafe skidded to a stop beside the car. He snatched Cap's gun as red blossomed across the man's white shirt. Sweat poured down the injured man's face as he grimaced.

"Get it over with," Cap said on a growl.

Rafe set the guns down on the top of the car and pulled out the cuffs he'd sprang himself from earlier and had pocketed. He secured the man to the steering wheel before frisking him. Wallet. Phone. Oh, and a little snub-nose revolver in an ankle holder.

"Unlike you, your partner, and the rest of Shoup's lackeys, I don't torture and kill people. But," he read the name on the driver's license inside the wallet. "Clark Alister Peterson, I know people who can make your life a living hell. So, you'll want to quit your job at Shoup and turn over a new leaf."

Rafe popped the trunk from the lever under the steering wheel, limped around back, and grabbed a t-shirt out of his bag.

"Use this. Hold pressure to stop the bleeding."

The man's face was draining of color even as he followed Rafe's instructions.

"I shot you," Clark said.

"You did. And it hurts like a bitch." Rafe's arm and leg would have some nasty bruises in a few hours.

"You're not bleeding."

Only on the inside, Rafe thought.

"Bullet-resistant suit."

Rafe held up the man's phone and unlocked it with facial recognition. He dialed Dia first.

No answer.

Mierda.

Next, he dialed Claire.

"Rider Security and In—"

"Claire, it's Rafe."

"You're calling into our emergency line, and you sound winded. What's going on?"

"Shoup's men came after me. Dia's not answering her phone. I need a ride out of here and an ambulance."

"Oh, crap. There was no mention of any attacks on Lucius' transcripts. Shoup must have planned this without him."

"I'm sending you my location, but I have to leave before the ambulance gets here."

"The ambulance isn't for you?"

"No."

"Okay. Ambulance to your current location. Can you hump it one and a half klicks to the gas station off Highway 56? That will put you close to I-88. I'll have Jackson pick you up."

"Got it. Leaving the phone on so you can trace me. Keep trying Dia."

He worked quickly, removing his luggage from the trunk. Using another shirt, he wiped down everything he'd touched—trunk, cuffs, and the man's gun and wallet, which he left on top of the car. He kept Lola's gun, sticking it in the back of his pants in case he needed it. If he didn't, he could ditch it later.

"Ambulance is on its way," Rafe told Clark. His tone sounded as weary in his own ears as he felt. He'd probably pass out the minute he was in Jackson's car. No, he needed to know Dia was safe first.

"Dia is your partner, right?" the man asked, voice hoarse.

Rafe's jaw tightened. "That's right." An icy fist squeezed his chest. He'd said he didn't torture people, but visions of doing just that to make Clark spill everything he knew flashed before Rafe's eyes.

"I heard plans for another team to go after her. We were supposed to torture you about details on the Rider team and where the Sizani family is hiding out. The other team has orders to torture your partner about the Sizani family."

A fresh wave of his own adrenaline surged through him at the thought of Dia taken and tortured.

"Where?" he took a menacing step toward Clark.

"I don't know. We weren't told the other group's location. I swear."

Rafe unleashed a few colorful explicative in Spanish as he slung his bag over one shoulder and wheeled his luggage behind him. Despite his throbbing muscles, he jogged toward the gas station.

"Claire, I know you heard that and can hear me." He didn't have a free hand to put the phone to his ear. "You keep trying Dia, dammit. And tell Jackson to haul ass here."

20

$\mathcal{D}$ia paced her hotel room. She needed to leave in an hour for her flight. She had taken a walk down Michigan Avenue to clear her head, but back in her room, her mind fixated on Rafe again. Tension and irritability had settled between her shoulders.

She still hadn't texted Rafe back, and the guilt of not returning such a nice gesture gnawed at her. Space. She needed a little space.

She pulled out her nunchaku from her suitcase and whirled them. Sometimes, this type of workout helped her steer her mind off troubling issues.

Is this what her dad had gone through after a week-long intense relationship with her mom? Had the desire to see her weighed on him after he'd left her? It had, she knew. But he'd taken six years to decide to do something about it and return to Katie. That was six years of sharing their love that her parents had missed out on. But how was Dia to know if she and Rafe would have her parents' kind of love?

Her phone buzzed. "Hi, Claire."

"Hi, Dia. How are you? Are you good?"

"Yeah..." she drew out the word as she wondered where Claire's line of questioning was headed.

"Okay. Whew. Rafe wanted—"

"Rafe?" Dia snapped out the word. Had Rafe sent Claire to check on her since she hadn't texted back? "Claire, I know what Rafe wants, okay?" Couldn't she be left alone about him for a day to process her feelings? She didn't know if she could give him a relationship. She need time and space. They would be in a cabin living and moving in the same house for days to weeks.

Can I simply have a day or two to breathe?

"Rafe was attacked."

"What?" Dia froze.

"Shoup's men. Rafe's okay. He escaped and Jackson is picking him up. Rafe wanted me to check on you. So, uh, watch your back."

Her stomach knotted—not at her own safety, but at Rafe's. "Where is he right now?"

"Gas station off Interstate 88."

"I'll go."

"He's okay, really."

Dia had a powerful urge to hear his voice and know for herself. "I'll call him."

"You can't. They ditched his phone. He called me from one he stole from his abductors."

"Abductors? He was abducted?" Her chest tightened. She thought of a call she'd gotten a few minutes ago. She hadn't recognized the number, so she hadn't answer it.

"He's okay," Claire repeated.

Abducted by Shoup's men. That wouldn't have been an easy escape. Ugh. She felt like a selfish louse, with her brooding over whether or not to text him. He could have died at the hands of Shoup's men without knowing how she felt about him. Which was what exactly?

Focus, Dia.

"Is he hurt?" she asked Claire.

"He's ambulating. Jackson is picking him up," she repeated. "I'll tell Rafe to call you, but he said to warn you to watch out for an attack."

"Okay. I'll head to the airport now." She disconnected the call.

Time to vamoose.

Shoup had apparently found out where they'd been staying. That was unexpected, because Claire had booked the rooms under fake names, and Lucius hadn't been told of their whereabouts either. Rafe and she couldn't have been tailed; they hadn't left the hotel. That left Jackson. He'd been the one in and out of the hotel and working closely with Lucius. Yes, someone having followed Jackson was the most likely scenario, which would also explain why Rafe and she weren't attacked in their hotel room. Shoup's men didn't know their room numbers.

Dia considered how she'd gone for a walk and back with no problems, so either Shoup's men hadn't seen her, or they didn't want to attack her on a public street with heavy foot traffic.

Regardless, she needed to get to the safety of the airport. She secured her carry-on bag to the handle of her rolling luggage before slipping the rifle case over one shoulder. With her right hand on the case handle, she snatched up her nunchaku in her left hand. She could store those in her carry-on when she got to the taxi.

As she swung the hotel room door open, a massive fist barreled toward her face. Although she jerked back, worn, bony knuckles clipped her chin, snapping her head back. Pain reverberated through her jaw as her teeth clattered.

Filling the doorway stood a large, burly man in cargo pants and a polo shirt. Behind him bobbed and weaved a smaller assailant with a puckered face like a bulldog.

Had they followed her here after her walk?

Dia was trapped in the narrow hallway with her suitcase behind her and a beast in front of her. To her left was the sliding door of a tiny closet and to her right a dead-end bathroom.

She had nowhere to go.

As the man stepped into the room, another fist came at her. She tried to back up and block, but there was no slowing the momentum of those burly muscles driving the knuckles toward her. His punch landed in her gut and brought her down hard on her knees. She sucked wind as her eyes watered.

This opponent was definitely a step up from the Goombas and turtles of Mario Brothers. This man was Wario, she decided. The man had the build and only needed a flaring mustache and purple jumpsuit. His eager accomplice with the bulging eyes and green shirt behind him was hopefully nothing more than a stompable Koopa Troopa.

By the mirror on the hallway closet door, she could see Wario bending over like he intended to restrain her, probably trap her in those blocks of biceps.

With a quick flick of her wrist and shoulder, she snapped one end of the nunchaku up into his face. It impacted with a satisfactory crunch. Snarling, he clutched his nose and stumbled back.

She only had seconds to consider her options as she tried to catch her breath from having the wind knocked out of her. She could take the fight to the hallway, but that's where his partner was. If she backed up to the bedroom, they would both fill the space.

Two against one.

In the bathroom, however, the Koopa Troopa would have a difficult time squeezing around Wario to join the fight. Of course, they were probably packing, which meant they could shoot her at any time.

Maybe. Just maybe, they would want to avoid loud gunshots in a hotel. Or maybe. Just maybe, Shoup had instructed his men to take her alive and therefore wouldn't risk shooting her.

As she staggered into the bathroom, another ramrod of a fist barreled toward her. Normally, she would use an attacker's own momentum to throw him into the wall behind her, but if this brute moved past her, his tortoise buddy could maneuver into the bathroom. She didn't need to end up wedged between the two of them.

She dropped to her knees to avoid the oncoming blow and lashed out her nunchaku again, right between the legs. He snarled and grabbed his crotch, swearing, but not going down.

Shitballs.

Wario brought a fist down solidly on her back, between her shoulder blades. The force of it had her slamming into the hard tile floor with a shockwave of pain searing her body. Seeing stars, she curled into a defensive ball, knees up to her chest.

"The fuck, man? Grab her already," the smaller man said, trying to see around his partner.

Before Wario could do just that, she was already pulling out the ceramic knife from her boot. Uncoiling, she drove it into his calf and yanked it back out again in a spurt of blood.

Crying out, he stumbled back, clamoring into his partner and knocking him backward.

Ignoring the pain in her back and ribcage, she shoved to her feet, nunchaku in one hand and knife in the other. She drove the knife into his left hand, which he'd been using to grip the door frame and keep from falling backward.

His cry of pain turned into a gurgling noise when Dia lashed out with the nunchaku, striking his jaw and snapping it shut. He fell into his partner, knocking the little Koopa Troopa into the mirror on the sliding glass door of the closet.

He clung to Wario's shirt to keep upright, but only pulled him down with him. Together, they shattered the mirrored door completely and landed in a heap in the closet.

They wouldn't stay down for long, Dia knew. Grabbing the handle of her suitcase, she reached for the hotel room door and wrenched it open, dashing out into the hall.

"Fuck sake. Get off of me!" the turtle one cried.

"My hand," Wario sobbed.

Dia dashed to the end of the hall and frantically pushed the elevator button. More than once wouldn't summon it any faster, but it gave her something to do while standing there, an open target in the hallway.

The smaller man stepped out of the room, head whipping in both directions. He froze, clearly spotting her down the hall by the elevator. As he took aim, the metal doors slid open.

Dia shoved inside as a gunshot rang out. Heart thudding, she pressed the button for the lobby level, followed by the one to close the doors. They were two inches from closing in the middle when a muzzle of a gun fit between them.

She was already standing to the side when the roar of another shot threatened to rupture her eardrum. The doors, programmed as they were when they met resistance, reopened.

Shoving aside her pain and fear, she let go of her suitcase handle and readied her nunchaku. As soon as Koopa was through the doors and joined her in the elevator, she made three quick strikes—gun hand, temple, chest.

Dropping the gun with a curse, he stumbled back into the opposite wall of the elevator. Snarling, he pushed off the wall and lunged after her. Dia sidestepped and lashed out. The chukon-bu, middle part of the wooden shaft of the nunchaku, struck the back of his head.

His momentum took him into the other wall of the elevator near where his gun had fallen. He reached down, but she was quick to wrap her weapon around his neck, the kusari, or chain portion linking the two batons, crushing his windpipe and hopefully slowing the blood supply to his brain.

Knowing this man would kill her given a second chance, she pulled as hard as she could. He'd already clearly abandoned his abduction plan, as evidenced by shooting at her.

When his body went limp, she didn't let go for a good ten seconds to make sure he wasn't faking. At last, she loosened her white-knuckle grip on the batons. Reaching over, she pushed the button to keep the elevator door open and rolled Koopa's body out into the hallway.

She snatched the handle and dragged her luggage behind her while scooping up the gun on the floor. After moving her baggage against the hall wall, she took a moment for three deep breaths, watching the man for any signs of sudden movement. Feeling momentarily collected, she rummaged through his pockets and found a wallet, syringe, and twist tie.

Don't mind if I do.

She jerked his hands behind his back and secured them before checking for a pulse. Not dead. She wasn't sure how she felt about that. What if he came after her in the future with some twisted vendetta against the woman he'd failed to kidnap?

She slipped the nunchaku in her luggage and the syringe sideways between her teeth. With Koopa's gun in her right hand, she dragged him by the shirt collar down the hallway with her left, back to her room. Running away from two men and leaving them in her hotel room was one thing. Stepping out of an elevator on the lobby floor full of guests with an unconscious man at her feet covered in blood from mirror shards was another.

She was hurt and tired and pissed off, but she needed to wrap this up.

21

The 'Do Not Disturb' sign swung lightly on the hotel room door as Dia closed it. She slipped in her earpiece and called her boss.

"Sweeney."

"Midnight here. I texted the cleaners a location a few minutes ago."

When she'd returned to her hotel room, Wario had been wrapping his bleeding hand and leg in towels. He hadn't make a move when she entered with his partner in tow, probably because she pointed a gun at him. She let Koopa loose on the floor.

With a syringe in one hand and gun in the other, she'd asked the big guy which one he wanted her to shoot him with, reminding him that one would hurt a hell of a lot and the other would probably take the edge off the knife wound pain he suffered. Wisely, he'd opted for the sedative.

"I heard about your call," Sweeney said, tone grumpy. "We seem to clean up a lot of your messes recently."

Rifle slung over her shoulder, Dia walked wearily down the hallway toward the elevator, this time without fear that Shoup's men would start firing at her. "I wouldn't be doing my job if I wasn't uprooting trouble, right? Besides, if Shoup's men are desperate enough to kidnap people, then we rattled some cages. Desperate people make mistakes, and that's when opportunity strikes."

"Kidnap?"

"The two men I left in the hotel room tried to subdue me, and another team went after Rafe Alonso." At saying his name, a pang struck her. She wanted to hear his voice and see for herself that he was okay.

"I want a full report about the incident," Sweeney said.

"Yes, mum."

When the call ended, the doors chimed open, and Dia stepped inside the elevator, she held her breath for a few moments as the doors closed completely. Her mind flashed back to visualize the muzzle of a gun sliding between them. She suspected the image would stick with her for a while every time she rode in one of these contraptions.

On her way to the front of the hotel for a taxi, she called Claire. "Hi, it's Dia."

"You're calling to let me know you safely made it to the airport, right?"

"Getting in the taxi now. I had a slight delay."

"Slight delay as in the heel of my shoe broke and I had to find a new pair? Or a slight delay as in the same trouble Rafe ran into?"

"The latter. Two uninvited guests in my hotel room. I've called in a cleanup crew to deal with them."

A long pause lingered on the other line. "When you say clean-up crew..." Claire's voice trailed.

"The cleanup crew will manage care of the blood spatter in the room and take the two men in the custody. They will sort out if the men have any criminal background that would warrant turning them over to the police."

"Okay. That's a little less disturbing."

"I'm about to hop into the taxi. I'll touch base after my flight. Thanks for the warning, by the way. Things might've turned out differently for me if I hadn't been prepared for an attack." She disconnected the call, more than ready to sit on a plane for a couple of hours and blissfully close her eyes.

RAFE IMPATIENTLY STRUMMED his fingers on his knee as he sat in the passenger side seat. Jackson spoke with Claire as he navigated the DEPARTURES section at the airport. Rafe couldn't hear the call and wished Jackson had put it on speakerphone.

"Thanks, Claire. Bye."

"What did she say? Dia's okay?"

Jackson arched an eyebrow at Rafe's demanding acquisition. Let the man pass judgment. Rafe worried about Dia and needed answers.

"Shoup's men attacked, but she's fine. On her way to the airport now."

"Is she hurt? What does *fine* mean? How about her back?"

"I don't have those kinds of details, but she's taking a taxi to the airport. I think she's okay."

Rafe relaxed slightly. They should've stuck together. Traveling as a pair, this wouldn't have happened. Partners traveled together, a Rider rule when danger was high. But Dia didn't work for Rider. She worked for Interpol—and whatever other organization had given her the skills to fend off two of Shoup's men.

Damn, she'd impressed him again.

And her job would continually put her in danger, which was something he would have to accept. After all, the world needed more women like Dia who were willing to protect families in the face of danger.

"Mica is furious she didn't know about the attack," Jackson said.

"Since she has a bug on Lucius, this must be Shoup's doing without Titan's approval."

Jackson nodded. "She's worried about me. Wants me to take a step back and surveil at a distance."

"That's a good idea. Stick to the shadows from now on. You're on-site work is done anyway. And you shouldn't work alone."

"Maxine and Vladimir are in town." Jackson shook his head with a quirk of his lips. "Can't say I ever imagined I'd do a job with the former leader of the Russian mob."

"The story I heard was that he'd mostly taken over as mob leader as a way to protect his family during a fairly lawless time in Russia. When he and Maxine crossed paths, he fell in love. Then, an opportunity to fake his death arose and he took the escape plan. Only a few of his family know he's still alive."

"I'm just glad he's on our side. The last time I was in the same room with a crime lord, I was not long out of my FBI training course and sweating bullets, hoping my cover didn't get blown while dozens of armed Colombian cartel partied with drugs and alcohol."

"Oh, yeah?"

"Yeah, but that's a story for another day." Jackson pulled to the curb.

Elbow bent, Rafe extended a hand, and Jackson clasped it.

"Until then, watch your back," Rafe cautioned.

"Thanks, man. Have a safe flight."

<hr>

DIA DEBOARDED the plane at Hartsfield International Airport. She positively ached to see Rafe safe but didn't know what to do about her irrational need to see him well with her own eyes.

As she made her way to baggage claim, she slipped in her earpiece and called her mom.

"Hey, hon. A visit and a phone call all in the same week. What's up?"

"Do you ever resent dad?" Dia asked.

"For what?"

"Having to raise a child on your own? Or what about now? What about the long absences while he's working?"

A smile lit her voice as her mother said, "He gave me you, which I'm grateful for. He didn't know we had a daughter, and I couldn't resent him for that. As for our life now, we both work. I don't think either of us feels like we're missing out because we're not spending every waking moment of free time together. We make the most of the time we have together, and that's what counts. Travel for my job lets me sell more books and make more money. Likewise, travel with his job helps him earn a paycheck. Together, we use those funds to pay for enriching activities together. When we're not together, we phone and text. Or communicate with video chats. I don't feel deprived, and I don't think he does either." She paused before asking, "What's worrying you?"

Dia picked her way through the crowded terminal. "I met someone, and we have this amazing chemistry. From our first encounter. I like him enough he makes me think about long-term, but I don't know what that looks like when our globetrotting careers won't overlap all that much. I love my job and I think I'd resent anyone who made me give it up, even when part of me has the desire to do so."

"The right man who wins your heart wouldn't ask you to."

"He hasn't, wouldn't. Likewise, I wouldn't ask him to give up his career, which I know he loves."

"You'll make it work. If it's love, you'll make it work. You'll forge an unconventional relationship rather than a traditional one because it's what you both want, and you'll enjoy all those precious moments together that much more."

"Perhaps you're right."

"I'm your mother, of course I'm right. Now, who's this man who has my fearless crime fighter discombobulated?"

"Rafe Alonso."

"Strong name."

"Strong man. Tall, dark, and handsome. He has a small scar on his face he earned while defending his brother."

"Ah, loyal, too, then. I take it he doesn't work for Interpol."

"No."

"Is this the man your father mentioned who works with him?"

"Yes."

Dad mentioned Rafe to her mother? Something to ponder.

"Bonus points for finding a man your father likes. That's a first."

"It is? He never told me he objected to any of my boyfriends."

"Well, he can't say such a thing when you're fawning over someone without upsetting you."

"Oh."

"So, what are you going to do about Rafe?"

"I'm going to find out if he and I can make a relationship work."

RAFE UNLOCKED HIS APARTMENT DOOR, feeling exhausted from recent events. He needed to soak in an ice bath in order to reduce the aching and swelling over most of his body.

He wheeled his luggage inside to find his lights were already on and tensed for a moment before he saw a man walk toward him from the kitchen.

"Brother!" Rafe dropped his bags and wrapped Santino in a hug. "So good to see you."

Before he was ready to let go and before he shed the tears threatening behind his eyes, Rafe stepped back from Santino. He assured himself wet eyes reflected how tired he was, nothing more.

Santino looked good—happy, based on the lightness around his eyes and the ease of his smile. "Ava and I are in town for the week to see her father. I thought I'd surprise you."

"You did. I'm glad you did. You look great." Rafe scrubbed a hand through his hair.

"How are you?" Santino inspected the bruise on Rafe's cheek.

"Meh. We've both had worse. This job went from a family vacation to a whirlwind of offensive and defensive maneuvers. How was your last trip?"

"Ava and I were in Brazil. We found a lost gold Incan chakana." He whipped out his phone and showed Rafe a picture of a gleaming cross-like artifact.

"Fortune and glory." Rafe chuckled. He placed a hand on Santino's shoulder and squeezed. "Let's celebrate with a beer." He walked to his fridge and pulled out two cold ones.

"Thanks." Santino popped it open and sank into Rafe's couch. "So, why the haggard look?"

Rafe drank his Corona and sat in his recliner. He pressed two fingers to his tender right cheek where a bruise marred the skin. "We infiltrated Shoup's house. He retaliated." His brother didn't need to know Rafe had been abducted for almost an hour before escaping. He would save that story for a later time, when the fear wasn't so fresh in his bloodstream.

Santino shook his head. "That man is a threat to us all."

"Mica's trying to bring him down."

"As she should, but he'll have the upper hand when he works outside the law and she's limited by it."

"We do our share of breaking and entering," Rafe countered.

"She won't commit murder to stop him. He won't afford her the same courtesy."

And torture, Rafe thought.

Santino took another swig of beer. "As she shouldn't," he added. "But doesn't change the fact we're more vulnerable than he is."

"She'll bring him down," Rafe said.

"I'll toast to that."

They clinked their glass bottles and drank again.

After a moment, Rafe asked. "Your relationship is good? You're happy?"

"Of course. More than I ever thought possible."

Rafe took another long gulp as he wriggled deeper in the chair. "How do you feel like Ava's equal? How do you not feel unworthy to be with her? No, I'm not being clear about my meaning." He tried to consider how to reword his question—questions—without sounding offensive.

His brother cocked his head to one side. "*No hay que preocuparse.*" He told him not to worry. "I get it. Ava is smart, savvy, and the daughter of a billionaire. You and I were raised differently from women like her."

"Yes."

"Simple." Santino leaned back and crossed his legs. "Ava doesn't see me as less than her equal, so why should I see myself as less? Also, I focus on the things I bring to the relationship—support, safety, and fun. Am I damn lucky to have her? Yes. Does that mean I think I'm somehow less? No."

Rafe digested his brother's words in silence, thinking again of Dorian's acceptance of him.

"Why do you ask?"

"Do you remember I told you I spent the night with a woman in Cusco?"

"I do." Santino nodded.

"That same woman saved my life at the mines and again when Shoup's men came after the Sizani family." He paused for dramatic effect. "That woman is Dorian's daughter."

Santino's brow furrowed. "I didn't know she was in the game."

"Yeah. Neither did Dorian. Dia is Interpol and has joined us for the Sizani case. And I'm in love with her." He had realized that when he feared for her life. The knowledge saturated him every time the craving to see her rose to the surface. He might as well admit it to someone.

His brother's jaw dropped open. "You're in love with Dorian's daughter?"

"Yeah."

"*Dorian's* daughter?"

"A kick in the balls, right?"

Santino chuckled. "You always did take the hard road. What does Dorian have to say about it?"

"He doesn't object to me wanting to date Dia."

Santino let out a low whistle. "That's huge. That's respect, man. You and Dia are dating?"

"Not exactly."

Santino sucked in a breath. "Tell me you're not just sleeping with her. You said you loved her."

"Give me a little credit, will you? I'm ready to date. She's not." Rafe rubbed his neck. "I even turned down her offer for casual sex."

Santino gaped at him. "Who are you and what have you done with Rafe?"

Rafe snorted. "I know, right? I told her I didn't want casual, but I'm here when she's ready for something serious."

His brother's expression filled with compassion. "What will you do if she doesn't accept your offer?"

Rafe shrugged. "Suffer in silence." He took another drink of beer. "I'm not being passive, though. Every time I see her, I'm showing her what she's missing." He winked.

"I'm stoked to see you happy about something. Someone. I want it to work out. If you need Ava and I to arrange a romantic getaway, we would love to help with something like that."

"I'll think about your offer," Rafe said. "For now, we have a family to keep safe." Tomorrow, he needed to pick up equipment from Claire and head to the cabin outside Allatoona.

First, he wanted that ice bath.

22

Dia knocked on Rafe's apartment door. Pulling her hand back, she felt flutters ripple through her stomach. Claire had told her his address when she'd asked. Dia probably should have called first, but she wanted to see him. She'd gone to her hotel first and cleaned up, stalling to see if this urge to see him would subside. It hadn't.

After the slide of a chain and click of a lock, the door opened. Rafe stood in jeans and t-shirt, looking gorgeous with his hair damp as if not long out of a shower.

Light danced in his tiger eyes as his mouth curved in a smile. "Dia?"

"I was worried about you." Dia kept her voice low. "When Claire told me Shoup's men had attacked you, I was worried."

He leaned on the doorway, looking her up and down from head to toe as if making his own assessment that she was well. "I was worried about me too. I've never had to pick handcuffs in the dark trunk of a moving car."

She gave him an impressed look. When she noticed the bruise on the side of his face and some on his arms, she wondered how hard he'd had to battle his attackers earlier. Her stomach knotted at the thought of him fighting for his life.

His brow furrowed. "When my captor told me they'd sent a team after you as well, I was worried we wouldn't warn you in time. Seems you handled your attackers better than I did mine. I shouldn't be surprised. After sparing with you at Cadillac Ranch, you showed your superior skills."

"I wasn't kidnapped because you gave me the heads-up. And your sparing session wasn't fair to you. You were trying not to hurt me, and I made a cheap shot."

He grinned. "We're in agreement on that."

She chuckled and shook her head. "Anyway," she sobered. "I'm glad you're okay."

Her fingers itched to reach for him, but he seemed intent on keeping his distance. He hadn't invited her inside his apartment. She didn't want to leave without touching him. The closer, the better.

"Thank you. It's nice to be cared about. And that you took the trouble to stop by."

Nerves had her adjusting the bag on her shoulder—an overnight bag because she hoped to put it to use at his place. Since she was still in his hallway, her drop-in wasn't going as planned.

"Are you going to invite me in?" she asked.

He pursed his lips. "I'd love to, but I'm not sure I'll be able to keep my hands off you." He shook his head. "You in my space. That's a fantasy I've had more than once."

She rolled one shoulder and licked her lips. "So don't keep your hands off me."

At her words, he snaked an arm around her waist and drew her into his apartment, closing the door as he did. "I thought you'd never ask."

His body felt warm and his lips hot as he pressed against her. She drank down his kiss, returning every motion with her own. She lost herself in the delightful sensation of their mouths and tongues colliding.

Floating.

She floated on air. Or maybe he was carrying her. Or maybe she was clawing her way up his body as her own throbbed with need.

"More," she said when they broke the kiss. She tugged his shirt off and over his head.

Oh, this torso. She ran her fingers along the formed biceps and firm abdominal muscles.

Yes, this. This man and this body. So many bruises though. She wished she could kiss them all away.

They kissed again, deep and sultry. His calloused hands moved under her shirt and over her bra, tantalizing fingers trailing over then under the fabric.

He pulled away and lifted her shirt over her head. "When I met you, my life was all gray scale. You brought this vibrant burst of color into my world."

She realized they'd somehow moved into his bedroom. The space had a few clothes on one chair, but otherwise it looked remarkably tidy for someone not expecting company. She glanced at the bed— king size. Reaching behind her, she unclasped her bra and let it fall to the floor.

His eyes went hooded as he gazed upon her. "*Tu serás mi muerte.*"

You'll be the death of me. She knew that one.

No, Rafe. I'll be the life of you.

When he didn't move, she finished stripping. He followed suit.

Bruised and battered by his attackers. But safe now. And hers.

Whoa. Where did that possessiveness come from?

She walked toward the bed and beckoned him over to her. He crawled over her as she backed onto the duvet. The predatorial way he crept over her and gazed upon her sent tingling, dancing flames along her skin.

Leaning down, he kissed her slow and tantalizing, like he could spend all day with their lips pressed together. One hand held him up, and the other trailed down her neck, over her breast and lower.

She groaned into the kiss and shifted to give his probing fingers access. He moved his lips down to her breasts and caressed them with his mouth. Intoxicated by his touch, she arched up to feel his body against her.

He chuckled. "I'm trying to go slow and enjoy myself here, but I'm sensing urgency from you."

"Life is short, and I need you now." Her voice was husky with desire.

She raked fingers along his back, causing him to suck in a breath.

"Slow next time," he agreed.

Reaching over into his nightstand, he withdrew a condom. He had it opened and on in seconds. His warm body hovered above her as their eyes connected. She thought she might drown in the depth of the affection in his gaze.

Her body thrummed with excitement as he drove into her. She gasped, and to let him know he was giving her everything she wanted, she arched up to kiss him.

With bodies merged, he gave her what she craved—not slow and not tender. Some other day when worry over hearing he'd been abducted hadn't wrecked her mind, they could take their time together. Because there would be a next time. And many more.

With every thrust, he took her to the brink—the precipice she'd denied herself. Together, in writhing ecstasy, they plunged off the edge into bursting, vibrant colors.

She thought of his words, about how she'd turned his world from gray scale to full color—he'd done the same for her. Then, she couldn't think at all, only shudder with delight and hold onto him with her last bit of ebbing strength.

***

SUN STREAMED through the window as Rafe looked down at the love of his life. He knew it with every fiber of his body but wasn't about to make such a confession and scare her off. He'd only recently managed to woo her close again.

He'd wanted her so badly, he hadn't clarified if her intentions had been to take both the physical and emotional plunge with him last night. All three times. He'd opted to enjoy a romantic night of love-making without pinning her down on commitment for fear of chasing her away.

He pulled on his jeans and t-shirt before checking his Glock and dropping it in his overnight bag. He could broach the subject of their relationship another day, when they didn't have a mission to complete. The Sizani family needed their protection.

Dia rolled over in bed, short hair a sexy, spiked mess. The outline of her naked body with the sheets stretched over her had him wanting to strip and join her in bed.

"You're dressed." She smiled at him.

"I'm assigned to go to the cabin this morning. Your father is picking you up to take you there later today. Probably better that he pick you up from Rider headquarters or your hotel rather than my place." Rafe slipped on his boots before adjusting his hair back into a low ponytail.

Her brow furrowed. "I thought he was already up there. I can't ride with you?"

"He drove back down specifically to bring you up there. I think he wants a little father-daughter time. I'm sure he heard about your scuffle. If he experienced anything like what I went through learning you were in danger, he needs to see you." He sat on the edge of the bed and ran a hand tenderly through her hair. "This won't be our last night together."

"No, it won't."

He smiled at her agreement. That would suffice for now. They could talk later about long-term plans.

Leaning down, he kissed her again. "Okay. See you soon."

"What's the status of the team?" Mica arrived at Bones at eight am.

She carried a large coffee, needing the extra caffeine because she wasn't sleeping well since Rafe and Dia had been attacked. The backlash caught her off guard, and she could have lost employees. The realization sickened her. She had immediately pulled Jackson back to covert monitoring only and as back up to Maxine and Vladimir's upcoming mission.

"On schedule to infiltrate," Claire said.

Mica's stomach knotted in anticipation. Lucius had known and tattled to Shoup about Rider's plans to infiltrate his house, but Lucius didn't know about Rider's plans to infiltrate Shoup's office. That scheme had taken more planning.

On the several occasions when Jackson had been with Lucius in Shoup's office, he'd stolen Shoup's key card long enough to copy the electronic signal before putting it back in the men's bathroom where Shoup would think he'd left it. Jackson also planted listening devices and a device of Claire's own design to disrupt the building's electrical system. When Claire activated it, Shoup's security team called in the glitch to an electrician. Claire recorded the call, and so knew the company they called and the scheduled day and time the electrician would arrive.

That was when the clock started ticking. Maxine and Vladimir already had a white van ready. They had taken a day to prep the vehicle with a matching electrician company logo on the side. While the paint dried, they'd bought plain blue overalls and stitched the company logo on the front.

Today, the real harrowing work began. Maxine and Vladimir had to show up in full disguise and convince the security team the electricians had a job cancellation elsewhere and were arriving a day early. With Shoup's level of security, they couldn't take guns, and they couldn't turn on their communication devices until after they'd been inspected. If anything went awry, Mica and Claire wouldn't know about it until Max and Vlad were trapped.

"Jackson is in the van parked in Shoup's lot and transmitting for us. He's also ready if we need an emergency escape for our fearless duo." Claire clicked her computer mouse. "You can listen through this."

Mica sipped her coffee and waited.

"We're in."

She jolted at the sound of Maxine's gravelly voice.

Time for Maxine and Vladimir to steal Shoup's files. Shoup's *real* files and not some malware viral worm thing like their decoy theft had earned them the other night. The duo had three replicas in their toolbox that had to work to pull off this plan: Shoup's face printed in 3D, his badge, and his fingerprint.

Nothing stolen would be admissible as incriminating evidence in a court of law, but if Rider could learn about Shoup's jobs and clients, they could find opportunities to either link him to past acts of indiscretion to prompt an investigation or have the FBI drop in mid-crime and make an arrest, the latter of which had worked to take down Lucius.

"Showtime," Claire said.

DIA SAT beside her father as he drove one of the Rider team's company SUVs North on I-75 toward the cabin where the Sizani family was staying.

His gaze slanted to her, eyes appraising her face and probably the bruise on her chin. "How bad was the attack?" he asked in a tone suggesting he wasn't sure he wanted to know.

"Two against one, and I spent most of it unsure who would win. I prefer sniper work to facing two attackers. Even one attacker. Hell, I'm not even supposed to be in combat situations. I'm cybersecurity."

"You handled yourself well."

She scoffed. "You weren't there."

"You walked away from the fight and they didn't. You did well."

His compliment turned her insides to mush. Some badass she was. The thought made her smile. "Thanks, Dad."

"You're all healed from your back injury?" her father asked.

"Yes, the muscles had seized up, but ibuprofen, heat packs, and massage seem to have helped." Heat crept into her cheeks at the word 'massage' and the memories of Rafe's hands on her that the word conjured. Her father didn't need to know his mentee had had his hands on her bare skin.

Again.

Or his tongue.

Is it hot in the car?

She resisted the urge to tug on the collar of her shirt or turn up the vehicle's air conditioning.

Dorian must have sensed something, because he let out a long sigh. "I don't know where you're at in your relationship with Rafe. And I don't need to know unless you feel compelled to share. But I will add that we're on a job at the cabin. We are professionals. And all under one roof. You and Rafe are both more than capable of doing your job officially and competently, and no doubt have the maturity to compartmentalize."

He rolled his shoulders. "I'm not sure I do. For the sake of your father, I would ask that you refrain from open displays of affection in my presence, with the caveat that should you enter into a serious relationship with Rafe, you provide me with sufficient notice to adjust to the idea of seeing the two of you demonstrate public displays of affection."

She chuckled. "I promise, no kissing Rafe in front of you, and I promise to give you ample forewarning should we become involved in a long-term relationship." She had committed last night, but she and Rafe still needed to discuss it.

"Excellent. Now, how did things go with your mother? She told me she was accepting of your career choice. I know that couldn't have been an easy conversation."

"She wasn't mad. She also thought Interpol suited me better than a medical device company job. I think there's an edge of pride, though I am sorry for lying to both of you. And I'm sorry I can't tell mom about MI6."

"We are proud of you."

A lump formed in her throat at his heartfelt words. "Thanks, Dad."

She laid her head back on the seat rest. As grueling as these last few days of travel, car chases, gun fights, and hand-to-hand combat had been, she was looking forward to a quiet, secluded cabin.

23

"Off the beaten path," Dia noted.

They wound over a paved, narrow drive that snaked up the side of a mountain. Black walnut, American beech, and chestnut oak towered over them. Pentas with clusters of tiny red and pink flowers dotted the underbrush. Purple angelonia bloomed vibrant.

A sturdy, dark wood cabin surrounded by tall pines came into view. It had large windows and a thick brick chimney.

"This is the safehouse?" Dia asked.

"It belongs to Mica's dad, but the deed is in neither of their names to keep it a secret. Circumstances as they are around Rider clients, they've had to use this location on multiple occasions."

"I'm surprised you didn't blindfold me for the trip," she quipped.

He snorted. "You're mostly trustworthy."

When her father put the car in park, she hopped out and went around to the trunk, pulling out both of their luggage bags. As she approached, she noted the security cameras watching all angles of the house and key-coded door locks.

The door swung open, and Rafe stood with a greeting smile on his lips.

Damn. That man could wear blue jeans like a movie star. She'd told herself she would keep the interactions professional, but her traitorous mind drifted back to last night in his apartment, and she couldn't help but smile in return.

Her father stepped forward and extended a hand, which Rafe shook. "Everything's in order here?"

Rafe's smile flattened. "Yes, sir. I got here two hours ago, and Ryan and Reece recently left. Hiba is reading a book, and the kids are watching, or technically fighting over what to watch on TV. They could all use some outdoor time."

Dorian nodded. "Why don't you and Dia take them through the trails? That will let everyone stretch their legs, unleash a little pent-up stress, and allow Dia to get the lay of the land."

Dia came up beside them. "If you show me to my room, I can drop off my luggage and change into some boots for the walk."

Rafe nodded and stepped aside. She entered, bringing her luggage up behind her, and her father followed. Rafe glanced at her luggage but didn't take it. Sweetly, part of him seemed to want to assist, but perhaps he wasn't sure how accepting her father would be at the gesture, or perhaps he was uncertain how accepting she would be of chivalry.

She continued inside, taking in the cabin's beauty with its large fireplace, high vaulted ceilings, and stairs with a ledge view of the living room.

"You're in the room up the stairs on the left with Ada. There are four bedrooms. Hiba has the master bedroom down here. Jabari and I will share one upstairs, you and Ada the other. Your father is up and to the left."

"Hi, Dia!" Jabari wore a huge grin when he saw her. He left the couch to greet her with a hug.

"Hi there, champ. How do you like this place?"

"It's cool. I like playing in the woods, but I can't go out without supervision. Rafe's here now. I had to share a room with mom, but she said now that Rafe's here, I can share a room with him."

"That sounds fun." She turned towards Rafe. "Give me ten minutes, and I'll meet you back down here to take the kids for a walk."

She was changed and ready to walk in five minutes, so she wandered into the study where she found Hiba reading.

"Oh, Dia!" Hiba slammed her book shut and pushed up from the sitting chair. Walking over, she wrapped her arms around Dia. "So good to see you."

Dia returned the hug before taking a step back. "I talked to my boss earlier. There are plans to take action against General Passable. I hope this means an end soon to your isolation and your ruined vacation."

"What a relief. Oh, we're all settled and feeling safe here. It's the worry. Worry about what all of this is doing to the children. Worry over my husband's safety. Worry of the integrity of our democratic society."

"I'm sorry. It's an awful situation to have to endure." She placed a hand on Hiba's shoulder and squeezed. "Rafe and I planned to take the kids for a walk through the trails. Do you want to join us?"

"Yes, I think I could use a little fresh air and exercise."

RAFE WALKED on the dirt path beside Dia. The trail spanned wide enough for two people side-by-side. Ahead of them, Jabari zig-zagged back-and-forth, constantly searching for pebbles and sticks. He would replace the stick in his hand if he found one he thought made a better sword. He was especially excited when he found thicker, L-shaped limbs he could pretend were guns.

Hiba scolded him from time to time against pointing the imaginary guns at people, so he pretended to shoot squirrels out of trees. Ada walked beside her mother with her hand stuffed in her pockets and kicking a toe at the loose gravel here and there.

Dia's gaze roamed the landscape, obviously absorbing the layout and committing it to memory. Rafe resisted the urge to hold her hand or start a conversation, because she needed to focus and mentally map the area.

She was beautiful. He loved her smile—soft when she was serene, coy when she teased, lucious when she flirted. He liked all facets of her—casual and relaxed at a bar, fierce in combat gear holding a rifle, elegantly decked out in an evening gown and heels, and bare before him in the heat of passion.

He wanted more of this woman.

"We should talk," she said.

He tried to gauge her soft expression to discern if he needed to brace himself for disappointment or let his heart swell with relief. "Okay."

"Last night—"

"Dia! Dia!" Jabari called. "Come look at the size of this toad." He waved to her beside a stream off the beaten path.

She chuckled. "I'm coming," she called. Before she left, she turned to Rafe and took his hand for a brief squeeze. Her eyes shone brightly, like she would embrace him or kiss him if the moment hadn't been inappropriate for a show of affection.

Watching her walk away and knowing she would walk back and finish that conversation made his chest flush with warmth.

⁂

AFTER A NIGHT ON DUTY, Rafe joined Dorian in the kitchen and poured himself a cup of coffee. Between Dorian's presence and Rafe's bodyguard role, he hadn't had a chance to circle back to Dia to finish their conversation.

Dorian had set up the griddle and splayed ingredients for pancakes on the counter.

"I'll help." Rafe measured the pancake mix into the bowl. He eyed Dorian as the older man cracked eggs into a separate bowl. "You and

Katie are happy? I mean, you don't seem bothered by spending time apart for your job."

Dorian's lips drew in a thin line. He clearly knew the basis for Rafe's question. As if transitioning his thoughts to Katie, his expression softened. "Every day with Katie is a gift. We can talk endlessly about any topic—her books, politics, music, food. She's my bright beacon in an often dark world. But we find fulfillment in our careers." He poured the eggs into the bowl with the dry ingredients.

Rafe stirred. "And missing each other for weeks at a time is manageable?"

"Sure." Dorian retrieved bacon from the fridge. "We text and call. Rafe, there are plenty of couples who work relationships around careers. Think of the entire military service. You and Dia can have a relationship with you working for Rider and her working for Interpol. Why are you grinning?" He placed strips of bacon on a skillet.

"I expected more opposition to me pursuing your daughter." Rafe had envisioned Dorian directing a quiet sort of vehemence toward him at the idea of him wanting to date his Dia. Aside from Dorian's anger the first day, which Rafe suspected reflected his emotions regarding his daughter's career secrets, Rafe hadn't felt any animosity, only acceptance.

"That's your own insecurity, Alonso. I told you I had no objections if she didn't, and I meant that. You're an honorable man, and I know you'd protect her with your life. Not that she's a woman in need of protection." Dorian pushed sizzling strips of meat around the pan. He smiled, adding, "Despite your attempt to hide a softer side, I've seen you let down your guard with Hiba and the children. There's compassion inside you. So, although you've had an unconventional upbringing that might have shattered the minds of lesser men, you've important attributes."

Awed into silence by Dorian's words, Rafe quietly processed them as he scooped batter onto the griddle. He'd always considered his past had made him lesser, but Dorian judged his character by Rafe's ability to have become a good man despite his past. A lump formed in his throat.

He felt the weight of his harmonica in his pocket. His own father had never expressed this type of praise. "My father always made me feel as though I fell short of his expectations for me."

Dorian flipped the bacon in the hot pan. "So I gather. I'll never comprehend why some parents use disappointment as a motivating tool. It's a toxic way to perpetuate poor self-esteem. Children need praise and encouragement for success."

Rafe considered how Dorian's rearing tactics had created a remarkable and self-confident daughter happy with her career choice.

"Are you dating my daughter?"

Rafe grinned. "Yes."

"As I expected. Very well. I suppose it's time for the unveiled fatherly threat. If you hurt her—"

"I won't." He didn't want Dorian to finish that sentence.

"I was referring to emotional damage," Dorian added.

One by one, Rafe flipped the pancakes. "I have no intention of that either, but relationships take work. Sometimes there is emotional pain and bumps in the road."

Dorian took a deep breath. "I find your assessment accurate."

⁂

SHOUP PULLED his knife out of Clark's chest and wiped the blood off the blade on a handkerchief. Ugh. Now there was blood everywhere. At least he had people to clean up the mess.

Looking down at the limp, lifeless body, Shoup's eye twitched. Shame. He'd liked Clark as he'd been one of his more competent and level-headed employees. But a blunder of Clark's magnitude—letting the target slip through his fingers—couldn't be tolerated.

Actually, the entire situation was infuriatingly intolerable. Shoup had neither the man nor woman who'd dared steal from him in his possession. Sure, they'd only taken what he'd allowed them to take, but they still deserved punishment.

Trying to inflict damage on the Rider team was like firing rubber bullets at a tank. Hadn't Lucius warned him that they were no simple adversaries?

How to destroy them then?

As Shoup slipped his knife back in the sheath on his cargo pants, he considered Clark's recap of Rafe Alonso's escape. Clark and his partner had abducted Rafe as he was getting into a taxi with his luggage.

"Why pack up and leave the day after my party?" Shoup asked.

Nick stepped around the blood congealing on the basement floor of Shoup's building.

"I don't like the timing," Shoup continued. "With the data from my laptop stolen, they should have been skipping town immediately after the party. Mission accomplished. Conversely, Mica—who's proven herself a savvy adversary—would keep her team in Chicago until she confirmed the USB contained the information she sought. I have the a virus, so they would have remained in the city and tried a new tactic."

"What are you thinking?" Nick asked, typing a message on his phone, probably scheduling a body dump with their disposal team.

"Why were Rafe Alonso and his partner leaving town?"

"You outsmarted them. Tail tucked between their legs, they were heading back to regroup."

Shoup shook his head. As much as his ego liked the idea of crushing defeat, none of the events since the Sizani fiasco had felt like a win. His mind lit with an idea. "They have another team." He snapped his fingers. "It's like hunting big game. Flash distracting prey at them over here," he wriggled his hand in the air, "while you shoot him dead with your Mauser 98 magnum."

He paced around Clark's dead body. What would be the play? Probably his office, not his home. His office was impenetrable. Unless someone on the inside helped Rider.

Lucius Titan.

Shoup's gaze snapped to Nick. "I want video footage of my building for the last five days."

"Of your office?" Nick startled. "We haven't had any security breaches."

"I highly doubt that."

24

After breakfast, Dia sat on the cabin porch, watching the sun dance through swaying leaves and pine needles as she sipped Earl Grey tea.

She'd received notices from both Interpol and MI6 that the UN was launching a counteroffensive against General Passable. That meant she neared the end of her time with the Rider team. She'd enjoyed working with them, but she was also ready to return to her Interpol and MI6 duties, which were piling up.

An end to her time with the Rider team also meant an end to her time with Rafe. The tougher pill to swallow knotted her stomach.

A farewell.

She thought about her conversation with her mom and how time apart from him would only make their time together that much more special. Not everyone needed to live under the same roof to have a fulfilling relationship. They could make the most of the time they had when they had it, and between those bouts, they could enjoy and maintain their careers, while keeping their interests. She had her career goals, but wouldn't they be so much more fulfilling to achieve if she shared her life with someone?

Checking her watch, she polished off the last of her tea before heading back inside the cabin where Hiba and the kids were slipping on walking shoes.

"We're taking a stroll," Dorian explained. "After this, I'll head to town for meal supplies."

The house fell instantly quiet when the four of them left. Rafe had had night duty, so Dia knew he napped upstairs. She should let him sleep, but she didn't want to let the next forty-five minutes of opportunity pass.

She took the stairs two at a time and knocked. "It's Dia."

"Yeah, come in."

When she opened the door, Rafe stretched in his bed before sitting up. He straightened his t-shirt and ran a hand over disheveled hair. She stepped inside and closed the door behind her.

Breathless from the stairs and her intrusion, she wrung her hands together. "I want to try this dating thing. I don't know where it can go long term or how, but I want to try."

He puzzled for a few seconds. "I don't think I can give you suburban life with routine. Even if I wanted that, I'm not sure I could fabricate it. I love spending time with you. We have incredible chemistry."

"Agreed." She ran a hand through her hair as she paced. "I'm not sure what you consider an ideal relationship. I don't want two point five kids and a house in the suburbs. I love my job. I love travel. Relationships are give-and-take, but I would never ask you to give up a career you love, either. I've seen you with the Rider team. They're your family."

"You think we can be a dating couple while holding onto the careers we love?"

She stopped pacing to look at him. "I don't need a Hallmark movie channel ending. There's you, Rafe. Only you. As long as we're exclusive and we make every effort to see each other regularly, I'll have the relationship I want. That's enough for me. We talk every day and we see each other every chance we get. We won't live under the same roof for now. Someday we might. Is that enough for you?"

"Yes." He smiled. "I like that. It doesn't have to be all or nothing."

"I was afraid it had to be, but I think we can have the careers we love and the relationship we crave. I don't need all day every day. But I do need you."

"Then you have me." He patted the bed beside him.

She glanced over her shoulder. "Everyone is out for a walk. We have a limited amount of time."

"Then we'll make the most of it."

After quickly tugging off her shirt and pants, she crawled toward him on the bed. "If we're doing this, and we're serious, you need to know I work for more than Interpol." Her voice shook with the fear and uncertainty of sharing a secret that could endanger both of them.

He pulled her closer so her body was over his. Arching up, he kissed the exposed skin between her breasts.

"Beautiful Midnight. I may not know a lot about all the organizations around the world, but I know Interpol liaisons don't go around shooting people. They don't have that kind of authority, and I don't think you're some type of rogue liaison. So, I gather you work for some other organization—CIA, MI6, or some other secret international group. You can tell me when you're ready to tell me. Preferably not when we're about to have incredible sex—on a time crunch."

She chuckled, her whole body warming at her proximity to Rafe and the anticipation of accepting each other into their lives.

"WHERE THE HELL IS HE?" Shoup demanded into his phone as he exited the elevator into the parking garage beneath his office building.

He had men trailing Lucius in the event that the son of a bitch did a double cross. Which he had.

Nothing was unfolding as planned. Shoup's team hadn't snatched the man or woman who had the audacity to steal from his own home. He didn't have the whereabouts of the Sizani family. Now this.

His man answered, "The abandoned auto warehouse off South Fulton Parkway. He's meeting with some shady characters. The way they greeted each other, I'm guessing the two men with him know him. Could be some of his former employees before his business went under."

Vision red with rage, Shoup pressed the key fob and unlocked his Ferrari. Once in the seat, he dropped his electronic tablet in the passenger seat beside him and peeled out of the garage in Lucius' direction. The midday sun blasted his eyes, until he retrieved the sunglasses from the passenger side visor and slipped them on.

Shoup had been compromised, just like that, in the blink of an eye. He wouldn't have even known if he hadn't had back up cameras.

Posing as electricians, a man and a woman had infiltrated his office and copied his files. He rarely encountered this level of sophistication. He'd taken several moments after seeing the footage to let the reality of the theft sink in. He didn't yet know what information they'd stolen, but they'd been in the room long enough to download gigabytes of data.

My data.

Stomach acid churned in his gut and up to the back of his throat as he made the turns toward his destination. He had an advanced security system and guards. Enough to deter his average enemies. And that was only leading up to his office which was protected by fingerprint and facial recognition. This infiltration was above average.

It had to be the Rider team. He hadn't had enough of a view of the older man and woman who'd infiltrated him to identify them, but he knew the Riders and they had no members meeting those people's descriptions. They must have contracted out the job. He would find them all and kill them.

Lucius had to be scheming with the Rider team. Inside intel was the only way they would have had a layout of his office, his cameras, and theft of Shoup's print and face. In addition, Lucius must've planted something to cause the electrical glitch that prompted his guards to call in the fake electricians. He had claimed he'd thought of taking down Rider by targeting their clients. Instead, the weasel was helping Rider plot against him.

Shoup phoned his surveillance team as he pulled into the parking spot outside the warehouse. "How many men are inside?"

"Still only the two. And Lucius."

"Hoyle?"

"No. He took a flight out of O'Hare earlier today."

Shoup stepped out of his car and slammed the door shut.

"Wait, boss. We'll come with you and back you up."

"I don't need backup for two and half men," he ground out the words. He also wasn't waiting for his men to arrive. This ended here and now.

He strolled in to see two men seated in chairs around three dozen crates talking to Lucius.

"Shoup, this is an unexpected surprise," Lucius said.

At his words, the men who'd started to stand in alarm at the approaching stranger relaxed back into their seats. Shoup pulled out his .45 and shot them before they had a chance to draw their weapons.

"What the hell is the matter with you?" Lucius growled. "Those men were part of my team. They were damn obedient soldiers."

Shoup brought up his tablet to show Lucius the screen. "You dumbass. I told you what would happen if you double crossed me."

He played the video of the fake electricians accessing his hard drive, but instead of watching the video again, he watched Lucius' expression.

"I had nothing to do with this." Lucius scowled as he turned his attention to the screen.

"That's two people stealing my information—clients, finances, confidential files. The works." Or so he suspected. He had Nick looking into what had been copied.

And there it was, Lucius squinting at the two people as his mouth parted slightly in surprise and his pupils dilated.

Yes, the traitor clearly knew these people and was entrenched in their scheme.

Shoup took two steps back and pointed his gun at Lucius' head, savoring the panicked look in the man's eyes.

"Wait. Wait a damn minute. I didn't know about this," Lucius blurted. "I know where the Sizani family is hiding out. I tracked some roof repair work Mica's father paid for on cabin in North Georgia. Ask Hoyle. He knows." His voice shook as sweat trickled down the side of his face. "I sent him there with three of your men. They'll grab them tonight. You and I are working together on the same side."

Shoup sure as hell wouldn't believe a claim to know where the Sizani family was hiding when spoken in desperation so Shoup wouldn't kill him. Lucius would turn the lie into another chance to manipulate him. Well, the joke was on Lucius.

Shoup pulled the trigger. The traitor's head snapped back as his whole body went limp. Nobody double crossed him.

Agonizing pain flared in Shoup's leg as he stumbled back. He drop his tablet and placed his left hand over his thigh, pulling his hand away to see blood staining his palm. Gaping down at Lucius' corpse, Shoup saw a gun in his limp hand.

No, no, no.

His men rushed into the building as his vision grew gray and blurred.

"Boss? Oh no. Boss?"

"Shit, that's a lot of blood."

"Call an ambulance."

"No ambulance," Shoup barked. He wouldn't let a bullet to the leg stop him. He wanted revenge more than ever.

"You," he pointed and barked. "Clean up the crime scene. No prints, no casings. Leave the bodies. You," he began to the other moron, "you're driving me to my airstrip."

"But your leg?"

"I'll patch it up in the car. Move!"

Before he left, he had one of the men find Lucius' pocketed phone. Using facial recognition—good thing it worked on corpses—Shoup unlocked it and reset it to a numbered code password. Once he stopped his bleeding leg, he would search Lucius' texts with Hoyle to find the location of the Sizani family.

Mica Rider had fucked with the wrong man. She and her team were dead. They just didn't know it yet.

MICA SETTLED into her office chair at her desk on the third floor of the Rider offices and took a slow, savoring sip of her caramel latte, indulging in a moment of low stress. She would regret having caffeine in the early evening, but she wanted to stay awake to wrap up some overdue charting in her files.

Today, she'd finally shed the angst of everything building between Shoup, Lucius, and the international crisis of the Sizani family. Maxine and Vladimir had completed their mission without a hitch and would be returning this morning.

The UN was pressuring General Passable to end his coup, apparently with some force behind the request according to texts from Dia. Hopefully that meant the family's isolation was coming to an end.

Rafe and Dia were safe after frightening and unanticipated attacks. Shoup must have had Jackson followed—this was the only explanation Mica could conjure on how Shoup had found both of them at the hotel. After that, she had pulled Jackson back to safety, not wanting him to be abducted also. She would think of a different way to handle Lucius.

To be sure, the road ahead would still be peppered with danger like a minefield. Mica also had to sort out how to take Shoup down. But she had time, and now she had leverage. If he threatened her, her team, or anyone's family, she had incriminating evidence against him. He had nothing against her.

Although she'd broken Lucius out of prison, orchestrated by Maxine and Vladimir, and Lucius had told Shoup of the Rider team's involvement, no one had any proof. As far as anyone could trace, Russian convicts had sprung Lucius from prison. Even if the state department offered a deal for information, the convicts could only attest that the commands had come from the Russian mafia. Vladimir still had his friends in low places, even though he was out of the game.

For one quiet evening, Mica would savor the serenity.

She logged onto her computer, and as soon as the screen flickered to life, Claire's face appeared. She had been at Bones all day working and appeared to be still there.

"Uh, good evening?"

"Mica, we've a serious problem." Claire's worried face loomed large on the screen before it flickered over to what looked to be a transcript. "This is the feed from the bug planted in Lucius' wheelchair. I can't listen to it twenty-four hours a day, and I had it set to dump the recordings in the transcript file every two hours, so it wouldn't drain the battery."

"Okay, Claire, slow down. I wouldn't be upset with you if there's something we're delayed learning about. None of us can work twenty-four hours nonstop. What has Lucius been up to?"

"Listen to it. Just listen. I'm sending an alert to the team at the cabin."

At Claire's words, Mica's chest spasmed. She opened the audio file and played it.

Lucius: *"Shoup, this is an unexpected surprise."*

Two gunshots sounded.

Lucius: *"What the hell is the matter with you? Those men were part of my team. They were damn obedient soldiers."*
Shoup: *"You dumbass. I told you what would happen if you double crossed me."*

A pause.

> Lucius: *"I had nothing to do with this."*
> Shoup: *"That's two people stealing my information—*
> *clients, finances, confidential files. The works."*

Another pause.

> Lucius: *"Wait. Wait a damn minute. I didn't know about*
> *this. I know where the Sizani family is hiding out..."*

Mica's stomach plummeted. They had been so careful to keep the cabin a secret, but she remembered a leak in the roof her dad had had repaired. The cabin was compromised.

Another gunshot.

No, two nearly simultaneously.

After Mica read the words, she checked the time at the bottom of the transcript against her computer clock. This was several hours ago.

Sh...sugar.

"He said Hoyle knows," Claire said, squeaky voice on the verge of panic.

"Where is Hoyle, right now?" Mica asked.

"I don't know. I don't have a tracker on him. Should we move Hiba and the kids?"

"Where is Jackson?"

"Flying back now, like you ordered."

Whew. One less teammate to worry about.

Mica scooped her keys off her desk and headed for the door as she slipped in her Bluetooth earpiece. "Call me on my cell phone."

Seconds later, Mica answered her phone. "I don't know yet if we need to move the family," she told Claire. "The cabin is fully equipped with firepower and a safe room, but three Riders against an unknown number of attackers. Risky either way."

She shook her head. "I'm heading out to the cabin. We've got nobody closer and everybody else on assignment. I need you to get in touch with Dia and her Interpol contacts. They'll have the connections and authority to check passenger flight logs and see if Hoyle took a plane down here and find out what time he landed."

And did Hoyle know his boss had died? If he did, what were the chances he'd blame the Rider team and come after them?

"Okay," Claire warned, "but you need to listen to the rest of the recording."

25

The mood felt lighter as Dia joined everyone at the dinner table. Rafe serenaded the children on his harmonica with *Two of Us* by The Beatles, a song about going home.

General Passable would cave soon under UN pressure, and Hiba and the children could return to their father and their country. Dia and Rafe had officially entered a relationship.

She planned to arrange for Rafe to go with her to escort the family home, and perhaps she and Rafe could steal a few days together before returning to their respective jobs.

"Smells delicious," she commented as she sat.

"Pot roast," her father said. "Rafe and I prepared it."

Rafe finished his song and tucked the harmonica into the breast pocket of his shirt. "There was minor squabbling about how much garlic to add, but no one was injured during the meal preparation process."

"I set the table," Jabari said.

"And I made all the water glasses," Ada chimed in.

"Everything looks fantastic," Dia said with appreciation.

After Hiba's prayer and food was splayed on individual plates, everyone ate.

Through dinner, conversation flowed about what the kids would do when they arrived back home.

Toward the end of the meal, all three Rider phones pinged simultaneously.

Dia had hers out first. She felt the color drain from her face. "We've been found. Hoyle and Shoup's men are on their way here." Four men, according to Mica's text

"Unknown ETA," Rafe added, blinking at his screen.

Dorian stood abruptly. "Evac plan in place. Everyone has exactly three minutes to gather belongings and meet back here. Move!"

RAFE THREW on his suit pants and jacket in a rush and grabbed his gun, phone, and Claire's EMP device. When he arrived back in the kitchen, Dorian was checking his weapon, also dressed in the Rider bullet-resistant suit. The Sizani family shuffled in, hastily packed bags in tow.

Dia emerged dressed in black with a hijab on. She had a chador over her bullet resistant vest and leggings. "Dad, you and Rafe can take the family in your car. I'll pose as Hiba in a second vehicle and see if I can lure away the attackers."

Before Rafe could protest her plan, his phone buzzed—three quick, sharp bursts.

Dorian already had his in hand. "Perimeter breech. They're already here."

"We can't risk running everyone to the vehicles, which they may have already sabotaged," Dia said.

Rafe nodded his agreement.

The lights flickered off. In only a few seconds, the generator kicked on. Hiba and the kids huddled together, the fear on their faces gripping Rafe's heart. Their attackers would cut the generator power soon.

"New plan," he said. "Dorian, take them the family to the panic room. Dia and I can fend them off on the main floor."

Jaw firm, Dorian glanced once at his daughter before leading the family away.

Dia adjusted her cloak with her gun in one hand as she walked toward the back porch. "I'll lure whoever I can away from the house with my disguise and thin them out for you."

He followed, hating her plan, but understanding this was who she'd chosen to be, like him. She was trained for this, and although he would worry, he trusted her skills.

"You have your nunchucks?"

She gave him a sly smile. "Naturally."

I love you, he thought.

Rather than laden the scenario with an ill-timed, heavy declaration such as that, he said, "You are the sexiest woman I know."

She placed a hand on his shoulder and a kiss on his cheek. "Be safe. I have plans for us when this is over."

He grinned as she slipped away and out the door. Locking it behind her, he steeled himself for the next part. He took the stairs two at a time to the balcony overlooking the living room.

From his vantage point, he had a view of anyone coming through the front door, the living room glass windows, or the back porch. He crouched down to make himself as small as possible in the dark.

Setting the EMP and gun down, he pulled out his phone and logged into the security app, which showed him the cabin's cameras. They had an hour of battery, so they continued to function even though the power and generator had been sabotaged. Three men approached by all three points.

Glass shattered, followed by a clunk, clunk, clunk of metal on wood. Smoke erupted into the living room, diffusing to the air rapidly. Any self-respecting pre-apocalyptic survivor could recognize tear gas. Fortunately, the vapor was heavier than air and would settle to the ground, making Rafe's higher position was ideal.

The three dark figures with semi-automatic weapons converged, wearing protective masks on their faces.

Rafe powered down his phone. He was probably twenty feet at an angle above and away from them, in range of Claire's EMP device. He pushed the button.

Nothing happened.

What had he expected would happen? Magnetic pulses were silent, and because the power to the house had already been cut, including the generator, there was nothing for the EMP to wipe out except for the gunmen's weapon.

The upside was the silent nature of the detonation that meant his location was still unknown to the assailants. The downside was he couldn't be sure it definitely worked without them trying their guns. Now he had three men to contend with who may or may not have active weapons. And even if the EMP worked, they may have backup weapons.

Rafe had two options—wait for an opportunity to take them one at a time or stand up, guns blazing, and take down as many as he could while they clustered in the living room. The latter would've been his father's approach—be the first to shoot and kill and don't give them the opportunity to kill you later. Survivalist mentality.

Rafe waited, crouched and still, letting them search through the main level of the house before they broke off—one heading probably toward the basement, another finishing his sweep of the ground floor, and the third creeping up the stairs.

Rafe considered his attack. A limb wound would leave the man free to attack another way, a torso shot would hit his vest, and a head-shot would ruin the mask Rafe needed to go downstairs and venture into the tear gas. Any gunshot would alert the other attackers.

How long does it take for tear gas to clear?

DIA PLUNGED into the darkness of the forest, running swiftly with senses attuned to every sound and movement. At the snap of a twig, she jerked her head to the right. By the faint moonlight, she glimpsed red hair.

Hoyle.

Excellent, he'd followed her.

She aimed and fired, but he'd already vanished. She'd known hitting him at this distance in the dark was unlikely, but she hoped the threat of a bullet wound would keep him moving away from the house.

She dashed in Hoyle's direction, trying to get her bearings in the woods she'd walked in daylight. Moonlight granted her enough of a glow to keep her from running into trees or smacking her head on low-hanging branches, but with the forest undergrowth, she couldn't see precisely where her feet were landing. One misstep on a jagged rock, hole, or tree root, and she'd be down with a twisted ankle at best and a broken one at worst. Either injury would make her easy pickings for Hoyle.

When she crossed over the pathway, she spotted a familiar boulder. Crouching behind it, she took a moment to listen and breathe as she slipped out of the hijab.

She took large breaths, trying to fill her lungs while simultaneously not sucking the air in loudly. Her calf muscles burned from her sprint through the woods.

The sound of splashing water had her ears perking. The ravine. She had an idea of Hoyle's location if he stuck to the path around the perimeter of the house, which would've been the least hazardous route. However, the trail would lead him back to the house.

Unacceptable.

She would have to cut him off to prevent him from returning to the cabin. If she circled around through the woods, she could get ahead of him. She moved swiftly, granting him a wide enough berth so her movements wouldn't be overheard—at least not to the extent that he could identify her location.

Ducking behind a tall pine, she worked to catch her breath. Gun in hand, she waited.

Where were his crunching footsteps? Had he taken a different path? Had he heard her and circled away from her or retraced his steps back to the cabin in the other direction? Or was her own breathing and heavy heartbeat interfering with her powers of perception?

A rustling sounded, but she couldn't tell how far away it was. She leaned over to look around the tree, only to discover Hoyle was right there.

The look of shock on his face revealed she had startled him as much as he had startled her. With lightning-fast reflexes, he raised his gun to shoot. She could've taken aim also, but that would keep her in his line of fire, and they might have shot each other at the same time.

Instead, she pivoted and kicked a leg at his wrist. The blow caused his hand to jerk upward before he had a chance to fire. She kicked again, this time solidly contacting his knee. No matter how big the man was, torn ligaments would bring him down.

Grunting, Hoyle fell to one knee, giving Dia the time she needed to aim her gun. This wasn't the type of man you left breathing to hunt you down another day. She had people she cared about who he could go after—her father, Rafe, the Sizani family, and any of the Rider team.

The bulk around his torso suggested Kevlar, so she needed a head shot. A millisecond away from pulling the trigger, Hoyle launched himself at her, springing like a crouched tiger intent on his next meal. The weight of the redheaded beast slammed into her chest.

Wrapping his arms around her torso, he took her to the ground, and the air whooshed out of her lungs as her back protested the jarring impact. The ringing in her ears told her she'd fired her weapon, though she had no idea where the bullet went.

This was no ordinary goon—no villain's peon. She was fighting Bowser himself—all raging muscle, spiked shell, horns, and fangs. King of the Koopas. But she didn't have three lives to spare in trying to beat him.

26

Before the gunman reached the top of the stairs, floorboards creaking lightly, Rafe ducked into a nearby room, waiting as the man to approach.

Lightning fast, Rafe stepped out of hiding, spun, and punched out a fist, landing his knuckles in the man's throat. Shoup's man recovered faster than expected as he turned to aim his gun, but Rafe slapped it away.

He didn't yet know if the EMP had worked, but he was fed up from having his body covered in bruises from the gunshots to his bullet-resistant suit from his last encounter. The man had another gun strapped to his thigh, an odd-shaped thing Rafe deduced was a tranquilizer gun.

Of course, Rafe thought, the men were equipped with sedative darts for their anticipated kidnapping victims. Did the tranq gun hold the same mixture used on him the other day? He had no intention of finding out.

When Rafe kicked a leg out, planning to land a blow to his midsection, the attacker wrapped a beefy arm around Rafe's torso and pivoted, launching Rafe up and sideways into the stair railing. His back viciously smacked against the beam, which fortunately splintered without outright breaking. If it had, Rafe would've fallen into the living room and likely broken more than one bone.

Pain seared through his back as he brought an elbow down above the man's clavicle. The man grunted and collapsed down to one knee. He bent his wrist and pulled the trigger of his biosensored semi-automatic handgun.

When nothing happened, Rafe breathed a sigh of relief even as he jerked his knee upward into the man's jaw. He wanted to land a solid punch in the face to stun his opponent, but the action in this case would actually be a fist to the teargas mask, and that might break some hand bones Rafe wasn't willing to spare.

Despite the damage done to his jaw, the man rose, driving a fist toward Rafe's midsection. He blocked, spun, and threw a karate chop backward into the man's cervical spine. The assailant flew forward into the banister, which splintered further.

Kicking, Rafe lashed a foot directly into the man's back. The banister broke completely, snapping like a dry bone, and the man grasped onto the ledge to keep from falling below.

"I need to borrow this." Rafe pulled the gas mask off the man's head before shoving a boot in his face, making him fall down into the living room.

He crashed half on the couch and half on the side table, which collapsed. After limply rolling onto the floor, he lay unmoving.

Rafe slipped on the gas mask before making his way downstairs, where much of the vapor had cleared.

Ah Dios. The plastic smelled of stale cigarettes.

The commotion must have alerted the man on the first floor, because he moved out of the bedroom and took aim at Rafe before pulling the trigger.

Hoyle's body crushed Dia, pinning her to the ground, flattening her like a pancake. She barely had room to breathe, and the stench of his body odor was additionally suffocating. He had one meaty hand squeezing around her throat and the other around the right wrist of her gun hand, pressing it to the ground.

She wrapped her left hand around his right wrist, digging her fingernails into the tendons to try to cause enough pain for him to release her before he strangled her.

But his grip didn't budge.

Something hot and wet trickled onto her neck. At first, she thought the man was drooling on her, but the copper scent betrayed the truth.

Blood.

He was bleeding, which meant she'd shot him.

With only seconds before she would certainly lose consciousness, she brought her left hand down to her cargo pant pocket and retrieved her nunchaku. She flicked her wrist, whipping one end to his temple.

When he reared back, his grip loosening slightly in surprise from the blow, she jabbed one konto—metal end of one baton—into his side where his shirt glistened the wettest.

Hoyle screamed, his grip on both hands slacking. With the slight give, she bent her right wrist and pulled the trigger at the same instant he tried to roll off and away from her.

As the smell of sulfur settled on the air, Hoyle's limp body settled on the ground.

She scooted away from him, gasping for air and fighting to keep the blackness around her peripheral vision from plunging her into unconsciousness. She kept the barrel of the gun trained in his direction though hand shook wildly. She wasn't sure she could hit him accurately if she had to fire again. In her other hand, she clutched the bloodied nunchaku.

Although he didn't move, she could see the rise and fall of his chest. Not dead yet.

She didn't know if he was playing opossum or too injured to move. Perhaps she'd only hit his bullet-resistant vest. No way would she get close enough to roll him over and find out.

Letting out a huffing breath, she felt steadier. Confident enough she could stand and her legs to support her. She pushed to her feet.

Time to let her guard appear down and see what Hoyle would do. She leaned her head against a tree trunk, raising her left hand to rub her exquisitely sore neck that would no doubt be covered in purplish bruises by tomorrow. Luckily, he hadn't completely crushed her voice box.

From her peripheral vision, Hoyle leaped up, knife blade in his left hand glinting in the moonlight. A wild snarl contorted his face.

Dia fired—direct shot between his eyes.

Hoyle crumbled to the ground.

Her aching body begged her to do the same, but people she cared about were in danger. In the distance, the muted sound of a crash came from the direction of the cabin.

Rafe.

NOTHING HAPPENED. The gun didn't fire.

The man looked incredulously at his gun, and Rafe was once again relieved to have used Claire's invention.

Rafe flipped the muzzle of his gun toward the ceiling a couple of times, signaling the man to raise his arms. He still didn't want to have to shoot his gun in case more men lurked outside, but his battered body wasn't up for another fight so soon. He'd shoot him if the need arose.

The man dropped his gun and lifted his hands, but as he did so, he pulled a knife from a sheath strapped to his thigh and hurled it. The glint of silver flickered as it sped toward Rafe's face.

Raising his left arm but keeping his gun pointed, Rafe blocked the knife with his left arm. The weapon hit the suit fabric but didn't penetrate. Instead, it clattered to the floor.

"Last chance, jackass. Hands in the air or I shoot you down."

The man raised his hands.

"Now turn around so I can cuff your hands behind your back."

The man did as he was told, but Rafe didn't have any cuffs. Instead, he bent down to the unconscious man on the floor and pulled out the tranquilizer gun.

Aiming, Rafe fired. A tiny projectile landed in the man's neck. He snarled and reached backward even as he became unsteady.

Rafe inspected at the weapon. Single use only, but it took effect faster than he would have expected. He wondered what concoction these tranqs contained. He thought of how quickly he'd become immobile in the car when he'd been kidnapped.

Sure, in movies tranqs worked fast, but in real life, they were slow—as in minutes rather than seconds to take effect—making them less than ideal. He would have to see if Claire could analyze Shoup's concoction and replicate it as a means of non-deadly conflict resolution.

After several seconds, the man eased himself to the floor. Rafe dropped that gun and replaced it with the tranq gun from the sedated man's holster, then shot the thug who'd fallen from the second floor. No point in taking chances that he would wake and come after them.

Convinced these two men were no longer threats, Rafe crept toward the basement and down the stairs.

Even with his senses on high alert, he didn't detect any sound or movement. He paused to listen.

Silence.

Finally, deciding he would rather take his chances being attacked by the man down here than risk Dorian attacking him thinking he was one of Shoup's men, he eased off the gas mask, saying, "Dorian?"

Dorian stepped out of the shadows, gun in hand. "The one who came down here is managed. How many more?"

Managed? Rafe wasn't sure he wanted to know exactly what that meant.

He said, "Cameras showed three attackers into the house. I've immobilized two and you one. That leaves whoever has remained outside with Dia."

"How many vehicles arrived?"

"One."

"So Mica's estimate of four men could be accurate."

Rafe pursed his lips. "Let me do a sweep and confirm. You stay with the family." He didn't want to take a chance that a second car had arrived with more men during his skirmish.

Rafe raced back up the stairs to find Dia checking pulses on the men he'd downed.

He lowered his weapon, relief flooding him. "You okay?"

Her hair was disheveled and her clothes covered in dirt and leaves. Face flushed like she'd come fresh from a run, she smiled at him.

"I'm okay. These two you took sufficiently down. How about the third?" Dia asked.

"Your father *managed* him."

"I'm afraid to ask what that means."

"So was I. What about others?"

"I took on Hoyle." She scrunched up her nose. "He's... uh... managed."

"I'll call Mica as I finish sweeping the house."

DIA WENT DOWN to the basement to fetch the family. When her father opened the panic room door, she exchanged hugs with him and the family.

"We're all okay," she told everyone.

Poor Jabari and Ada looked terrified.

"Let's get them to the vehicle. Rafe is confirming our cars good to drive and calling Mica."

"Bless you for protecting my family," Hiba told her.

Dia suspected she looked rather haggard after her fight with

Hoyle and Hiba could probably tell her win hadn't been easily secured.

When they reached the main floor, Dia noted the bodies of the men Rafe bested had been moved. He'd evidently cleared a path for the family where they wouldn't have to see their attackers.

Rafe approached, and Jabari ran to him.

"You're okay!"

"Yeah, man. Just another day on the job." But he glanced around nervously, making Dia wonder if he suspected another attack so soon.

Rafe shrugged out of his jacket and wrapped it around Jabari. The apparel covered his body down to his knees. "We'll keep you safe." Rafe looked up at Dia and Dorian with a worried expression but like he didn't want to share bad news in front of the Sizani family.

What had Mica told him that had him concerned?

"Cars are functional. Engines are running. We need to go. Now."

Dorian nodded. "On my six," he told the family.

Dia shuffled behind them, alert for danger. Once outside, they quickly ushered the family inside the backseat of the SUV, where everyone strapped in. Dorian climbed behind the driver's seat.

Rafe approached. "Go with your dad. I'll be right behind you in the other car."

"What do you know?"

He lowered his voice. "Shoup shot Lucius. Last transmit from Claire's device had Shoup hopping on a plane."

"Mica thinks he's coming here?"

"Here or after her family. She has Maxine and Vladimir guarding them."

An engine gunned down the driveway.

Dia tensed as a vehicle approached.

"It's Mica," Rafe said. "Get in." He gestured to the vehicle with the Sizani family.

Dia relaxed slightly and turned to climb into the passenger seat beside her father. Rafe stepped in the direction of Mica's car as it came to a sudden halt.

From the shadows, a figure stepped out from the trees beside the cabin and lurched forward, dragging one leg behind him. Shoup was dressed in all black with mud and underbrush smeared haphazardly about his body. His face and bald head were scratched like he'd tangled with mother nature on his trek in the dark toward the cabin.

Rafe had turned to see the emerging monster, too. Dia and Rafe reached for their guns, but Shoup already had his leveled at Dia.

Rafe leaped a second before Shoup fired, putting his body between the bullet and Dia's head.

"No!" Dia screamed. She dove for Rafe, catching him in her arms.

He wasn't wearing his bullet-resistant jacket. He'd given it to Jabari.

Another shot rang out as Mica stepped out of her vehicle and shot Shoup. He fell to the ground with a bullet in his head.

"Rafe, Rafe, Rafe." Dia's hands frantically ran over his body, searching for the blood that would denote the source of his certainly fatal wound. They were miles from medical care and the bullet had hit him in the chest.

Tears filled her eyes and spilled down her cheeks. The world went blurry, like a melancholy Monet painting.

Her father arrived and knelt beside him, his hands moving over Rafe's body. Had he found the bleeding? Was he applying pressure?

Rafe coughed.

Oh, god, he was dying in her arms.

"Dia," Dorian said. He held something for her to see.

She blinked and swiped the back of her hand over her eyes to clear them.

Something silver glinted in her father's hand. Rafe's harmonica. The metal instrument was dented where the bullet had struck it. She recalled him pocketing it before dinner.

She choked out a part sob part laugh as she looked down at Rafe's face and stroked a hand through his hair.

27

———————

FIVE DAYS LATER

Rafe knelt down before Jabari inside the airport terminal. A dozen of President Sizani's security team surrounding them, waiting to whisk the family back to the presidential house. They had taken a series of private jets back to the islands, during which Rafe had spent time with the family playing card games.

When the kids were entertained with television, he spent the hours talking with Dia. They'd planned out several trips together already and how they would coordinate schedules.

"When you think back, try to remember the fun times, yeah?" Rafe told Jabari.

"Like this smore's," the boy said.

"Like that. Remember how brave you are."

"Maybe I'll be brave like you someday. Protect people. I'll be big and strong and fearless."

"Little secret?" Rafe lowered his voice.

Jabari lean toward him and nodded.

"Sometimes I'm afraid. And that's okay. You can be afraid and still do whatever you need to do to take care of the people you love." Truthfully, Rafe had spent much of this mission afraid for many of the people he cared about, especially when Shoup took aim at Dia. Rafe's world had tilted on its axis. No way he would ever let someone hurt his nunchuck wielding, badass girlfriend, Dia.

The boy nodded and swallowed.

"I hope I see you again next summer. And in preparation of that, I got you this." Rafe pulled a small box out of his pocket and handed it to the boy.

When Jabari opened it, his eyes went wide. "A harmonica! It's perfect. I will learn to play."

Rafe's father's harmonica had saved his life—the one thing Rafe kept and cherished from the troubled man. Despite his father's *trust no one, look out for yourself* mentality, his father's spirit had protected him one last time.

¡Dios le acoja en su seno!

Jabari surprised Rafe by wrapping his small arms around his neck. Rafe looked up at Hiba, who gave their embrace an endearing smile, and Dia, whose lips curled in amusement.

After the hug, Rafe stood and took a step back as his heart squeezed with a mix of emotions. He truly hoped Jabari would remember the fun of the vacation and not the fear. Rafe also hoped he would see the boy again.

"Thank you," Hiba said warmly, "Thank you for everything."

When Hiba turned away, Jabari on her right and Ada on her left, they were instantly surrounded by the Comoros presidential security team. The family disappeared in a conglomeration of black suits.

Rafe stood still, watching them go as Dia slid beside him and looped her arm in his.

"You're a good man, Rafe Alonso. And you'll make a good father one day."

He arched an eyebrow at her. "That so?"

She chuckled. "Easy, tiger. It's an expression and the truth but not yet an invitation."

"Here's an expression for you that is both truth and an invitation. I love you, Dia."

FIVE MORE DAYS LATER

"FIVE DAYS on a private yacht in the Mediterranean. I can get used to this," Dia said.

Rafe followed her down the narrow stairs, through the hallway, and to their cabin after a relaxing dinner with Santino and his girl-friend, Ava. The boat belonged to her father, and she sprang for the all-expense paid vacation for the four of them.

"Please don't get used to this," Rafe said. "It's not in my budget as a bodyguard." He opened the cabin door for her.

Dia laughed as she planted a kiss on his cheek. "You don't need to worry about that. Honestly, I'm going a little stir crazy on a boat. But I partially blame that on not having taken a real vacation or time for myself in way too long. I sort of plowed through college and agent training. Then there were missions, one after the next. Always another mission. I have to re-learn how to relax during my down time."

She patted his cheek. "You're an important part of reminding myself to take time to enjoy life. I have something to look forward to between the missions. I'll savor every getaway with you—even if it's some bungalow in Central or South America without electricity."

"Stir crazy, huh? We should probably work out that extra energy you're feeling." He sidled up next to her even as he pulled off his collared shirt.

Her gaze instantly heated his body and sent a sizzling zing of desire through him. "Didn't we do that last night?"

"We certainly did. But I plan to give you enough heated passion in five nights to warm you all the way through the next mission." He purred out the words, loving the way his enticement drew her closer.

"I love you," she said. Reaching back, she unzipped her black dress and let it fall to the floor.

Mica sat at the coffee shop, enjoying her macchiato with Jackson, when Eddie Finch arrived. He shook Jackson's hand, who'd stood to greet him, and smiled in the first show of affection she'd seen from the stiff FBI agent. Jackson sat back down.

Eddie's warmth chilled quickly as he sat carefully across from them before placing his sunglasses on the table.

He adjusted his impeccable suit before turning a pair of irritated eyes on Mica. "Well, this is a damn mess." He deflated slightly. "Lucius escaped prison only to join forces with Shoup. I'm guessing that was an effort to team up against the Riders, because you've clashed with both of them."

Mica nodded. "They sent a combo team after the Sizani family at my cabin." Of course, Eddie already knew this because he knew Mica had killed Peter Shoup after he'd shot Rafe, but she felt the need to emphasize how she and her team were defending themselves this entire time.

"Did Jackson tell you Lucius is dead?" Eddie asked.

"I did hear that," she confirmed.

"Some type of shootout in a Chicago building. Several dead including Lucius. We have some witnesses willing to say Shoup was the shooter. They're probably only coming forward because he's not around to threaten them to stay silent. Maybe that shootout was some type of double cross. You have any insight into that clash of the titans?"

Mica shrugged. "Two men with large egos." She wanted to say good riddance, but Eddie was all about justice, and not the poetic kind. "Jackson had been there to spy on Lucius because the moment I knew of his prison break, I suspected he would come after us again. I pulled Jackson back before that incident in Chicago. Didn't feel safe leaving him there."

They were late learning about Shoup's showdown with Lucius, Lucius sending Hoyle to her cabin, and Shoup's flight to Atlanta because she'd pulled Jackson back from his direct surveillance. However, if Jackson had been tailing Lucius at that time, he might not have survived Shoup's shooting rampage.

Eddie nodded. "Yes, Jackson told me as much. I told him he should have reported an escape convict to me, not just surveil the asshole."

"Fair point," Mica conceded. "I was hoping we could catch the pair of them in some act that would send them both to prison."

Eddie narrowed his eyes as if doubting she was providing him the full story.

She stared at him impassively.

Don't dig, Eddie. Just take your ignorant bliss and your wins.

That was their unspoken agreement.

"The Sizani's are home safe?" he asked, moving on from the topic of Lucius' death.

"Yes."

Eddie reached into his jacket and pulled out a jump drive. "Did you send me this?"

She cocked her head to one side. "I work in security. I send information to different people at different times. You'll have to be more specific."

Eddie rolled his eyes, sculpted brows raising. "Did you send me Shoup's client files?"

Mica raised one eyebrow as she crossed her arms. "When you receive useful information anonymously. It probably means the person or persons supplying the information don't want to be identified."

"What am I supposed to do with illegally obtained information?" He blinked at her, still holding up the USB.

"That's up to you. Could be Shoup kept a lot of dirty secrets on people in positions of power. You can take the safe road and look the other way, or you can investigate as your job title suggests taxpayers expect you to."

With a grumble, Eddie pocketed the USB once more and slipped on his glasses. "Jackson, you're good?"

"I'm good, man, thanks."

"I wish the bureau could have kept you on," Eddie said as he stood in a more sincere tone than he'd ever used addressing Mica.

Jackson didn't say *me too*.

She watched Eddie disappear.

"Do you miss it?" Mica asked Jackson when Eddie had left the coffee shop.

"The FBI? No. Rule number one... don't embarrass the bureau. I broke that rule."

"You want to tell me what happened?"

Jackson shook his head with a grin but sad eyes. "Nope. I'll never see her again, so we'll leave that pain to the past."

****QUICK NOTE FROM THE AUTHOR****

I HOPE you enjoyed *Sizani File*!

Want to find out what secrets are hidden in Jackson's past and how he'll need to face those who seek to destroy the one woman who captivated his heart? *Rivera File* is coming soon. Join my newsletter HERE to get both a free Rider File novella and be the first to know when *Rivera File* is available.

Haven't read the other Rider File novels? Join new couples in each full-length romantic thriller.

Meridian File / Masters File / Box Set 1

McMillan File / Maltisse File / Box Set 2

Storm File / Sullivan File / Box Set 3

Sharp File / Sizani File / Box Set 4

COMING in 2024: *Rivera File / Rucker File / Box Set 5*

YOU CAN SAMPLE other books in my series through my *Samet Sampler*. Only 99c for four variety novellas—romantic suspense, thriller, magical romantic suspense, and urban fantasy romantic suspense.

THE RIDER FILES SERIES

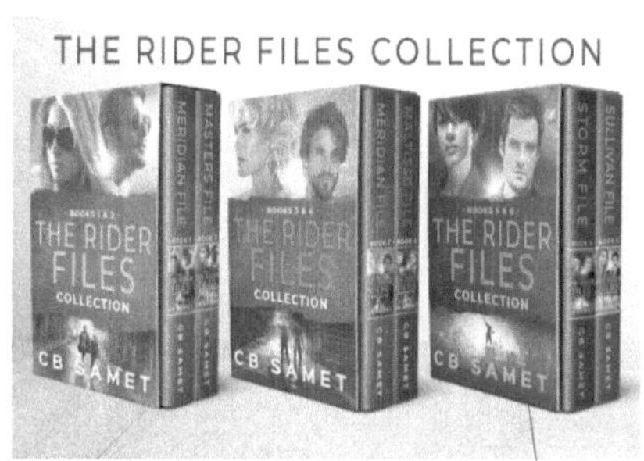

Meridian File / Masters File / Box Set 1

McMillan File / Maltisse File / Box Set 2

Storm File / Sullivan File / Box Set 3

Sharp File / Sizani File / Box Set 4

2024: Rivera File / Rucker File / Box Set 5

DEAR READER

Want to keep in touch?

If you enjoyed this book and want to know about future releases by CB Samet you can CLICK HERE to sign up for my mailing list! I promise I won't spam you. I only send an email when I have a new book released, giveaways, or special discounts. You can also unsubscribe at any time.

If you loved this book, kindly let others know by posing a brief comment on social media or leave a review where you purchased it so readers can find their next favorite romantic suspense series.

Even more ways to follow me below!

Thank you for reading,
CB Samet

OTHER BOOKS BY CB SAMET

Looking for more romantic suspense? How about with an urban fantasy twist? Check out The Shadow Guardians trilogy.

Get *Raven's Flight, a prequel novella* for FREE. In my newsletter, you'll learn about me, special discounts, and new releases.

Raven's Flight, prequel novella

Raine Down, Book 1

Rosalyn's Run, novella

Storm Surge, Book 2

Anka's Orb, novella

Sky Fall, Book 3

The Dr. Whyte Adventure Novels

Thriller Series

Black Gold

Whyte Knight

Gray Horizon

The Avant Champion: Honor

The Avant Champion: Ashes

Brothers' Bond: An Avant Champion Malakai Story

The Avant Champion: Conquest

Isabel: An Avant Champion novelette

The Avant Champion: Redeem